Deemed 'the father of  ard
**Austin Freeman** had a t as
a writer of detective fiction. He was born of a
tailor who went on to train as a pharmacist. After graduating as
a surgeon at the Middlesex Hospital Medical College, Freeman
taught for a while and joined the colonial service, offering his skills
as an assistant surgeon along the Gold Coast of Africa. He became
embroiled in a diplomatic mission when a British expeditionary
party was sent to investigate the activities of the French. Through
his tact and formidable intelligence, a massacre was narrowly
avoided. His future was assured in the colonial service. However,
after becoming ill with blackwater fever, Freeman was sent back to
England to recover and, finding his finances precarious, embarked
on a career as acting physician in Holloway Prison. In desperation,
he turned to writing and went on to dominate the world of
British detective fiction, taking pride in testing different criminal
techniques. So keen were his powers as a writer that part of one of
his best novels was written in a bomb shelter.

19/8/15

£4.29 + £0

BY THE SAME AUTHOR
ALL PUBLISHED BY HOUSE OF STRATUS

# For the Defence:
# Dr Thorndyke

R Austin Freeman

HOUSE OF
STRATUS

This edition published in 2001 by House of Stratus, an imprint of
House of Stratus Ltd, Thirsk Industrial Park, York Road, Thirsk,
North Yorkshire, YO7 3BX, UK.

www.houseofstratus.com

Typeset, printed and bound by House of Stratus.

A catalogue record for this book is available from the British Library
and the Library of Congress.

ISBN 0-7551-0359-9

To
My Brother Robert

# CONTENTS

# CHAPTER ONE

## *The Letter*

It was about four o'clock on a summer afternoon when Andrew Barton, pipe in mouth and garden shears in hand, suspended for a moment his operations on the privet hedge in his front garden to glance down the lane at the postman, who had just turned into it from the road at the end. It was a glance of no special interest. He was not expecting any communication. But as there was no other house in the lane – which presently petered out into a footpath across fields – it was obvious that his own residence was the goal of the postman's peregrinations.

He observed the man's approach intermittently, punctuating his observations with perfunctory snips at the hedge and speculating vaguely and incuriously on the source of the letter which the messenger was presumably coming to deliver. He was not particularly interested. Yet even a rural postman, though less portentous than the telegraph boy, embodies untold potentialities of good or evil, of joy or sorrow, of fortune or disaster. But Andrew was not particularly interested; and thus he watched, unmoved and unsuspecting, the approach of Fate's special messenger, charged with a message the significance of which was only by degrees to be unfolded.

The man strode up to the gate with a letter in his hand and ran his eye critically over the half-cropped hedge.

"I see you are havin' a bit of a tidy-up, sir," he remarked as he handed the letter over the gate; "and none too soon. He was getting

1

rare straggly. But Lord! How the stuff do grow this weather! 'Tis out of bounds almost afore you've done a-trimmin' of it."

As Andrew showed no sign of rising to this conversational bait, beyond a vague assent, the postman wished him "good afternoon", took another glance at the hedge and turned back down the lane, a little disconcerted by Mr Barton's unwonted taciturnity.

"Didn't seem to like the look of that letter," he mused as he swung along in his heavy, nailed boots. "Someone dunning him for money, maybe."

It was a simple and reasonable explanation of the sudden change in Andrew's expression as he read the address on the envelope and glanced at the postmark, and not so very wide of the truth. But "dunning" was not quite the right word, since that implies a demand for payment of a lawful debt. Of such demands Andrew Barton had no experience, being a scrupulously prompt paymaster. But a glance at the too-familiar handwriting prepared him for a demand of another kind, and the only question was, "How much does he want this time?" He tore the envelope open with angry impatience and read the answer to that question.

16, Barleymow Street,
Crompton-on-Sea.
21<sup>st</sup> August, 1928.

My dear Old Chappie,

What a time it is since I had the felicity of looking at your blessed old mug! Years and years! I am just pining for the sight of you; and no doubt you are equally pining for the sight of me. I hope so. Because I am going to satisfy my yearning and I should like to satisfy yours at the same time. In short, I propose to pop over this day week and shed the light of my countenance on you and Molly. I shall turn up to lunch.

Your affectionate and devoted,
though unfortunate cousin,

Ronald.

P.S. I have just got the offer of a top-hole job in the North. £300 a year and commission. But the fly in the ointment is that they want me to deposit £50, and I haven't got it. I hope you will be able to help me to that extent, for it would be a thousand pities to miss a chance like this. Of course, I shall be able to let you have it back in a month or two, with five per cent interest if you like. Further particulars when we meet. By the way, if you should be writing to me, please address me as Mr Walter Green. I am adopting that name temporarily, for business reasons.

R.B.

Andrew read the letter through twice, returned it to its envelope and put it away in his pocket-book. Then he resumed his operations on the hedge, with increased energy but diminished attention, whereby its symmetry was somewhat impaired but the job was more speedily completed. When the last savage snip had done its work, he hastily raked the cuttings together, conveyed them to the destructor in the back garden and deposited the shears and the rake in the tool-shed. Then he sauntered down to the studio which he had built at the bottom of the garden and let himself in with his key. A half-finished picture stood on the watercolour easel, the palette, brushes and water-dipper reposed invitingly on the table alongside, and the Windsor chair seemed silently to offer its services. He sat down wearily. He even dipped a brush in the water. But it would not do. Painting is no occupation for a mentally preoccupied man. Finally he rose, and, leaving the studio, walked up to the house, where he scribbled a note to his wife and laid it on the hall table (they kept no maid, and the daily "help" had gone after lunch), put on his hat and went forth, turning to the right as he emerged from the gate and taking his way along the footpath that led across the fields.

His cousin's letter had given him matter for serious and somewhat difficult thought. As to the money, the nominal loan – which would certainly never be repaid – was an inconvenience to a man of his modest means. But it was not that which disturbed him. He was used to being "milked" periodically by this thriftless scallywag, who was always in low water and always on the point of making his fortune. But these transactions had been conducted through the post. They involved no personal contact. It was the threatened visit that was the cause of his trouble and that gave him so difficult a problem to solve. For on one point he was resolved; that visit must not be allowed to take place. And, furthermore, Molly must not become aware that it had been proposed. He would, if it must be, submit to the extortions of this wastrel, if not with pleasure, at least with resignation. But he would not have him in his house. And thereby hangs a tale which may as well be told now, to the end that the reader of this narrative may start with a clear understanding of all the circumstances.

Andrew Barton's life lay under the shadow of a tragedy. The origin of that tragedy was insignificant even to triviality. But so it is in the affairs of men; from the merest trifles consequences develop which bear no reasonable proportion to their determining antecedents. The chance burrowing of a mole robbed a nation of its king; a trivial error of our most remote ancestress "Brought death into the world and all our woe." The tragedy that darkened Andrew Barton's life was due to nothing more impressive than a misplaced cricket ball.

But, on occasion, a cricket ball can be a formidable missile. This one, driven by a vigorous stroke of the bat, impinged with a terrific impact on Andrew's face between the eyes, just below the level of the brows, and laid him on the field insensible and gory. Perhaps something in the way of plastic surgery might have been done; but, for a time, his condition was so critical as to occupy the whole of the doctor's attention in the effort to save his life; and when at length his recovery was assured it was too late. The fractured nasal bones had united firmly in their displaced position.

It was a tragedy indeed. The Andrew Barton who had gone to the cricket match was a rather strikingly handsome young man. The convalescent who came out of the hospital was one at whom the passing wayfarer cast one curious glance and then looked away. The fine Grecian nose was flattened level with the cheek-bones, excepting the uninjured tip, which jutted out from the face like a sparrow's beak.

The disfigurement alone was tragedy enough, especially to an artistic young man who had been accustomed to take an innocent pleasure in his own good looks. But his exaggerated disgust of his uncomely face and the self-consciousness that it engendered were not the worst results of the disaster. There was his wife. To do her justice, she made heroic efforts, in her pity and sympathy, to appear unaware of the change. But her efforts to seem not to notice the disfigurement were misinterpreted. To him, with his morbid conviction that he was a curiosity of hideousness, the fact that she seemed to avoid looking at his battered nose conveyed the impression that she could not bear the repulsive spectacle. In short, in respect of his personal appearance, Andrew suffered in an intense degree from what it is fashionable to call "an inferiority complex"; and that complex led him to take a perverted view of his relations with his wife.

The marriage had been a typical love-match; but, in its beginnings, very largely based on physical attraction. The beautiful girl and the handsome young man had fallen in love with each other's good looks; which, as they were both amiable, kindly and pleasant mannered, was not a bad start. But at that their relations had tended to remain. They continued to be lovers, mutually devoted; but the deeper comradeship of man and wife seemed slow to develop.

The fault was undoubtedly with Molly. Unconsciously, she made the fatal mistake of failing to enter into her husband's chief interest. Andrew was devoted to his art. She was aware of the fact and took it for granted, but she made no attempt to share his artistic interests. She admired his pictures, was pleased with the recognition that they received and praised them in somewhat inexpert terms; indeed, the rather naive and ignorant comments that she made jarred on him, so that he unobtrusively discouraged her from frequenting the studio. So she tended to live her woman's life apart, treating the studio and its activities as matters outside her province. The love and mutual admiration that had brought them together had continued unchanged and undiminished during their married life up to the time of the accident; nor was there, even then, any sign of a change. But still, they were little more than lovers.

Hence, it was not perhaps unnatural that, when the misfortune befell, Andrew should experience a certain sense of having failed to keep his covenant. Molly had married a handsome man and had given her beauty in exchange. And now the bargain was, on his side, unfulfilled. He still received, but had nothing to give. Still, he could delight in her loveliness and charm; but she must put up with a husband who was a monster of ugliness. It was rather unreasonable and perverse, and it was largely untrue. But that was what he felt. And he felt it bitterly.

But his fatal misadventure had yet another unfortunate effect; which brings us back to our story. Andrew had but one near relative – his cousin Ronald. Ronald, however, was a very near relative indeed. He was, in fact, a cousin twice over; for, not only was his father a brother of Andrew's father, but his mother was a sister of Andrew's mother. In view of this double relationship, it is not surprising that the two men were a good deal alike. Actually they were as much alike as a pair of twins. But the remarkable resemblance was masked to some extent by the one point of difference. Andrew's nose had been of the straight, or Grecian type; Ronald's was curved on the bridge – a definite Roman nose. Now, a Roman nose imparts a very distinctive character to a face, particularly in profile; and hence this really trifling difference served effectually to disguise the fact that these two men were almost identically alike.

Nor was the resemblance limited to the facial characteristics. As in the case of twins, it pervaded the whole personality. They were of much the same colouring, stature and figure. Their voices and intonations were recognizably similar; and even in those elusive muscular habits which express themselves in pose and gait, there was in each man a suggestion of the other.

Their mental similarity was less marked. But yet it was distinguishable. For Ronald was not devoid of artistic aptitude. He painted in a somewhat dilettante fashion, and could have done better if he had taken more trouble; and in other respects he showed a certain mental affinity to his cousin. But just as the almost uncanny physical resemblance was masked by a single salient dissimilarity, so,

6

but in a much more marked degree, were the mental resemblances masked by a profound contrast in the moral qualities. It seemed as if, in Ronald, some "recessive" moral taint, which had lain dormant for a generation or two, had suddenly come to the surface. He was an undeniably "bad egg". To the precise, thrifty, conscientious Andrew, his thriftless, slippery cousin was an object of puzzled contempt and, moreover, a source of constant anxiety. For Ronald Barton was an inveterate cadger, a confirmed borrower; and, as is the way of the habitual borrower, as soon as the loan had been obtained, the transaction was finished and the incident closed so far as he was concerned. Thus it happened that at the end of each year, Andrew found his bank balance substantially eaten into by the "trifling loans" that this plausible rascal had wheedled out of him.

But, as we have already hinted, it was not the drain on his resources that was troubling him now. He had accepted Ronald – his only near kinsman – as a sort of troublesome younger brother and was resigned to his extortions. What was disturbing him so profoundly was the fear that he might not be able to stave off the proposed visit. He loathed the very idea of having his cousin under his roof; and especially did he loathe the idea of any association between Ronald and Molly.

That was the real trouble. It was not that he was in general a jealous man or that he had the slightest mistrust of his wife. But he distrusted Ronald profoundly. Of that gentleman's mode of life he knew nothing; but he suspected a good deal. And he was very clearly convinced that this shabby knave was no fit associate for Molly. And there were certain special reasons why he disliked the idea of their meeting.

They had met twice. The first time was shortly after the wedding, and, then, Andrew had been not displeased by Molly's warm admiration of his cousin. For Ronald was an undeniably fine-looking young man, and he had been on his best behaviour.

But the second meeting had been a very different affair. The experience had been one of which Andrew could not bear to think. It had occurred soon after the accident, when the "inferiority complex" was at its worst, and Andrew had found himself constantly following Ronald with his eyes, noting with envy the strikingly handsome face and the swaggering, confident carriage, and contrasting them with his own hideousness and insignificance. And he suspected that Molly was making a like comparison, and he knew that Ronald was. For, on this occasion, that gentleman had been somewhat less discreet. Ostentatiously respectful, with a certain oily civility, he was nevertheless disposed to assert the privileges of cousinship with an insinuating familiarity that made Andrew squirm. And, beneath his deferential manner there seemed a sinister suggestion of a new consciousness of power; a suggestion that he had discovered a new way to put on the screw if the need should arise. Andrew had then and there determined that he should never come into the house again.

To that resolution he still held firmly. But the problem that he had to solve was how, decently, to evade the proposed visit. He could not write bluntly refusing it, and, even if he did, the thick-skinned Ronald would pretty certainly come, notwithstanding. In any case, there would be a letter in reply, which Molly would probably see; and then he would have to tell her of the proposal, and it would be difficult to explain his objection. But he wanted to keep the whole affair from her knowledge. In this he was, perhaps, unwise. It would certainly have been simpler to accept the visit and prepare Molly with a few words of advice and caution. But he could not do it. Deep down in his soul was a feeling that bade him keep Ronald completely out of her life.

Thus he turned his difficulties over and over as he strode along the footpath through the fields. And gradually a plan shaped itself in his mind. It was quite a simple one. He would first send Ronald a postcard acknowledging his letter but making no comment. Then, on the day before that of the proposed visit, he would send a letter stating that he had some business in Crompton – which was only thirty miles distant – and would call on Ronald to talk over the financial situation. There would be no time for an answer to his letter, and, if he agreed to the "loan" – which experience told him he probably would – the matter would be settled and the reason for the unwelcome visit would cease to exist.

There was only one detail at which he boggled. If he went to Crompton, he would be away from home all day, and he would have to give Molly some sort of explanation of his absence. And it could not be a true explanation. It seemed a small matter. But Andrew hated the making of a directly untrue statement at any time, and especially did he hate the idea of telling his wife a lie. However, it seemed that there was no choice. The only way in which his day's absence from home could be simply and naturally explained would be by saying that he was going up to London to show some of his work to a dealer; and that was the course that he decided to adopt.

When he arrived home, he found, rather to his relief, that Molly had not yet returned. With his decision fresh in his mind, he went straight to the writing table in the sitting-room and wrote a brief note to Ronald, acknowledging his letter. Having sealed and stamped it, he dropped it into his pocket, ready for posting later, and then went into the little kitchen to make preparations for tea. But still, as he filled the kettle and set it on the gas ring, collected the tea-things and arranged them on the tray, his perplexities and the plans he had made to solve them continued to revolve in his mind as a sort of background to his present occupation. Impatiently, he tried to dismiss them. He had decided what to do, and further thought was but a useless, purposeless travelling back and forth over the same ground. But the emotional jar that Ronald's letter had inflicted, with its vivid revival of unpleasant memories, had disturbed him profoundly; and, strive as he would to concentrate his attention on what he was doing, he could not silence the running accompaniment of futile reflection. Nevertheless, he carried out his task quite efficiently and with careful consideration of Molly's very definite views on the niceties of the tea-table. The embroidered tea-cloth was spread on the table in the sitting-room in exactly the correct manner and garnished with little top-heavy flower glasses, artfully disposed so as to develop the maximum of inconvenience and liability to capsize. The tray, symmetrically set with its proper appointments – excepting the teapot and hot-water jug, which lurked in the kitchen awaiting the co-operation of the kettle – was placed at the head of the table. Biscuit box, cake basket, butter dish, jam and preserve jars and other minor articles of "family plate" were posted with the strictest regard to their customary stations (and with no regard at all to the fact that the biscuit box was empty and there was no cake). In Molly's mind the "five o'clock tea" tradition still lingered, and the occasion was one of some ceremony.

When he had laid the table, Andrew surveyed his work critically, and, having decided that all was in order, proceeded to cut some wafery slices of brown bread and butter, which he adroitly rolled up into little sausage-like scrolls. Of these he prepared quite an imposing pile, in view of Molly's partiality for them and of the fact that she usually returned from her expeditions in a state of ravenous hunger (she had gone over for an afternoon's shopping to the little town of Bunsford, some two miles away).

At length he laid down his knife, and, having taken a glance at the kettle, went out to the garden gate and looked down the lane. His wife had just turned into it from the road and was now advancing briskly with an enormous parcel in either hand and a smaller one tucked under her arm. For a moment he was disposed to run and meet her and relieve her of her burdens, but, experience having taught him that Molly's parcels usually ran to bulk rather than weight, he turned back into the house, leaving the garden gate and the front door ajar, and went to the kitchen to make the tea.

He had just placed the silver teapot and hot-water jug on the tray when he heard her coming up the garden path, whistling cheerfully to announce her approach. He went out into the hall to welcome her, and, when she had held up her face for the customary kiss, she tenderly deposited her parcels on the hall table.

"You seem to have been going it," Andrew remarked, with an eye on the parcels.

"I have," she admitted. "I've had a lovely time – a regular beano. They were simply giving the things away, so, of course, economy suggested that one should take the opportunity. And I did. I've bought no end of things. You shall see what I have brought with me, presently;

the rest are being sent. Do I smell tea? I hope so, for I am simply starving."

She entered the sitting-room and stood for a moment regarding the arrangements with smiling approval.

"How nicely you've laid the table, Andy," she exclaimed, "and, my word! what a heap of roly-polys you've cut."

She picked one up and bit off half. Then she continued, with slightly impaired enunciation: "There are some pastries in a box on the hall table. Puffs and things. I hope I haven't squashed them under my arm. I was nearly eating them in the train. Shopping *does* make you hungry."

Andrew fetched in the box and transferred its contents – bilious little tarts and cakes and three-cornered puffs, apparently produced with the aid of a pair of bellows – to the cake basket. Then he lifted Molly's hat off – it came off quite easily, being of the coalscuttle-extinguisher type then in vogue – while she placidly poured out the tea with one hand and fed herself with the other, continuing her cheerful babbling, punctuated with mastication.

Andrew sat down at the table, and, as he sipped his tea, looked thoughtfully at his wife. Perhaps a little furtively, too, with an unpleasant and guilty consciousness of the letter in his pocket. But principally his mind was occupied, half-unconsciously, in admiring contemplation of his beautiful wife. Her charm seemed to him always new, as something freshly discovered. To look at her was a pleasure that never staled. It was not only that he was as much, or even more, in love with her as ever, but as an artist, and a figure-painter at that, he was peculiarly sensitive and appreciative of human beauty, and especially the beauty of women.

"So you've had a good day's sport," said Andrew.

"Rather!" she replied, in a tone of deep satisfaction. "Of course, Bunsford is not like London, but there are quite a lot of good shops there. And didn't I turn them upside down! And didn't I make the money fly! You'll have to hurry up and sell some more pictures or we shall be on the rocks."

11

Now, Andrew knew quite well that this was all nonsense. Molly's little raids on the Bunsford shops were dissipations of the most inexpensive sort. She never nearly spent the hundred pounds a year that had come to her on her father's death. Nevertheless, he seized the opportunity.

"Yes," said he, "it is about time I raked in some fresh supplies. There are one or two small things that I have got on hand, ready for the market. I must take them up to Montagu and turn them into cash."

"You needn't, Andy," she said, with one of her delightful dimpling smiles. "I was only joking. I didn't really spend much, and I've got quite a lot in the bank."

"I know, dear," he replied. "I wasn't such a mug as to take you seriously. But still, I think I may as well take those things up to Monty. It's no use keeping stuff in the studio cupboard. I think I will go up one day next week, probably Tuesday."

She made no comment on this proposal, and their talk drifted into other channels. After tea she produced the two hats – the principal spoils of the raid – and exhibited them to Andrew; who looked at them as Lord Dundreary looked at the chimpanzee, with surprise and incomprehension. (The feminine hat is usually outside the scope of the masculine intellect, and the hats of that period were beyond belief as things intentionally created.) Then Molly went about her lawful domestic occasions, and Andrew sneaked out to drop his letter into the postbox down in the village. It was a harmless letter, devoid of significance and committing him to nothing. Yet, as he held it in the slit of the postbox, he felt an unaccountable reluctance to let it go; and when at length he released it and heard it fall to the bottom of the box, he had the sense of having done something portentous and irrevocable.

# CHAPTER TWO

## Alarums and Excursions

The days that followed slipped by slowly and wearily, charged for Andrew with anxiety and unhappiness. Unhappiness because he had, for the first time in his married life, a secret which he was withholding from Molly. And in his heart he felt that it was a discreditable secret, of which he would be ashamed if it should ever leak out. This was the chief occasion of his anxiety. For there was the chance that something might upset his plan; and, if it did, he would have to explain. But what could he say? To Molly it would appear as if he distrusted her, and who could say that she would be wrong? Was there not some distrust implied in his repugnance to her meeting Ronald? It was a dreadful thing to think of, for, hitherto, the most perfect confidence had existed between him and his wife; and no woman could be more irreproachable in her conduct than Molly.

Still he went on making the few preparations that were necessary. From his bank at Bunsford he drew out fifty pounds in cash (paying in an equivalent cheque on his London bank) in case Ronald should be unable to deal with a cheque; and, to meet the alternative case, he drew a cheque on the London account to the order of Ronald Barton, Esq., and put it in the attaché case that he kept in the studio cupboard. Then, with great care, he drafted the letter which he proposed to send to Ronald. He dated it the 26th of August – Sunday – though, in fact, he proposed to post it early on Monday, so that it should be delivered on Monday evening or by the first post on

Tuesday morning – in either case in time to prevent Ronald from coming, but not in time to allow of a reply. It was but a short letter, and, in its final form, ran thus:

Willow Cottage, Fairfield.
26th August, 1928

My dear Ronald,

It happens by a fortunate chance that I have to run over to Crompton on business. I say "fortunate" because we shall have certain matters of a rather private nature to discuss and we can do that better in your rooms than here.

I don't know quite how long my business will take, but I shall turn up at your diggings punctually at one o'clock, when we may, perhaps, go somewhere and get some lunch, before beginning our discussions.

Yours ever,

Andrew.

It was not without some qualms that he concocted this mendacious epistle, and when he had finished it and addressed and stamped the envelope, he hid it away securely in the attaché case until the time should come for posting it. Finally, into the same receptacle he put one or two small and trivial paintings – little more than sketches – which he had hardly thought worth offering to his dealer. Of course, he was not going to offer them now. Their presence in the attaché case was merely a concession to sentiment. He didn't want to tell more lies than were absolutely necessary.

Now that he had made all his preparations, it would have seemed reasonable for him to dismiss the matter from his mind until the time for action should arrive. But this he was quite unable to do. The emotional upset, which was at the root of the whole rather foolish business, kept his mind unsettled and exaggerated the effect of his guilty consciousness of his secret and his anxiety lest some unforeseen hitch should occur. The result was that he found himself everlastingly revolving the details of his plan, considering what he should say to

14

Ronald and what he should do if, by any disastrous chance, his scheme should miscarry and his deception should become known to Molly.

In order to be alone and free to think his futile thoughts, he spent much of his time in the studio. He tried to work. He had a rather important picture well started, and, in his normal state of mind, it would have been easy and pleasant to carry on. But after a single attempt he had to desist for fear of spoiling what he had already done.

In the evenings, his restlessness and a curious shyness of his wife's society drove him out to stride impatiently across the fields or along the little-frequented road, chewing the cud of useless and purposeless reflection. He had better have stayed at home and listened to Molly's cheerful gossip, for thereby he would have avoided a world of trouble. But no man can foresee the little surprises that Fate has in store for him; and so it was that Andrew, taking his way along the darkening road, walked straight into the ambush that chance had prepared.

The week had nearly run out, for it was the Monday evening, the evening before the appointed day of his visit to Crompton, when he set forth in his old studio jacket, hatless and unadorned by the spectacles that he wore in more populous places to mitigate the effects of his disfigurement, to tramp along the road and think out once again the details of his proceedings on the morrow. He had posted his letter to Ronald in time for the eleven o'clock collection and everything was ready for his journey. By this time tomorrow, he thought, his difficulties would be over. He would have paid out the money, have disposed of his wastrel cousin and would be free to take up again the normal course of his life.

Thus preoccupied he swung along, taking little note of his surroundings. At long intervals the headlights of an approaching car started out of the gathering gloom, glared on him for a moment and were gone; or overtaking him, cast his attenuated shadow along the lighted surface of the road with increasing intensity until it culminated in an instant of dazzle, a whizz, a hum of mechanism and a dwindling red light fading into the darkness.

It was at the crossroads, known locally as Ribble's Cross, that the incredible affair happened. Preoccupied as he was, a stationary car drawn up at the corner of the side road made little impression on him, though he saw it and could hear the engine running, and was dimly aware of two men lurking near the car. But wrapped in his own thoughts, he gave them but a passing, inattentive glance and straightaway forgot their existence. A few moments later, a bright light streamed past him from behind, then a car came abreast of him and drew up abruptly with a shriek of the brakes and an irritable voice demanded: "Well, what is it?"

Andrew gazed in astonishment at the speaker – a hard-faced elderly man who appeared to be addressing him – and stepped up to the open window to ask what he meant. As he put his head in at the window, the light of an electric torch flashed full in his face; but in spite of the dazzling light he could see that the man had his other hand thrust into his hip pocket. He could also see a middle-aged woman grasping the driving wheel and staring at him with an expression of consternation. He was about to put his question – in fact he had begun to speak – when he felt both his wrists seized in a vice-like grip and held together behind his back. Simultaneously, a hand grasping a pistol was thrust over his shoulder and a voice from behind him commanded:

"Put 'em up. Both of you."

Exactly what happened during the next few seconds Andrew never clearly knew. As he felt his wrists grasped, he struggled to turn round and became aware of two men whose faces were hidden by black masks. At the same moment, the man in the car made a quick movement with his farther hand. An instant later there was a double report with the sound of shattering glass; a piercing scream from the woman, a grinding noise from the engine, and the car leaped forward. In another moment it had gathered speed and was receding swiftly into the darkness. As the reports rang out, Andrew felt his wrists released, and, turning quickly, he saw the two men running furiously towards their car and heard a whimpering voice exclaim:

"You blasted fool! Couldn't you see it was the wrong man? And you've done him in."

Andrew stood, bewildered and half-stupefied, looking at the retreating bandits. They were still talking excitedly but he could not hear what they were saying. Soon, they reached their car, tumbled in hurriedly and slammed the door. Again, there was a grinding sound; the car started forward, turned up the side road, and was quickly lost to sight between the hedgerows. The hum of the engine soon died away and Andrew was left standing alone in the silence of the deserted road.

He tried to collect his scattered wits and to realize what had happened. It was an astounding affair. The audacity of these ruffians in attempting a highway robbery in the presence of a witness seemed amazing. Yet, but for the circumstance that the passenger in the car had been armed, it might easily have been done. The presence of an unarmed stranger would have offered no hindrance to two armed and masked men.

But what had really happened? Was it true that that stern-faced elderly man had been "done in", or was this only a frightened man's conjecture? Almost certainly the latter, for there had been no time to ascertain the effects of the shot. Perhaps there was no harm done, after all, beyond the smashing of the windscreen. Meanwhile, the question arose as to what he ought to do. At first he was disposed to hurry back to Fairfield and give information to the police; but on reflection, that seemed a futile thing to do, for, long before he could reach the village, the woman who was driving the car would have reported the outrage to the police, at the next town. Moreover, there was no police station at Fairfield and only a police patrol who was sent out to the village from Bunsford. Finally, he decided to notify the police at Bunsford on the morrow, though even that would be of little use, seeing that he would be totally unable to identify either of the men or give any description of them.

While he had been turning these questions over in his mind, he had been retracing his steps along the road; for the shock that he had sustained had effectually diverted his thoughts from his domestic troubles and the solitary countryside ceased to attract him. Presently he came to a stile at the entrance to a footpath which led in a nearly straight line to the village. Here he paused for a few moments and looked back along the road. In the far distance the headlights of a car appeared as bright sparks of light on the dark background. He watched them, as he stood with one foot on the lower step of the stile, with a feeling of faint dislike. At the moment, the idea of a motorcar seemed to have unpleasant associations. After looking for a few seconds at the distant lights, which grew brighter as he looked, he mounted the stile, and, stepping down on to the footpath, set forth on the short cut across the fields.

There was no lack of matter for conversation with Molly that night. As he poured out the thrilling story of his adventure, she almost lost interest in the hat, on which she was performing some kind of minor operation, in the wonder and horror of the tale.

"But what impudence and bravado!" she exclaimed. "They seem to have gone on just as if you hadn't been there."

"I shouldn't have been much good in any case," said Andrew. "They were probably both armed. At any rate one of them was, and he was pretty ready with his pistol."

"Yes," said she, "I am glad you weren't able to interfere. You might have been lying dead at this moment. I wonder if that poor man in the car was really killed."

"I hope not," said Andrew, "but I am afraid he was hit. He could hardly fail to have been seeing that the muzzle of the pistol was within a foot of him. I suppose I had better drop in tomorrow morning at the police station at Bunsford and give my name and address in case they want to call me as a witness."

Molly laid down her work and looked at him anxiously.

"Do you know, Andy," she said, "I don't think I would if I were you. Why say anything about it to anybody? You have got nothing to tell that would help the police. You wouldn't know the men again if you saw them. It is a horrible affair. There may have been murder done. Don't you think it would be better for you to keep right out of it? Nobody knows that you were there, and nobody need ever know."

"The woman in the car saw me, you know," said Andrew.

"Yes," retorted Molly, whisking about with that mental agility which is the peculiar gift of woman, "and she probably took you for one of the gang. And if she did, she will swear through thick and thin that you were. You know how positive women are when they have got an idea into their heads."

He did – Molly, herself, having contributed some striking instances; and he realized that she had put her finger on the one possible complication. Nevertheless, he did not like the idea of lying low when it was certain that inquiries would presently be made.

"Well," she urged, when he pointed this out, "wait till they are made, and see what sort of inquiries they are. If the police advertise for the witness who saw the attack, you can come forward. In the meantime, keep your own counsel; and don't go out of the house without your spectacles."

The serious view that she took of the matter tended to transfer itself to him, though the conclusion of their talk still left the question unsettled in his mind. But as to the wisdom of her advice in regard to the spectacles he had no doubt. Until he announced himself, he had better remain unrecognized. And the spectacles were a very efficient disguise, having, in fact, been designed expressly for that purpose. The horn rims enclosed lenses which were virtually plain glass, to offer the least possible obstruction to Andrew's excellent vision. The part of them which really functioned was the bridge; which was provided with a broad, saddle-shaped guard of flesh-coloured celluloid which occupied the hollow where the bridge of the nose should have been, and, to a great extent, concealed the deficiency. He almost invariably wore them out of doors; and it was due only to the failing light and his mentally disturbed state that he had gone out this evening without them.

The morning found him still undecided as to what he should do, though Molly renewed her admonitions during breakfast. But now the unpleasant business that he had in hand once more began to occupy his thoughts to the exclusion of everything else. The guilty consciousness of the deception that he was practising on his wife worried him intensely and made him impatient to be gone.

19

Immediately after breakfast, he fetched his attaché case – packed in readiness on the previous day – from the studio, put on his spectacles and made ready to depart.

"I suppose, dear," said Molly, as she accompanied him to the outer door and gave him a farewell kiss, "you won't be very late home tonight?"

"I don't expect to be," he replied. "Still, you had better not stay up if I am not home by about ten."

With this he kissed her again, and, turning away, strode briskly down the path. At the gate he looked back and waved his hand. Then he started at a good pace towards the station, with a sense of relief at having got so far without a mishap. Only a few hours more, now, and he would be clear of his worries and would be his own man again. And once again as he swung along, he debated whether he should or should not call at Bunsford police station.

But the question was decided for him by circumstance. As the train on the little branch line from Fairfield drew up in Bunsford Station, he found that a train from London to Crompton was signalled and already in sight down the line. It was a full three-quarters of an hour earlier than the one that he had intended to travel by and would bring him to Crompton that much before his time. Nevertheless, in his impatience to get clear of his own neighbourhood, he welcomed it, and hurried across to the booking office. A couple of minutes later, the train drew up at the platform. It was only moderately full and he was able to secure a first-class smoking compartment to himself. While the train lingered in the station, he peered out anxiously, but no one came to disturb the solitude for which he yearned. At length, the guard's whistle sounded and the train began to move.

He heaved a deep sigh of relief, and as the train gathered speed he proceeded deliberately to fill his pipe. Then he took out Ronald's letter from his letter-case, read it through slowly from the address to the signature and tore it into minute fragments, which he allowed to flutter out of the window. Then he opened his attaché case and carefully checked its contents; and when he had done this, he leaned back, relighted his pipe and once more began to revolve in his mind the problem of how he should deal with Ronald.

The money question did not trouble him appreciably. He had in the attaché case, in two blank envelopes, a cheque for fifty pounds drawn to Ronald's order and a bundle of fifty pound notes. He took it for granted that one of those two envelopes would be transferred to Ronald – preferably the cheque; or, if it had to be the notes, he would tear up the cheque and cancel the counterfoil. That was all plain sailing, and, though it irked him to pour his earnings into the bottomless pocket of this worthless spendthrift, he would accept the loss with resignation. The real problem was how to keep Ronald away from Fairfield. Supposing that even after the money had been paid, he should persist in his intention of making the visit? What was to be done? Could Andrew tell him bluntly that his presence would not be acceptable? It would be very uncomfortable. And even so, Ronald was uncommonly thick-skinned.

He would not be easily put off if he wanted to come.

It was a difficult problem; and Andrew had not solved it satisfactorily when the train rolled into the station at Crompton and came to rest at the platform.

# CHAPTER THREE
## In the Midst of Life

Andrew's first proceeding on coming out of the station was to make enquiries at the baker's shop, which was also a post office, for the address of a picture dealer. Of course he knew that there would be no picture dealer, as he understood the term, in a town like Crompton; nor had he any expectation of transacting any business whatever. The enquiry, like the pictures in his attaché case, was a mere concession to sentiment. He had told Ronald that he had business in Crompton, and he felt that he must make some pretence of business. It was mere foolish make-believe, and he knew it; but to a man habitually truthful, as he was, there is perhaps a shade of difference between a statement, true in the letter though false in the spirit, and one without even a foundation of truth. At any rate, that was how he felt about it.

"A picture dealer," the woman in the shop repeated, reflectively. "I don't know of any regular picture dealer in Crompton. There's Mr Cooper in the High Street, he sells pictures. He calls himself a carver and gilder. He's the only one I know of."

"I expect he will do," said Andrew, with literal truth this time, and, having thanked the woman, he went forth in search of the High Street and Mr Cooper.

The former was found easily enough, and the latter after a very brief exploration. Andrew stood for a while outside the shop and examined the contents of the window. There were a few brushes and tubes of colour, several empty frames and half a dozen "original

22

watercolours." As the most ambitious of these was priced at eighteen shillings the pair, including the frames, the prospect of any business grew still more remote. Nevertheless, Andrew entered the shop, and, by way of breaking the matter gently, began with the request for a tube of Winsor and Newton's cobalt. When this had been handed to him, he laid his attaché case on the counter and opened his "business".

"Do you do anything in the way of buying pictures?" he asked.

Mr Cooper was cautious. "I don't buy a lot," said he, "but I am always ready to look at samples. Have you got any with you?"

Andrew opened his case and produced his "samples", which the dealer took in his hands and looked at suspiciously.

"Are these originals?" he asked. "They look like reproductions."

"No," replied Andrew, "they are originals; my own work."

Mr Cooper examined them again with renewed interest. After a prolonged inspection, he inquired: "How much?"

"Five guineas each," Andrew replied.

The dealer stiffened and cast a startled glance at the artist.

"Did you say five guineas each?" he demanded, incredulously.

Andrew repeated the statement, whereupon the dealer hastily deposited the paintings in the open attaché case and shook his head sadly but emphatically.

"I don't say they may not be worth it," said he, "but I have to sell pictures cheap, and find the frames myself. Five shillings a drawing is my outside price."

Andrew was not surprised or disappointed. The interview had served its purpose. It had been a business transaction and had conferred a quality of literal truth on his statement to Ronald. Satisfied with this make-believe, he repacked his pictures and closed his attaché case. Then, after a few minutes' amicable chat with the dealer, he wished him "good morning" and took his leave.

His premature arrival at Crompton left him with a full hour to dispose of before keeping his tryst at Ronald's lodgings. He was not inclined to call there before he was due, with the chance of finding his cousin absent and being brought into undesired contact with the landlady; and, moreover, he still had the foolish urge to consider over again what he would say to Ronald at the coming interview. Accordingly, he spent the time rambling up and down the streets, looking with rather wandering attention into the shop windows and examining the general features of the town.

First he proceeded to ascertain the whereabouts of the street in which his cousin lived, and, having found it, to locate approximately the number, 16. Barleymow Street was a respectable though rather shabby street, mostly consisting of private houses with a few shops. Near one end was an archway leading into a kind of alley, and, above the arch was a blue lamp bearing the words, "Police Station", while, on the space of wall beside the arch was a large board covered with printed bills containing announcements of persons missing, wanted or found drowned, and other similar police notices. Here he lingered for a while, reading these rather gruesome advertisements and once more considering irresolutely whether he ought not to step in and make his report of the incident of the previous night.

It was a more momentous question than he realized; but, fortunately, he took the right decision, though whether that decision was due to Molly's admonitions or his preoccupation with his present business it is impossible to say. At any rate, he decided to wait until he was back in his own neighbourhood and turned away in search of further objects of interest.

Such an object he found near the opposite end of the street, and the oddity of it diverted his attention for the moment from his immediate anxieties and preoccupations. It was in a large window – a sort of hybrid between a shop and a private house – and consisted of a handwritten placard executed in bold roman capitals announcing that these premises were occupied by no less a person than Professor Booley, late of Boston, USA (popularly believed to be the hub of the universe). It set forth that the said Professor was a specialist in the beautification of the Human Countenance, and gave in emphatic and even dictatorial terms a number of items of advice coupled with reasoned suggestions. Thus:

"Good looks are the surest passports to success. If nature hasn't given them to you, come in and let me make good her failure.

Why have eyebrows all awry when the specialist can set them fair and even?

Why have a wrinkled face? Don't. Come right in and have your skin made as smooth as a baby's.

Why have a crooked nose? Don't. Let me straighten it out.

Don't be content with a back seat because you were born homely. Come into my parlor and be made fit for a place in the front row."

Andrew stood before the window, reading these adjurations and commands with a faint smile, in which, however, there was more of wistfulness than amusement. Doubtless, the Professor was a quack of the deepest dye; but he had set forth a truth of which no one could be more sensible than the spectacled reader who stood before the window. Dimly as he had realized the value of good looks when the precious gift was his, his loss had made it but too clear. What most men experience only with advancing years, he had experienced in the heyday of his manhood.

He sauntered on, musing whimsically on the Professor's procedure. How did that redoubtable operator set about smoothing out wrinkles? A flat iron hardly seemed to meet the case. And how did he straighten out a crooked nose? The question evoked a ridiculous picture of the Professor tapping out the patient's proboscis on an anvil, or bringing it to a straight line by means of a screw clamp. If only the Professor's claims could be taken seriously! Though, to be sure, even Professor Booley had not claimed to be able to create a new nose on the foundations of one that had been battered out of existence.

Slowly his saunterings and shop-gazings consumed the time, as he noted by an occasional glance at his watch; and punctually at two minutes to one he turned again into Barleymow Street. There was no need for him to check the numbers afresh, for, at the middle of the street, where he had located number sixteen, his cousin was already waiting, slowly pacing up and down before his doorway, and at the moment with his back turned towards Andrew. Then he swung round, and, catching sight of his cousin, started forward briskly with a smile of recognition and greeting.

As the two men approached, they regarded each other critically, and Andrew noted with something like a pang of envy what a really fine-looking man his cousin was; such a man as he, himself, had been but a year or two ago.

"Here you are, then," said Ronald, grasping his hand effusively, "punctual to the minute as usual. You ought to have been a business man instead of an artist."

"There is no reason why one should not be both," said Andrew.

"Answered with your customary wisdom," rejoined Ronald. "And, speaking of business, have you polished off the little affair that brought you to the unlikely region of Crompton-on-Sea?"

As he asked the question, Ronald's face exhibited a faint smirk which brought an angry flush to his cousin's cheek. Obviously, Ronald was slightly sceptical of the business appointment; but he might have kept his scepticism to himself.

"Yes," Andrew replied, "it didn't take more than a few minutes."

"I hope you brought off the deal," said Ronald.

"No," replied Andrew, "there was nothing doing; at least, not at my price. Better luck next time, perhaps. Do you know of a likely place where we can get some lunch?"

"I know a place that will suit us exactly," answered Ronald. "But you won't want to lug that attaché case about with you all day. We shall probably go for a walk after lunch. Shall I plant it in my digs until you want it again?"

Andrew accepted the suggestion gladly, having already had enough of the case, and handed it to Ronald, who let himself into the house with a latchkey and disappeared for a few moments. When he re-appeared, he linked his arm in Andrew's and led him away in the direction of the approved restaurant, which was situated at the farther end of the High Street and turned out to be a place of some pretensions. As they walked, Ronald chatted with the easy volubility of an accomplished salesman or cheap-jack on every subject but the one which was the occasion of their meeting, while Andrew listened half impatiently but with a certain grim amusement. He knew this trick of Ronald's of old. That slippery gentleman could never be brought to make a plain statement of the circumstances which called for the particular loan which he happened to be seeking. Instead, he managed with really remarkable skill to keep up a sort of conversational solo on all kinds of indifferent topics, always discreetly avoiding the one concerned with the financial transaction.

On this occasion, he got an excellent start as they passed the arched opening that led to the police station; for, at that moment, a bare-headed policeman was engaged in sticking a new bill on the notice board. They had only a glimpse of it in passing, but they were able to see that it was headed in bold type: "Wanted for Murder." That bill furnished Ronald with material for discourse – one could hardly call it conversation – until they reached the restaurant.

Andrew made no attempt to counter these manœuvres. In a contemptuous way he was slightly amused by his cousin's evasions; and he had no curiosity as to the "top-hole opening" which was the nominal occasion of the need for fifty pounds. Probably it was a myth covering some gambling transaction. That was really of no consequence. He had brought the money with him and he knew that presently he would hand it over. The only thing that mattered was that there should be no arrangement for a visit to Fairfield.

The lunch was a complete success. Andrew, himself, was pretty sharp set and Ronald's exploits suggested a recent period of abstemiousness. In fact, his concentration on alimentary activities hindered his conversation to an extent that enabled Andrew to get in a question or two on the subject of the "opening". But Ronald was not to be drawn.

"Yes, old chappie," said he, "we shall have to talk things over presently, though it's all pretty simple to a man of your business acumen. We might take a stroll in the country where we can talk at our ease. There's some quite pleasant country along the north coast. Quiet, too. Most of the visitors seem to keep to the south. By the way, those spectacles of yours are an excellent idea. You hadn't got them when I saw you last. I suppose you don't really want them for your eyesight, but that wide bridge covers up the scar so that you look quite like your old self."

Andrew noted the evasion with amused exasperation, but he made no further attempt to "get down to brass tacks". He sipped his coffee and assented passively to Ronald's suggestion of a green Chartreuse "to give the festivity a final kick". Then he paid the bill and went forth with his companion to see what the country walk might bring in the way of explanations.

It brought what he had expected; an endless stream of talk on the most diverse topics with a discreet avoidance of any references to the golden opportunity. Only once was that subject approached, and then merely in respect of that aspect of the transaction which to Ronald was the only one that mattered.

"By the way, old chappie," he said when Andrew had put out another feeler, "I suppose you have brought the rhino with you?"

"I have brought a cheque," Andrew replied.

Ronald's face fell. "That's a bit awkward," said he. "The fact is I haven't got a banking account at the moment. Didn't find my bank satisfactory and haven't got a new one yet."

Andrew made no comment; but a vision of the initials "R.D." arose before "the eye of his mind". Bankers are apt to develop an "unsatisfactory" attitude towards customers whose cheques have to be "referred to drawer", which, as Andrew knew, had happened in Ronald's case on more than one occasion.

"You see," Ronald continued, "it would hardly look well if I had to hand in your cheque for my deposit. They'd see that I had no banking account of my own, and that's just what I don't want them to know. I want to give the impression of a financially substantial person, as I shall have some of their money passing through my hands."

Andrew noted mentally the appropriateness of the phrase, "passing through my hands", and saw unpleasant possibilities looming in the future. He only hoped that "they", whoever they were – supposing them to have any real objective existence – would make suitable arrangements for "their" own security. Meanwhile he replied:

"It is an open cheque; but if that doesn't quite meet the case, I dare say I could manage to let you have cash. But I should like to know a little more about the business."

"Of course you would," Ronald agreed heartily, "though the essential fact is that I have to lay down fifty pounds as security before I can take up the appointment. Look at that jolly old windmill. What a pity they have taken the sails off! Makes it look such a ruinous affair. But they nearly always do, if they don't pull the whole thing down. Soon there won't be a complete windmill in the whole country."

Here he broke off into a discourse on windmills in particular and the deterioration of the countryside in general, and, for the time being, the subject of the security lapsed. It being obvious that he did not mean to be drawn into any intelligible account of the business transaction, real or imaginary, Andrew resigned himself to the inevitable and accepted the conversational lead; with the reservation that no arrangements for a visit to Fairfield were entertained.

Apart from its unpleasant antecedents, the walk was agreeable enough. They had soon left the little town behind, and the country, though not romantically beautiful, offered a pleasant rural prospect. The cornfields, it is true, were denuded of their crops, which now, in the form of rows of ricks, lined the hedgerows at the bottom of the fields. But the stubble, now faded to a soft purplish grey, was enriched by the daisies that had sprung up since the harvest, and the groups of scarlet poppies. The only drawback to the landscape was the scarcity of trees and the lack of any relief from the glare of the hot afternoon sun. For, late as it was in the year, the summer continued with unabated heat and brilliancy. The sky was cloudless, a tremulous haze hung over the ground, and the sea, which was visible over the edge of the cliffs, was still of the clear summer blue.

"It's deuced hot," said Ronald, taking off his hat to wipe his forehead. "How would it be to get down to the beach and have a stroll along the sands? It would be fresher there than up here."

"Can we get down?" asked Andrew.

"Yes," replied Ronald. "There is a sunken road leading to a gap-way that opens out on to the beach. I found it by following a couple of seaweed carts, and I've been there once or twice since for a bathe. Nobody ever seems to come there, so you don't have to bother about bathing suits."

He turned off the road and led the way across a stubble field, and, after walking about a quarter of a mile, they came to a shallow sunken road, marked by deep ruts in its chalky surface made by the wheels of the heavily laden seaweed carts. Gradually the road sank deeper as it declined towards the sea level until it took on the character of a narrow gully enclosed by lofty walls of chalk. Down this gully the two men picked their way over the rough road in the deep, cool shadow until they reached the bottom of the slope and stood looking out on the sun-lit sands.

Ronald cast a glance at the two lofty headlands which enclosed the little bay and remarked:

"We shan't be able to walk very far along the beach. The tide is coming in, and it won't be long before it is up to the cliffs where they jut out. We mustn't get caught on the hop."

"Well," said Andrew, "there's a good stretch of smooth sand in the bay. It will be quite pleasant to walk up and down by the sea without going out of the bay; and it will seem cooler by the water's edge, even if it isn't."

"Yes," Ronald agreed, "there is something cooling in the very sound of the waves breaking on the beach. But I don't see why we need stop at the sound. A dip would be a good deal more refreshing. What do you say? The sea looks just perfect for a bathe."

Andrew cast an approving glance at the calm blue sea and the lines of creamy white where the little surf broke with a gentle murmur on the shore.

"It does look rather inviting," he admitted; "but it seems a bit primitive – no bathing suits and no towels."

"As to the suits," said Ronald, beginning to slip off his jacket, "you can see for yourself that the place is as solitary as the Sahara; and what do you want with towels when you have got a roasting sun like this to dry you?"

He settled the question by backing into a shallow recess in the cliff and proceeding rapidly to divest himself of his clothes, when Andrew, after a moment's hesitation, followed suit. As both men were rather scantily clad in the ubiquitous grey flannel suits that were then the vogue, the process was not a long one. In a couple of minutes they were scampering across the sand towards the surf in a condition which Mr Titmarsh would have described as "naked as a pair of Hottentots", Ronald taking a certain satisfaction in the defiance of convention and Andrew slightly self-conscious.

The breach of the proprieties, however, was only potential, for Ronald's description of the place was so far justified that the nearest approach to a spectator was a small fishing lugger with dark brown sails which was beating up the coast some three or four miles away. Meanwhile the two cousins swam up and down in the calm water outside the surf, with intervals of resting and wallowing in the shallows or basking in the sun on the dry sand before once more splashing into the water.

In these disports the best part of an hour passed. At length, Andrew suggested that it was time to be turning homeward, and they emerged for the last time, shaking themselves as they stepped out on to the wet sand, and took their way across the beach to the place where their clothes were deposited close under the cliff. Ronald led the way at a brisk run, and, on arrival at the "dressing station", sat down and reclined at his ease on one of the heaps of clothes – it happened to be Andrew's, and the similarity of the two suits may possibly have misled him; but the enjoyment with which he rubbed his wet body on the dry garments strongly suggested an intentional "mistake". It would have been like Ronald. Andrew followed, shivering slightly, and sat down on the other heap in an upright posture, to catch as much of the sun's heat as possible; for the afternoon was drawing out and the sun was now appreciably lower.

For some time neither of the two men spoke. Ronald lay stretched at full length with his eyes closed, enjoying the warmth of the sunlight which played on his rapidly drying skin, while Andrew sat absently watching the fishing lugger, now tacking out to sea and now going about to make a tack inshore. At length, Ronald spoke, in a drowsy tone and without opening his eyes.

"So you think you will be able to manage cash in place of that cheque? I hope you will. It will be a lot more convenient for me."

"Well," replied Andrew, "I'll see what can be done. But you haven't given me any particulars, you know."

"What's the good?" protested Ronald. "I don't know much about it myself. It's an insurance job. I shall have to rout out new clients and, when I get a bite, I shall have to take the first premium. That's why they want a deposit. So that I shan't mizzle with the takings. Isn't that enough for you?"

As it was all the information he was likely to get, Andrew assented with a grunt and once more fixed his eyes on the distant lugger. Another interval of silence followed. Then Ronald inquired, sleepily:

"Molly send me any message?"

"She doesn't know I was going to see you; and I don't want her to know anything about this transaction. She mightn't be best pleased at my dropping money in this way."

"Don't you believe it, dear boy," said Ronald, with a faint smile. "Molly is quite fond of her cousin. She would be only too delighted to help him out of a difficulty. She knows what an affection he has for her. And, by Jove! What a good-looking girl she is! I don't know of any girl that I admire so much. You're a lucky beggar. But I'll remember that mum's the word when I come over to see you."

"I think," Andrew said, huskily, "that it would be as well if you did not come over just at present. In fact, I would rather you did not."

Ronald opened his eyes and looked curiously at his cousin. Then he shut them again and smiled a smile of deep cunning.

"So that's how you feel, is it?" said he. "I suspected something of the kind when you had this very opportune business appointment in Crompton. However, I can take a hint. I should be devilish obtuse if I couldn't take one of that breadth."

He spoke without anger but in a tone of undisguised contempt which brought the hot blood to Andrew's cheeks and which made it clear that he grasped the position exactly. Andrew squirmed with shame and anger; shame of the paltry, unreasonable jealousy of which Ronald evidently suspected him, and anger at the suspicion. For a moment he looked down at the face of the man beside him, with its closed eyes and the sinister, cunning, insolent smile; and an impulse surged through him to batter it with his fists until it was even as his own. But he conquered the impulse and looked away, fixing his eyes once more on the lugger, which was now tacking inshore and would soon be hidden by the projecting headland. He followed it with a dull interest as it drew nearer and nearer to the headland, idly watching for the moment when it should pass into eclipse, or should go about and head again out to sea.

Gradually the distance between the vessel's bows and the jutting promontory contracted, and Andrew still watched with a strange, foolish eagerness to see whether she would vanish or turn about. At last the dwindling space dwindled to extinction and the boat's bows and the dark brown mainsail began to slip out of sight behind the promontory; and at that moment, Andrew was startled by a heavy thud at his side, a rattle and clatter above and around him and a volley of falling fragments of chalk, one of which struck him a shrewd blow on the shoulder. With a cry of alarm, he scrambled to his feet and raced away for dear life across the sand, pausing only to look round when he had run a full thirty yards.

What he saw when he did at last look round, seemed to turn him to stone. Beside the place where he had been sitting was a litter of fragments of chalk and one great block which rested where Ronald's head had been. Out of the litter the naked legs projected, moving with a slow, twitching, purposeless motion which was horrible to look on, and which, even as he looked, slowly died away and gave place to a dreadful limp stillness.

For some moments, Andrew stood gazing with starting eyes at this awful spectacle without conscious or intelligible thought. He was literally stunned. Presently, regaining some semblance of consciousness, he began to creep back towards the place where his cousin lay with some vague idea of help or rescue. But when he drew nearer, that idea faded from his mind. The way in which the great

33

block sat on the flattened clothing, to say nothing of the gory oozings around it, told the horrible story. That block, weighing perhaps a hundredweight, had come down on the smiling face with the closed eyes with the impact of a steam hammer. It was useless to think of trying to move it, even if that had been within the compass of one man's strength. The head that had been there was a head no longer.

Still confused and bewildered by the suddenness of the catastrophe, Andrew stood with his eyes riveted on the great block, shaking like a man in the cold stage of an ague. He was aware of a dreadful feeling of faintness and nausea and of a cold sweat that had broken out on his face and trickled down in chilly drops. But, for a time, his power of thought seemed to be in total abeyance. He could only stand and stare vacantly at the great block and the naked, motionless legs.

Suddenly, he became conscious of his own nude condition; and with that consciousness his faculties awoke. With a nervous glance up the face of the cliff to the white patch which marked the spot from which the block had fallen, he ran to the heap of clothes, and, snatching them up, backed away from the cliff and began to huddle them on as quickly as his shaking limbs would permit. But still, his actions were those of an automaton, for, all the while, his eyes strayed continually to the motionless form under the litter of chalk fragments and the great block which rested where, but a few minutes ago, had been that comely head with the closed eyes and the sinister, insolent, smiling face.

When he had dressed himself, he looked around for his hat, but he could only see Ronald's panama. His own hat must be somewhere under that gory heap, which he would not even dare to approach. With a shudder at the very thought, he picked up the panama and flung it on his head, careless of the fact that it came down nearly to his ears. Then, with a last look at the figure that reposed with such dreadful stillness at the foot of the cliff, he turned and walked away quickly towards the gap that opened on to the sunken road.

As he entered the now sombre and gloomy gully, the dark silhouette of the lugger stole out from behind the headland and began to shape a course towards the bay.

# CHAPTER FOUR
## The Shadow of the Gallows

---

Andrew stumbled up the rough sunken road with an appearance of haste and speed which was in curious contrast with his actual lack of conscious purpose. Vaguely, there was in his mind an intention to give information to somebody of the terrible mishap, and a desire to get back to the town to that end. But he was still shaken by the horror of what he had seen, was still haunted by the vision of that great block of chalk resting so flatly where a head had been that there had seemed to be no space underneath it. Quickly as he went, his knees trembled weakly, the faintness and nausea were only beginning to subside and a chaotic whirl of thoughts surged through his mind. To the bearing on the future of the thing that had happened, he was as yet unable to give any consideration. His whole attention was focused on the dreadful disaster that had befallen in the twinkling of an eye; the heavy thud of the falling block, the rattling down of the fragments, and, above all, the sight of those horrible, twitching legs.

When the sunken road at length reached the surface, it strayed away across the fields as a rough, chalky cart-track which seemed to lead in the direction of a distant farm. As it was the only road visible, Andrew followed it automatically without giving any thought to its direction. At least, it led away from the sea and that terrible haunted bay. As to the whereabouts of the town he had only a confused idea; for, during the walk out with Ronald, his mind had been so preoccupied that he had taken no note of the way they had come.

Ronald had selected the route and he had followed Ronald. Now nothing impinged on his vision with any kind of familiarity. So, for a time, he walked on rather like one in a dream, clearly conscious of nothing and only dimly aware of a certain feeling of discomfort, particularly in his feet.

He had followed the cart-track for close upon a mile when it opened on a road; a small by-road enclosed by dust-whitened hedgerows. The necessity of deciding which way he should turn aroused him from his dreamy, half-conscious state. He wanted to get to Crompton, but he had only the vaguest idea as to the direction in which it lay; and the sinuous road, curving away on either hand, gave little indication as to whither it eventually led. After a few moments of hesitation, he turned towards the right and once more set forth at a quick pace, spurred on to haste by the agitation of his mind rather than by any conscious purpose.

He hurried on along the road for more than half a mile before he met any human creature. Truly, Ronald had been right as to the scarcity of wayfarers in this part of the country. At length there appeared at a bend of the road a miller's cart with its tarpaulin cover raised, in the old-fashioned way, on a sort of ridge-pole, and the driver dimly visible in the dark triangle underneath. As it came in sight, Andrew decided to hail the driver and ask for a direction to Crompton; and then, becoming aware for the first time that his spectacles were not on his face, he instinctively thrust his hand into the pocket in which he usually carried them. But they were not there. Instead, he brought out a cigarette case which was certainly not his.

For a few moments he stood staring foolishly at the case in his hand and wondering how it could have come into his pocket. Then his eye caught the wristband of the shirt which projected from the end of his sleeve; and he saw that the shirt also was not his. On this, with a sudden suspicion that something was amiss, he examined critically the clothes which he was wearing, including the shoes. Of them all, not a single item was his own. In his hurry and agitation, he had put on Ronald's clothes; indeed, he could not have done otherwise, for his own were under that dreadful heap which he could never have brought himself to disturb.

The discovery gave him a shock which was somewhat disproportionate to the occasion. Naturally, he was surprised; but there was really nothing in the affair that need have disturbed him. The clothes were almost exactly like his own, and they fitted him well enough to pass without attracting notice. The error could be easily explained, and he would probably be able to recover his own clothes, or at least the contents of the pockets. But the incident jarred on his already strained nerves as if there were something incriminating in it. Perhaps the need for explanation which would presently arise unnerved him; and certainly the loss of his spectacles and the necessity for going abroad with his hated disfigurement exposed affected him profoundly. So much so that he let the miller's cart pass unhailed and started forward once more, trusting to chance to find the right direction.

By this time, his thought had become a little more coherent, and he began to look about him with some anxiety; for the afternoon was waning, and, at this time of year, the evenings begin to draw in. It was, therefore, with a sense of relief that he found himself approaching a crossroad and perceived at the crossing a four-armed finger-post. But, if he was relieved at the prospect of getting a reliable direction, he was rather disconcerted when he reached the post and read the inscription on the pointer; for it then became clear that he had been walking almost directly away from Crompton from the time when he emerged from the sunken road.

He turned away from the post and started on what appeared to be the direct road to the town, though even this was only a larger by-road. But its surface was better than that of the one on which he had been travelling, and he set forth at a swinging pace to cover the three miles that, according to the finger-post, lay between him and the town, regardless of the slight discomfort due to the strange shoes. In spite of the unpleasant surprise of finding himself in the wrong clothes, the halt and the necessity for thought had done him good by diverting his attention from the horrors of his late experience to his present condition and the question as to what he would be called upon to do. He had found a wristwatch in one of the pockets of the coat, and, as he now strapped it on his wrist and noted the lateness of the hour, he turned this latter question over in his mind.

Someone would have to be informed of the accident and, when he asked himself, Who? the obvious answer was, the police. He knew where to find the police station, and he decided to make straight for it as soon as he entered the town. The story that he had to tell was perfectly simple. There would be no need for any elaborate questioning on the part of the police. At least, he hoped not; for he was conscious of a very definite shrinking from any discussion of his relations with Ronald. Perhaps he might take the opportunity to mention the incident of the motor bandits. He considered this point, and, possibly influenced by Molly's warning, eventually decided that he had better keep to the subject of the accident and say nothing of the other matter.

Presently another question intruded itself on his mind. At the time of the disaster, the tide was coming in and the margin of the advancing waters was not so very distant from the base of the cliffs. Would there be time for the body to be recovered? And, if there were not; if the corpse should be borne away by the waves and carried out to sea, how would that affect the position? He considered this point at some length and not without a shade of uneasiness, but could arrive at no conclusion, excepting that it would involve disagreeable explanations to Molly. But, in any case, he would have to account for his presence at Crompton.

So, as he strode along the road, his thoughts rambled from one to another of the innumerable consequences of the tragedy that came crowding into his consciousness. Mostly, they were unpleasant to contemplate; and if, in the dim background of his thoughts, there was some faint feeling of relief at the disappearance from his life of this troublesome parasite, he put it away from him with something like a sense of guilt.

When, at last, he entered the town, the light was already failing. Nevertheless, he pulled his hat even further down over his face as he

FOR THE DEFENCE: DR THORNDYKE

yearned for the protection of the lost spectacles, and looked about him furtively. At first, the place seemed to him completely unfamiliar; but, after wandering up one thoroughfare and down another, he came into the High Street and was then able to take his bearings. The police station, he knew, was at the end of Barleymow Street and thither he at once directed his steps. He found it without difficulty and turned into it gratefully out of the glare of the High Street with its illuminated shop windows. He crept along in the shade of the houses, glancing uncomfortably at Number 16 as he passed it, and thinking of the fine, manly figure that he had seen standing outside it when he arrived, and of the corpse around which the waves were perhaps already clamouring. But he hurried on and presently came to the archway that led into the passage or alley in which the station was situated.

Here he paused irresolutely, suddenly aware of an unaccountable feeling of nervousness and a reluctance to speak to strangers of the awful thing which he had witnessed. The lamp had been lit outside the arch and it cast its light brilliantly on the notice board and the various bills that were pasted or tacked on it. Conspicuous among these was the bill that he had seen the constable sticking up as he and Ronald had passed. Again his eye caught the heading, printed in bold type: "Wanted for Murder", but he was too much preoccupied with his present business to feel any curiosity as to this crime, whatever it might be; in fact, he was on the point of turning away when two other words in large type arrested his attention. Halfway down the sheet, occupying an entire line, were the words, "Ribble's Cross". Then there had been a murder; and he was a principal witness.

He turned back and rapidly ran his eye down the bill. Not the whole way though. After a brief and dry statement of the actual circumstances, the announcement went on:

"It is believed that more than one man was concerned in the crime, but the only one who was seen was the man who actually fired the shot. He is described as a somewhat fair man with grey eyes, about thirty years of age and easily recognizable by reason of a remarkably deformed nose, which appears to have been broken and is completely flat excepting at the tip, which is rather prominent."

He read no farther, but, backing away hastily from the area of light under the lamp, crept into the shadow of the houses and stole along the darkened street, trembling so violently that his legs seemed ready to double up beneath him. The description in the bill had struck him with the force of a thunderbolt. For the moment, he was on the point of mental and physical collapse, conscious of nothing but an overwhelming terror and a horrible feeling of sickness; indeed, so near was he to actually fainting that he was fain to lean against the wall of a house and rest awhile on the low sill of a darkened window.

His terror was natural enough and not without ample cause. For, stunned as he was, the essential position presented itself clearly and unmistakably. There had been two persons in that car. One of them was dead – murdered; and the other, the woman, believed that she had seen him commit the murder. Even in his dazed condition, Molly's words recurred to him; when a woman holds a belief, she knows no doubts. This woman would be ready to go into the witness-box and swear that she saw him fire the shot that had killed her companion. But what answer could there be to the testimony of an eye-witness? There could be none. Nor could there be any extenuation. It had been a cold-blooded murder without provocation or excuse of any kind. He had but to be caught to be set forthwith on the direct road to the gallows. And caught he would assuredly be. The woman had given a correct description of him and she would recognize him instantly and with certainty. And as to escape; how was a man to escape arrest whose face advertised his identity to any chance stranger?

He rose shakily from the window-sill and began once more to creep along the street in the shadow, pulling down his hat over his eyes and lowering his head when he came within the range of a street lamp. His state was pitiable. He was as one already condemned. Hope he had none. He saw the rope dangling before his eyes, the drop of the gallows yawning at his feet. Like some hunted animal, he looked around wildly for some place in which to hide. But where could he hide in this wilderness of men? where every stranger was a possible enemy? Supposing he should make his way back to the country and lurk in the unfrequented fields? To what purpose? Sooner or later he must be found. Someone would see him and report his meeting with the man with "the remarkably deformed nose". He could not hide in the fields for ever. He must have food and drink; unless he could find some remote and obscure place where he could lie in hiding until he should die of starvation. It was a poor chance, though perhaps it was better than being hanged.

As his thoughts rambled on thus, he continued to creep cautiously along the street. In so far as his mind was capable of forming a decision, he had decided to make his way out of the town, and he began to look warily ahead and scan the corner of the street as he approached it; and at this moment he found himself passing a half-lighted window which he recognized by the still visible placards as that of the Beauty Specialist.

He paused and gazed at the placards. There was not enough light to read the inscriptions, but he had no need to read them. He remembered them quite clearly. And as he recalled those ridiculous promises and exhortations, a wild hope sprang up in his heart. Of course, the fellow was a mere quack. But was it possible that he could do something? It mattered not in the least what he did. An additional disfigurement even would answer the purpose if only his appearance could be in some way changed so that his face should cease to be the face which that woman had seen at the window of the car. It was a chance – the only chance that he could see of escape from the gallows.

He looked up and down the street. Not a living creature was in sight. He made an effort to pull himself together. The pallor of his face he could not control, but he could try to muster up some composure of manner. But even in that moment of agitated expectation, one cautionary idea stole into his mind. Supposing the Professor had seen the bill outside the police station! He must be prepared for that contingency. Nevertheless, he determined to take the risk.

After another glance up and down the street, he approached the door, and, gripping the handle firmly to control the tremor of his hand, turned it deliberately, pushed open the door, entered and closed it after him. As he turned away from the door, he confronted a pleasant-faced elderly man in shirt-sleeves and a white apron, who was busily engaged in packing one or two large trunks, by the rather dim light of a single electric lamp.

At the sound of the closing door, the man looked up, and a shade of impatience or annoyance stole over his face. Andrew noted it with some misgiving as he inquired nervously:

"Are you Professor Booley?"

"I am," was the reply; "or, perhaps, I should say I was, as my professional career in this country has now come to an end. I am just putting my goods together ready for a start tomorrow morning. In twenty-four hours, I hope to be in Liverpool, if not actually on board ship. May I ask what you wanted with me?"

At the Professor's announcement Andrew's heart sank. For a few moments he was unable to answer; but, at length, recovering his outward composure with an effort, he replied:

"I had come to ask for your professional help, and I hope you will not refuse to do what you can for me."

"I am afraid that is what I shall have to do," the Professor rejoined in a tone of courteous regret. "You see how things are with me. I have finished up and am just making my preparations for departure. I thought I had fastened the door when I turned the lights out. I am real sorry not to be able to do your business, whatever it is. By the way, what was it that you wanted me to do for you?"

"If you will look at my face," said, Andrew, "I think that will answer your question; and I do hope you will try to help me if the thing is not absolutely impossible."

The Professor looked at him a little curiously; then, suddenly, his attention sharpened and a somewhat startled expression appeared on his face; whereat Andrew experienced a spasm of alarm. Had this man seen the police bill, and was he recognizing "the man with the remarkably deformed nose"? His terror was not diminished when the Professor strode forward and fixed a look of intense scrutiny on

42

that unfortunate member. But the next question reassured him to some extent.

"You were not born like that?"

"No," replied Andrew. "I once had quite a decent-looking nose. This is the result of a blow from a cricket-ball."

"Ah!" said the Professor, "nasty, dangerous things. You must have been a fairly good-looking fellow before you caught that biff."

"I believe I was," Andrew replied, modestly.

The Professor continued to scrutinize the injured nose with the most profound interest and attention. Then from inspection he proceeded to palpation. With an unmistakably expert finger and thumb he explored the sunken bridge, delicately tracing the edges of the flattened nasal bones and pinching up the loose skin which lay over them.

"It's an absolutely ideal case," he murmured, rather with the manner of a man speaking to himself. "A good firm base of solid bone and a fair amount of spare skin, all free, without any adhesions to the bone underneath. It's a case in a million."

Recognizing these observations as being of the nature of a soliloquy, Andrew forbore to interrupt. But when the Professor, subsiding into silence, stepped back a pace and stood, still with his eyes riveted on the deformed feature, as if taking in the general effect in relation to the rest of the face, he ventured once more to urge his case.

"I hope you are going to relent, Professor," he pleaded, "and give me the benefit of your skill. It means a lot to me, as you can judge for yourself."

How much it meant to him, the Professor was, naturally, unable to judge, having, apparently, not seen the police bill. But the hideous disfigurement of an otherwise comely young man must have seemed to him a matter of sufficient urgency, for he replied in a tone of kindly sympathy:

"I can see it does, sonny; and I can't find it in my heart to send you away like that when a bit of trouble on my part may make life a different thing for you. No, sir! We have our duties to one another;

and my duty is to let the packing go to blazes and put all the skill and knowledge that I have at your disposal."

Andrew drew a deep breath of relief, and, with a heart bursting with gratitude, he began to stammer out his thanks, when the Professor interrupted him.

"Don't be too previous," said he. "When I tell you what I propose to do, perhaps you'll think better of it. If I get busy, you won't enjoy it a little bit. I tell you it will hurt like blazes. It might be possible to use a local anaesthetic such as dentists use. I do sometimes, but I don't want to in this case because it might easily happen that the anaesthetic would just turn the scale the wrong way and make the operation a failure. And I don't want it to fail. But I give you fair warning. While I am working, you will feel as if you had molten lead running into your nose. And, mind you, you'll have to stick it and not move a muscle or the whole thing will be a failure. Now, what do you say? Can you stick it? It's up to you to decide."

Andrew had no hesitation. What the Professor was going to do, and what the result would be, he had no idea. But whatever the result might be, if only it were to alter his appearance, he would be saved from his present horrible peril.

"You can take it," said he, "that I am prepared to put up with any pain that you have to inflict; and I promise you that I will keep absolutely still until you have finished."

"Good!" said the Professor. "I take you at your word; and I think it will be worth your while. But there is one other warning that I ought to give you. There is just the possibility that something may go wrong after the operation. It isn't at all likely, but it has happened in one or two cases, so I think it only right to mention it. Will you take the risk? It's only a small one."

Even to Andrew, the change in the Professor's attitude was apparent. From reluctance to be disturbed in his preparations for his journey, it had changed into an evident eagerness to proceed with the operation, whatever that might be; and, when Andrew replied that he was fully prepared to accept the risk of subsequent failure and to hold the Professor unaccountable for any such failure, his answer was received with a grunt of satisfaction.

"We won't want to be disturbed," said Booley, when this point had been settled, "so I will just lock up and switch out the light."

He locked the front door and retired into an inner room where he switched on the light and invited his patient to enter. Then, having extinguished the light in the outer premises, he closed the inner door.

"Now," said he, "let me just explain in a general way what I propose to do. The method that I am going to employ is what is known as the subcutaneous wax method. I'll show you." He opened the drawer of a cabinet and took out a circular cake of a colourless, glassy-looking material, which he exhibited to his patient.

"Now, see here," said he, tapping the round mass with his knuckles, "this is paraffin wax; quite a hard substance, as you see, but not in the least brittle. Now, paraffin wax is a very remarkable material. It is one of the most inert substances known. It never changes of itself, it has practically no effect on any other substance, and it is not affected by contact with other materials. And it can be reduced to a liquid by heat – rather a lot of heat, unfortunately, in the case of hard wax like this.

"Now, what I am going to do is this: I shall melt some of this wax, and, when it is quite liquid, I shall inject a quantity of it into the space under the loose skin of your nose. That will produce a shapeless swelling over the place where the bridge ought to be. Then, while the wax is still soft, I shall model that shapeless lump to the shape that you want your nose to be. And now you will see why I am telling you this. I have got to do all the modelling while the wax is soft enough to pinch up into shape. When once it has set solid, it is finished for better or worse. Nothing more can be done. And it is only a matter of seconds before it sets. Consequently, the success or failure is in your hands. No matter how much it hurts, it is up to you to keep quite still until I have finished the modelling. You realize that?"

"Quite," replied Andrew; "and you can rely on me to stick it without moving, however bad it is."

"I believe I can," said the Professor. "You looked in a most almighty funk when you first came in; but you seem to be your own man now.

45

Which is rather singular. Most people are as bold as brass at first, but get the horrors when it comes to actual business."

The Professor was quite correct in his observations; but he was not in possession of all the facts. What had revived Andrew's confidence was the information that in any case, there would be some sort of hump over the sunken bridge of his nose. As to the shape of that hump he was not very much concerned. Any kind of hump would transform him so that the woman's description of him would be totally inapplicable. And the mere pain dismayed him not at all. Doubtless it would be extremely disagreeable; but it would be a good deal less disagreeable than being hanged.

Having delivered himself of the above admonitions, the Professor inducted the patient into a sort of modified dental chair and then proceeded to light the gas ring under a water-bath in which was a porcelain vessel containing a quantity of wax shavings. While the water was heating he made his other preparations, beginning by washing his hands very thoroughly in a lavatory basin and then laying out his instruments on a small swivel table such as dentists use. The most conspicuous of them was a hypodermic syringe of large size but fitted with a rather fine needle. From time to time he examined a chemical thermometer which he had placed in the vessel containing the wax, and, meanwhile, carried on encouraging conversation.

"By the way," said he, "we haven't settled on the sort of nose that you would like me to build up. We must be quite clear on that point before we start. What was your nose like before that cricket-ball came bumbling along? Was it a straight nose, or was there a curve on the bridge?"

Even while the question was being propounded, Andrew had come to a decision, and a perfectly natural and reasonable one in the special circumstances. In his terror of the gallows, his one object was to shake off his identity – the identity of the man who was "wanted for murder". He would not go back even to what that man had been, if that had been possible. He wanted to break all connection with that man.

"It was a slightly curved nose," he replied.

46

"I thought so," said the Professor; "a moderate Roman. And very becoming it must have been – and will be again. You'll think it cheap at the price of a few minutes' discomfort."

He bent down over the porcelain vessel and again inspected the thermometer. Apparently, the correct temperature had been reached, for he now turned out the gas and placed the water-bath on the little table, which he swung round close to the patient's head. Having lighted a spirit-lamp on the table, he held the needle of the syringe in the flame for a few seconds. Then, dipping the needle into the melted wax, he slowly filled the syringe, emptied it into the vessel, and very slowly and carefully re-filled it.

"Now," said he, "get a grip on the arms of the chair and make up your mind to put up with a bit of pain. It will be over in less than a minute. Better shut your eyes."

The Professor had not exaggerated. It was an appalling experience. First, Andrew was aware of the prick of the needle in the loose skin over the nose. That was nothing to complain of. But it was followed immediately by the most horrible pain that he had ever experienced. The Professor's words exactly described it. He felt as if molten lead were being poured into his nose. In his agony, he held his breath and clutched the arms of the chair until his knuckles seemed to be bursting through the skin. His eyes were closed, but the tears welled up between the lids and trickled down his face in a little stream towards his ears. But, by a supreme effort, he resisted the natural impulse to shrink away from the torturing hand. Throughout the whole proceeding, he held his head rigidly still and uttered not a sound.

Meanwhile, the Professor, murmuring at intervals little phrases of sympathy and encouragement, went about his work with unhurried skill and concentrated attention, but yet with a certain air of suppressed excitement. Having completed the injection, he laid aside the syringe and made a critical inspection of the rounded, blister-like swelling which had arisen over the sunken bridge of the nose. After a few seconds, he began cautiously to manipulate it at the edges, persuading the liquid wax towards the middle line. Then, as the wax began to thicken, he proceeded quickly and deftly to model it to the desired shape, darting from one side of the chair to the other to view the growing member from its different aspects. Yet, in spite of his eagerness and excitement, his movements were quite deliberate and controlled. Evidently, in his mind, he had a perfectly clear picture of the state of the invisible wax, and, as its consistency increased and it gradually approached the solid condition, the touch of the flexible, sensitive fingers became firmer and more decisive.

It was, as he had said, only a matter of seconds, but to the unfortunate patient, sitting with the muscles of his neck contracted into tense cords and his hands holding the arms of the chair in a vice-like grip, it seemed hours before the Professor, straightening himself up with a gentle sigh, announced:

"There, my son; that's finished. The wax is set solid, though it won't be quite hard for an hour or two. How is it feeling?"

"Not as bad as it did," Andrew replied, faintly, "but it still hurts a good deal."

"I've no doubt that it does," the Professor rejoined, sympathetically, "but it will soon be all right now. You've been a good lad. You stuck it like a Trojan."

"What does it look like?" Andrew asked, without much eagerness and with his eyes still shut.

"You shall see for yourself presently," the Professor replied in a tone of deep satisfaction, regarding his work with his head on one side. "But don't move just for a minute. I must touch up the colour a trifle so that it shan't be too noticeable. At present it's as red as a strawberry."

Having recourse once more to the inexhaustible cabinet, he produced therefrom a stick of yellowish grease-paint and a little jar of powder. With the former he laid a fairly thick tint of opaque yellowish white over the restored nose (to the patient's extreme discomfort), smoothing it out with the tip of his finger until the tint was perfectly even. Then, with a tiny puff, he covered the greasy surface with a thin coating of powder, finishing off with a few delicate touches of a ball of cotton wool.

"There," he said, "I think that will do. It looks quite a natural colour now. When the irritation from the heat goes off and the redness dies away, it will look a bit queer and tallowy. Then you'll have to wash the paint off. And I need not warn you that, although the wax will be quite hard and firm, you've got to be careful in the way you handle that nose. It will stand any ordinary treatment in reason; but you've got to remember that it's only a lump of wax after all, and that if you knock it out of shape, it's going to remain out of shape. It can't be melted soft again."

"Yes," said Andrew, "I realize that; and you may take it that I shall keep out of the way of cricket-balls in the future. Can I see what it is like, now?"

"You can," replied the Professor, who still showed a tendency to dodge about from side to side of the chair and take ecstatic glances at the new nose from various points of view. "I am going to show it to you this instant."

As he spoke, he wheeled away the swivel table, and in its place wheeled up an appliance somewhat like a reading-stand with a largish mirror in the position usually occupied by the book-rest. Deliberately, he trundled it up to the side of the chair, arranged the mirror at exactly the correct angle, and then swung the brass arm round so as to bring the glass precisely opposite the patient's face.

"Now," said he triumphantly, "tell me what you think of the result."

# CHAPTER FIVE

## Black Magic

In response to the Professor's invitation, Andrew sat up in the chair and looked into the mirror. But, as his eyes were still full of water, he got but a blurred impression of what was before him. Even so, he was aware that the face which confronted him was not the face to which he had of late years become accustomed – the face of the "man with the remarkably deformed nose".

He took out his handkerchief and carefully and thoroughly wiped away the still-exuding tears, while the Professor hovered around, watching him in a transport of delighted expectancy. When he had dried his eyes as completely as was possible in the circumstances, he looked again into the mirror. And then he sustained yet another shock. It is impossible to guess what he had expected – if he had expected anything. But most assuredly he had not expected what he saw. For the face that looked out at him from the mirror was the face of his cousin Ronald.

He stared at it in blank amazement with a bewildered sense of being in a dream, or suffering some sort of hallucination, or being the subject of some kind of wizardry or enchantment. And the Professor, watching him eagerly, rubbed his hands and smiled.

The thing was astounding, incredible. It was no mere resemblance or similarity. The face was Ronald's face. Doubtless, if Ronald had been there to furnish a comparison, some difference might have been discoverable. But Andrew could perceive none; and when he moved his head from side to side, exhibiting the half-profile with a view of the Roman nose, the effect was even more impressive. For that was the view of Ronald's face that he had always found most striking and characteristic.

The Professor, watching him with an expectant smile, noted his astonishment and was deeply gratified. Well might the patient be astonished at the miracle that had been wrought in the space of a few minutes. But his kindly soul yearned for something more than astonishment; and the joy that he had looked for did not seem to be there.

"Well," he asked, at length, "what do you think of it? Will it do?"

Andrew pulled himself together with an effort and came back to the realities of the situation.

"I beg your pardon," said he; "but I was so amazed at the result of your skill that I could find no words to thank you. I can't even now. When I look into the mirror, I can't believe my eyes."

"Your eyes are all right," said the Professor, "or will be when they have done watering. Meanwhile, you can trust mine; and I tell you that you have got a nose that any man might be proud of. And, if you don't mind me saying so – I'm talking business, not paying compliments – you are an uncommonly good-looking young man."

The compliment, which his own eyesight confirmed, fell pleasantly on Andrew's ears even in the midst of his confusion. Why not? His repulsive ugliness had been the haunting trouble of his later life, and he had known the satisfaction of conscious good looks in the golden past. It was pleasant to realize that he would have no more to sneak about in spectacles and hide himself from the common gaze. But, furthermore, and especially, the change assured him that his main purpose was achieved. The deadly peril that had encompassed him was dissipated. He was saved. That woman might now shout from the house-tops her vivid description of the murderer. The more vivid and exact it was, the less would it apply to him. "The man with the remarkably deformed nose" had ceased to be. The police might search for him as they pleased; it was no concern of Andrew's.

"Naturally, I don't mind your saying so," he replied, "since the good looks – which I can see for myself – are your own creation. I only wish I could find words to thank you sufficiently. You can hardly imagine the misery of going about, an object of pity and disgust to every person whom one may meet, and the relief of having that disfigurement removed. I assure you that I am more grateful than I can tell you; and I do think it most generous of you to have put aside your own urgent affairs to render me this great service."

"Not in the least," said the Professor. "It has been a delight to me to exercise my art to such excellent purpose. We all like to succeed in what we try to do, and I feel that I have had a great success tonight, and I don't mind admitting that I'm mighty pleased with myself."

A less appreciative listener than Andrew might have felt a slight suspicion that the brilliant success was a somewhat novel experience for the Professor. But as the splendour of the achievement dawned on him by degrees and he realized its beneficent consequences, Andrew had no room in his mind for anything but gratitude.

"You have reason to be," he replied. "It must be a glorious thing to wield the power to change for the better the whole course of a fellow creature's life. I shall be your debtor to my dying day, and I shall never forget what I owe you. Which reminds me that, apart from the debt of gratitude, which I can never repay, I am in your debt in a pecuniary sense. May I ask what the amount is? I know in advance that whatever your fee is, it is quite inadequate to the value of the benefit bestowed."

Even as he uttered the words, he experienced a sudden pang of alarm. For in that moment he remembered that he was not wearing his own clothes. He had not yet searched the pockets of the suit that he had put on in error, but, as they were those of his thriftless and chronically impecunious cousin, it was quite conceivable that they might not contain the wherewith for him to pay even a modest fee. Hurriedly, he thrust his hand into the breast pocket of the coat and brought out the small wallet that he felt there. When he opened it he discovered, to his intense relief, that it contained two pound notes. They might not be enough, but they would be better than nothing.

52

As a matter of fact, they were more than enough; for the Professor, glancing at the wallet and possibly noting its scanty contents, held up his hand.

"Put it away, sonny," said he. "There isn't any fee. It has been a labour of love, and I am not going to spoil it for myself by taking money for it. Let me have the luxury of giving you a free and willing service."

Andrew was disposed to demur, but the Professor would listen to no protests, and, as he was obviously in earnest, Andrew refrained from pressing him any further.

"Very well," said he. "I am so much in your debt that a little more makes no difference. But it would give me very great pleasure if you would come as my guest and let us celebrate your triumph and my resurrection with a little dinner – or perhaps we might call it supper. You won't refuse me, will you?"

The Professor reflected, with a gloating eye still fixed on his masterpiece.

"I'd enjoy a little celebration," he said, at length, "if only for the pleasure of looking at you. But it will have to be a short one as far as I am concerned, for I still have my packing to finish. Where did you propose to dine?"

"I leave that to you," replied Andrew, "as you probably know the town better than I do."

The Professor knew of a respectable Italian café in the High Street close by; and, when he had doffed his apron, turned down his shirt-sleeves and put on a coat and hat, they went forth together, the guest leading the way and the host submitting to be led and secretly hoping that the café would not turn out to be the one at which he had lunched with Ronald. Not that it mattered much, since he had then been wearing his spectacles. But he was still under the influence of the police bill and accordingly anxious to avoid any connection with the man who was "wanted".

It was not the same restaurant, but a more modest establishment of the familiar Italian type. It resembled the other, however, in one respect; its walls were lined with large mirrors, to the evident satisfaction of Professor Booley, who was thus enabled to inspect his masterpiece from several points of view; which he did with such persistence that he appeared to consume his food by a mere mechanical and half-conscious act of ingestion.

To Andrew that dinner was a most uncanny experience. His mind was still in a whirl of confusion from the crowding events and the repeated shocks that he had sustained, and, above all, from the glimpse of his cousin's face looking out at him from the mirror. He had still the feeling of being in a dream or under some sort of spell of enchantment, of moving in a world of unrealities. The change that had been wrought in him had been too sudden and profound for complete realization. In the space of less than an hour he had become a different person. It was no mere matter of disguise. He was actually a different person. The Andrew Barton who had set forth from Fairfield that morning, had ceased to exist. In his place had been born an entirely new individual; and that individual was himself. It is not unnatural that an idea so opposed to all human experience should have been difficult to accept as a thing that had actually happened. It was not only amazing. It was incredible.

The sense of being in a dream or under some hallucination was intensified by the immediate circumstances. As he sat at the table he had a wall-mirror on either hand. By turning his head slightly in either direction, he was able to observe his cousin Ronald dining with Professor Booley. It was extremely uncanny. The first time he caught sight of that familiar figure, he started violently and looked away only to find that same apparition presented to his view in the mirror at his other hand. By degrees, however, his nervous tension relaxed and his mind became less confused, under the reviving influence of food and drink. He had, in fact, been badly in need of refreshment after his long walk, together with the repeated mental shocks finishing up with the severe pain of the operation; and though the latter had now subsided to a dull ache and a tenderness which made mastication slightly uncomfortable, he found distinct physical satisfaction in disposing of the carefully chosen dishes and the contents of a small bottle of claret.

He was but half-way through his meal when the Professor looked at his watch and stood up.

"Don't let me disturb you," said he. "Make a good dinner and don't eat too fast. But I must run away now and finish my packing. I am sorry that you did not come to me sooner, so that I could have seen a bit more of you. But I'm mighty glad that you came at last. I shall look back on this as a red-letter day. You've given me the greatest opportunity I ever had. No; don't get up. Finish your dinner quietly, and, as I told you before, be careful how you handle that nose."

The two men shook hands heartily, and, after cordial expressions of mutual good will, said a final "goodbye", when the Professor bustled away, pausing only for an instant at the door for a last fond look at his masterpiece.

When he had gone, Andrew resumed his attack on the food with a growing sense of bodily well-being. He even ordered a coffee and liqueur, and, while these were being obtained, he stood up and stepped over to the mirror to view himself at close quarters; to the indulgent amusement of the elderly waiter, who wrote him down a vain young dog – but not without some excuse for his vanity.

He gazed long and earnestly at the tall handsome man who looked out at him from the mirror. But his original impression remained unshaken. The man was Ronald – and yet the man was himself. Well as he knew his cousin, he could see in the reflection not a single appreciable point of difference. He and Ronald had been as like as twins, excepting for their differently shaped noses. And now the wizardry of Professor Booley had extinguished even that difference.

He went back to his seat, and, as he sipped his coffee and the liqueur, lit one of Ronald's cigarettes and set himself to consider the amazing situation, and his own course of action whereby to meet it. And, even then, he began to have some dawning perception of the complications that this situation might involve. But he was far from perceiving that the control of his future had passed out of his hands; that events were already shepherding him irresistibly in a particular direction without regard to his inclinations or desires. It was only by degrees, as he began to make his plans, that he realized how little choice he had; how completely he had become the creature of circumstance.

The first shock of discovery came to him when he essayed to settle his immediate proceedings. He had looked out the trains on the previous day and he knew that there was a train leaving Crompton at half-past nine. That would get him home about eleven. By that time Molly would have gone to bed, and, as he had no latch-key, he would have to knock her up. But the consideration that he had no latch-key – that his latch-key was in the clothes which were now, perhaps, washing about in the sea – brought him up against the realities of the situation. Suddenly, he realized that the Andrew who would appear at his door was not the Andrew who had left it in the morning. The figure that faced him in the mirror was the figure that would face Molly at the door. He would have to explain what had happened. But as the thought came to him, he put it away. The thing was impossible, absurd. Molly was not an intellectual woman, but she had a massive common sense. How would she react to the amazing story that he had to tell? He could not have a moment's doubt. She would see, standing on the doorstep, a man who, to all outward seeming, was cousin Ronald. She would hear him explain that he was her husband, strangely metamorphosed; that, having started for London, he had returned from Crompton; that he had, in error, put on another man's clothes, and that he had, in the course of a few hours, grown a new nose. Whether she would ever listen to such a statement was an open question; but it was quite certain that she would not allow him to enter the house at eleven o'clock at night.

Such being the case, it was obviously useless to think of going home that night. He would have to stay at Crompton; and he would have to make some arrangements for the night's lodging. As he debated this question, it suddenly occurred to him that Ronald's lodgings were available. He would have to go there to retrieve his attaché case; for that case contained a hundred pounds, and he began to perceive that he might want that hundred pounds rather badly in the course of the next few days. He felt in his pocket for the latch-key which he had seen Ronald use, and, having found it, took it out, inspected it curiously and returned it. But, simple as it seemed to enter this house and take his place as the tenant, he viewed the project a little apprehensively and considered it at some length. And all the time, as he sat there considering, the clock of Destiny was ticking on; the clock which no man can put back.

At last, when he had screwed up his courage to the sticking point, he beckoned to the waiter; and, having paid his bill, took up his hat and went out. He found his way easily back to Barleymow Street, and, entering that secluded thoroughfare, walked briskly towards the house. Suddenly, it occurred to him that he was not certain as to which rooms his cousin had occupied. When Ronald had run in with the attaché case, he had been absent for but a few moments, and Andrew, looking in at the ground-floor window, had thought that he saw someone moving within. But he was not quite certain; and the doubt gave him pause. It would be very awkward if he let himself into the house and then was unable to find his rooms.

He slowed down his pace to a saunter while he turned the problem over in his mind. As he passed Number 16 on the opposite side of the street, he looked across and noted a light moving about in a first-floor window. Otherwise, the house was in darkness. Still he could not bring himself to make the plunge; and, as he wandered on irresolutely, he came to the archway leading to the police station. The lamp still threw its light on the portentous bill, and he was moved, partly by curiosity and partly by a certain bravado, to stop and read it. He could do so now with perfect safety.

At this moment three men issued forth from the police station, one of whom looked like a fisherman while the other two were policemen; and the latter carried between them a folded stretcher. They advanced together and came out of the archway, when the two stretcher-bearers halted, opened the stretcher, fixed its struts and deposited it on the pavement. Then the three men turned and looked up the street.

"They ought to be here in a minute or two," said the fisherman. "I left 'em coming into the High Street." He stared into the gloom of the ill-lighted street for a few more seconds and then announced: "I think I hears 'em coming. Yes, here they are."

As he spoke, Andrew became aware of a faint rumbling in the distance, which suddenly grew more distinct as a dark object accompanied by a moving light appeared at the end of the street. With a sudden suspicion as to what that dark object might be, Andrew turned away from the archway and began to saunter up the street. Very soon the dark shape resolved itself into a two-wheeled farm cart, of which the horse was being led by a labourer, while two men, apparently fishermen, one of whom carried a ship's anchor-light, walked at the side.

As the rather funereal procession passed him, Andrew looked at it with a strangely detached interest. He could not see what was in the cart, but a few wisps of sea-wrack that clung to the spokes of the wheel told him that it was a seaweed-cart; on which, he turned once more and slowly retraced his steps.

The cart drew up opposite to the stretcher, which the policemen, one of whom was a sergeant, dragged close alongside. Then the three fishermen and the labourer proceeded to draw from the cart an elongated object wrapped in a boat sail which they carried to the stretcher and deposited thereon with elaborate care; notwithstanding which, the canvas became slightly displaced and a bare foot projected at the end. The sergeant, observing the foot, stooped and tenderly replaced the canvas covering. Then he turned back the canvas at the other end, glanced inside, ejaculated "Good God!" and hurriedly replaced it.

Meanwhile one of the fishermen had climbed into the cart and now descended with a bundle of clothing in his arms.

"Here's his clothes," said he, addressing the sergeant. "You'll want them to find out who he is."

"Yes, by the Lord!" the sergeant agreed. "There won't be much chance of identification otherwise. Bring them along."

Andrew watched with profound interest as the fisherman handed the clothes, garment by garment, to the sergeant, who, as he received them, laid them over the shrouded figure on the stretcher, excepting the shoes and the crushed hat, which he tucked under his arm.

"That seems to be the lot," he remarked, as he took these last articles. "There was nothing else? No walking stick?"

"No; that's the lot," was the reply.

"I suppose you don't know what is in the pockets?"

"No," the fisherman replied rather gruffly. "'Twasn't no business of ourn. We just grabbed 'em up and stowed 'em in the boat. Another five minutes and they'd have been awash."

"Well," said the sergeant, "we will go through them when we get them inside. Do you mind lending a hand with the stretcher as I've got these things to carry?"

The fisherman took his place at the foot end between the handles as the constable took his at the head. The latter gave the word, when they both stooped, grasped the handles and lifted, and then the whole procession moved off under the arch and disappeared down the alley, excepting the carter, who remained in charge of the horse and was now engaged in adjusting the nosebag.

When he had seen the last of the procession, Andrew turned away and began to walk slowly up the street, his retreat being somewhat accelerated by signs of impending conversation on the part of the carter. It had been a strange experience and he was conscious of a certain surprise at his own state of mind. As the clothes – his own clothes – had been transferred, he had watched with a curiously detached interest, checking each garment and making a mental note of the contents of its pockets, not without a passing thought as to the information that they would convey to the observer who should presently turn them out. Yet he had felt no sense of proprietorship in them. Once they had been his; but now they belonged to the corpse on which they lay. They appertained to a past which had been blotted out and had no connection with the present – at least with his present. And his mental attitude towards the corpse, itself, also surprised him in a vague way. The thrill of horror which had affected him at the time of the catastrophe had now no counterpart. In the whirl of events which had followed it, the tragedy had dwindled to a mere incident which concerned him only in respect of its consequences. And these consequences were what he would presently have to consider. But, for the moment, there was the immediately important question of the night's lodging.

When he arrived at the middle of the street, he perceived that there was now a light in the window of the ground-floor room of Number 16. This rather disconcerted him; but, since the thing had to be done sooner or later, he screwed up his courage to make the attempt forthwith. Taking the key out of his pocket, he crossed the road and walked boldly up to the door.

It was evidently the right key, for it entered and turned in the lock without difficulty. He pushed the door open softly and stepped into the hall. There was no light in it excepting what came through the open door of the room. He looked into the latter, which appeared to be a bed-sitting room, for it contained a bedstead, an easy-chair and a good-sized table. On the table was a shaded oil lamp and, what was of much more importance to him, his own attaché case.

As there could be no doubt that this was Ronald's room, he walked in confidently and was about to shut the door when a voice from somewhere upstairs called out:

"Is that you, Mr Green?"

He was on the point of replying "No," when he fortunately remembered Ronald's alias; whereupon he answered: "Yes."

"Oh!" said the voice, "so you have come back. I began to think you had gone for good."

The voice did not impress Andrew as an amicable voice; and when it took visible shape as a rather slatternly-looking middle-aged woman, the impression was confirmed.

"I thought that perhaps you'd hopped off," she explained, standing in the doorway and regarding him with a truculent eye.

"Now, why should you think that?" he asked in a conciliatory tone and wondering what the deuce her name was.

"Well," she replied, "you are not usually so late as this. Mighty punctual for your meals you are as a rule, and nearly a fortnight's board and lodging owing, and no luggage to speak of excepting this"

– indicating the attaché case – "if it belongs to you. I haven't seen it before."

Andrew thought it best not to discuss this point; but the arrears (which did not surprise him in the least) had better be settled at once. The difficulty was that the money was in the case, and, as his ownership had been questioned, it might be a little awkward to produce it from that source in the lady's presence.

"I am sorry to be so behind hand," he said, meekly, "but I can settle up now if you would be so kind as to let me have an account of what is owing."

"I gave you my bill days ago," said she. "You know I did."

"Yes," said Andrew, "but that was only for last week. I think I had better settle up for the fortnight. Would you mind making out a fresh bill?"

"Up to Thursday, the day after tomorrow? That will be the fortnight."

"Yes, I think that will be best."

The lady thought so too, by the light of experience, and in a slightly mollified frame of mind retired, shutting the door after her.

As soon as she was gone, Andrew proceeded with some anxiety to open the case, which, fortunately in the circumstances, had no lock. But his anxiety was relieved by the first glance. Whatever the landlady's shortcomings were, dishonesty was not one of them, for the contents of the case were exactly as he had left them. Hurriedly, he took ten of the pound notes from the bundle and, having shut the case, bestowed the notes in his wallet. Then he began rapidly to consider his future movements.

There was no object in his remaining at Crompton and there was a very good reason why he should go up to London without delay. His main banking account was kept at the head office in Cornhill, and he was accustomed to keep a rather large balance there. The account at the Bunsford branch was only for local expenditure and he fed it with cheques on the London office. He had had to pay in a London cheque to get the fifty pound notes.

Now, the cheque that he had drawn for Ronald was drawn on the London office, and there he would have to go to cash it. He did not know much about banking, but it occurred to him that if he was to cash that cheque, he must do so without delay. On the morrow at some time there would be a rumour of his death, and he presumed that with the death of the drawer the cheque would be unpayable at the bank; and he did not want to be referred to the executors. What he would do about the question of his death, was a matter that he would have to consider later. At that moment, it was vitally important that he should have that fifty pounds.

By which it will be seen that his power of coherent thinking was reviving and also that he was beginning, even if half-unconsciously, to realize the compelling force of events.

The landlady's bill was not a masterpiece of calligraphy, but it supplied some indispensable information. It set forth that Mr W Green was indebted to Mrs Sarah Baxter in the sum of four guineas, being two weeks' board residence at the rate of two guineas per week. It seemed a modest charge, and he suspected that Mrs Baxter had not made an extravagant profit. He handed over the sum and, when the bill had been receipted, he dropped it into the attaché case.

"Shall you be staying on after Thursday?" Mrs Baxter asked.

"Well, no," he replied. "I have finished my business in Crompton and I have to go up to London tomorrow. Probably I shall have to stay there some time, so I shall take my luggage with me. If I should have occasion to come back, I will write to you."

"I can't keep the rooms vacant, you know," said she.

"Of course you can't," he agreed. "I must take my chance. Do you know how the morning trains for London go?"

"There's a fast train at eight thirty-five," she replied. "It's the best train in the day; gets to London at a quarter to ten. I should go by that if I was you."

"I think I will," said he, "if my going so early will not inconvenience you."

She looked at him with amused surprise.

"You're mighty considerate all of a sudden," she remarked. "But, Lord bless you, I am up before six every morning. You'll have your breakfast by seven o'clock and, if you'll put your shoes outside the door, I'll give them a brush. They look as if they wanted it."

Andrew thanked her (but not too profusely, as she seemed unaccustomed to excessive manifestations of politeness) whereupon she wished him "good night" and retired.

When he was once more alone, he sat down in the easy-chair and tried to think out his position. But the fatigues and agitations of the day, combined with the effects of his recent meal, began to make themselves felt. A comfortable drowsiness stole over him. The cigarette which he had lighted, went out and fell from his fingers. His thoughts grew muddled, and he felt a growing desire for sleep. After nodding in his chair for half an hour he got up, searched for Ronald's pyjamas and, having found them hidden under the bedclothes, undressed and turned into bed.

# CHAPTER SIX

## *Two Inquests*

It was but a quarter of an hour after the time for opening when Andrew presented himself at the bank. He entered with a studiously assumed air of unconcern, but with a curious feeling of unreality and a distinct and unpleasant consciousness of the fact that he was falsely personating the payee of the cheque which he was about to present for payment. He knew the place well – his own bank, where he had kept an account for years and where he had at this moment some four hundred pounds to his credit – and most of the clerks and cashiers knew him well enough by sight. Yet he was entering in the guise of a stranger; for though some of the cashiers had seen Ronald, it was unlikely that any of them would remember him.

Nevertheless, he maintained a calm exterior and, selecting a cashier who was a stranger to him, laid his cheque on the counter and pushed it under the brass screen. He had already endorsed it with a copy from memory of the too-familiar signature.

The cashier took up the cheque, looked at the signature, turned it over to see that it was endorsed, and then retired, presumably to compare it with the recorded signature in the book. But Andrew watched him with a shade of uneasiness lest there should be some other kind of investigation. He had not seen the morning paper and could not, therefore, judge whether his assumed death had yet become publicly known, or whether, if it had, the bank would take notice of it. Hence he waited in anxious suspense while the formalities were being disposed of; and he breathed a sigh of relief when the man, reappearing from behind a screen, approached the counter, laid the cheque on it and opened the drawer in evident preparation to pay.

"How would you like it?" the cashier asked. "Five pound notes?"

"Thank you," said Andrew, "but I think pound notes would be more convenient."

"Yes," the cashier agreed, "five pound Bank of England notes are not quite what they were when you could change them into gold."

He counted the notes out from a new bundle and passed them across the counter to Andrew; who counted them and bestowed them in his wallet. Then he wished the cashier "Good morning" and took his departure with a faint sense of having received yet another push from "circumstance" in a direction which was not that of his own choice. He had cashed Ronald's cheque, and thereby he had tacitly assumed the identity of the payee.

The sense of compulsion became more pronounced as he turned over once again the question of his immediate future. He had already decided that it was not practicable for him to go home at once. The identity of his clothes would have been already ascertained from the letters and visiting cards in the pockets, and, by this time, it was probable that the police had communicated with Molly. He might even find them at the house and become involved in the inquiries. But the very thought of any kind of contact with the police filled him with horror. The risk was not to be entertained for a moment.

But after the initial inquiries, there would be the inquest. Of course, Molly would have to attend; and she would have to identify the body. That consideration gave him pause, for it opened up fresh possibilities. He knew of no recognizable differences between Ronald and himself, apart from their respective faces; and as the body had, apparently, no recognizable face, comparison in that respect was impossible. But might it be that he had some bodily peculiarity which Ronald had not, whereby Molly would be able to decide that the body was not that of her husband? The thing was conceivable. It was not even so very improbable. And if she did so decide, or even express a doubt as to the identity of the corpse, matters would be greatly simplified for him in regard to his explanations to her, though a doubt as to the identity of the body would be an element of danger.

The conclusion which emerged was that he had better wait and see what happened at the inquest. Meanwhile, he had to make some arrangements for food and lodging. Hotels he dismissed on the score of expense and especially of publicity – for he still had an instinctive urge to keep out of sight as far as was possible. The alternative was a bed-sitting room or furnished apartments; and, having decided on the latter, he bought a morning paper and betook himself to a tea-shop to study the advertisements over a cup of coffee.

His choice settled on three sets of apartments, all in the neighbourhood of Hampstead, a locality with which he had been familiar before he married. Having finished his coffee, he tucked the newspaper under his arm and made his way to the Broad Street terminus, where he a took a ticket for the Heath Station and, selecting an empty compartment, opened the newspaper and searched its pages vainly for some notice of the Crompton tragedy. Apparently the news had not reached London when the paper went to press.

In the matter of lodgings he was fortunate, for his first essay brought him to a pleasant, old-fashioned house in a small close off the High Street, where he was offered a ground-floor room, with a bedroom over it, which seemed in every respect so desirable that he engaged them at once. Then, having paid a deposit to establish the tenancy, he returned to town to lunch and to collect his scanty luggage from the cloakroom at Cannon Street Station.

The latter part of the programme, however, he deferred until later in the day, for he had no object in returning to his lodgings before the evening, and he found some relief in walking about the crowded city streets while he turned over again and again the various possibilities of escape from the perplexities in which he was involved. He looked in, for a while, at the Guildhall Art Gallery and found some comfort in the companionship of the pictures. Then he had a late and leisurely tea, after which he repaired to Cannon Street Station, and, having redeemed his luggage – Ronald's suitcase and his own attaché case –

made his way to Broad Street Station. And here he had a most surprising and disturbing experience.

As he reached the top of the broad staircase, he observed that a train was waiting at the platform and he judged by the hiss of escaping steam that it was ready to start; an opinion that was confirmed by the ticket collector who urged him to "look sharp" as "she was just off". On this, he started forward at a run, threading his way as well as he could through a dense crowd of people who were waiting for the next train. But he nearly missed his passage, for, as he struggled towards the open door of an empty compartment, the engine-driver sounded his whistle and the train began to move. He barely managed to fling his luggage in at the open door and scramble up to the footboard as the protesting guard rushed at him, pushed him in and slammed the door.

As soon as he was shut in, he turned and thrust his head, out of the window to compare his wristwatch with the station clock. But the comparison was never made; for at that moment he met the eyes of a woman at the edge of the crowd and then only a few feet away, who was gazing at him with a most singular expression. As their eyes met, she uttered an exclamation and started forward, making as if she were about to try to board the train. She did, in fact, run alongside for a short distance until a porter, suspecting her intentions, firmly headed her off; and then Andrew, gazing at her in the utmost astonishment, saw her standing, still staring at him with that strange expression, until distance and a curve of the line hid her from his view.

It was an amazing affair. Who could she be? She was a total stranger to him – that is, to Andrew Barton. But he was Andrew Barton no longer. The reflection was a distinctly uncomfortable one. He had taken over the reversion of Ronald's nose. Might there be some other reversions of which he knew nothing? It seemed far from improbable, judging by the little that he knew of his late cousin's moral character and manner of life.

He tried to recall the woman's appearance. It was not difficult, for she was a somewhat unusual-looking woman; rather big, with a marked suggestion of energy and muscular strength and by no means uncomely. She had a good deal of hair of a coppery tint and eyes of a pale, bluish grey. Certainly not a woman whose appearance would be easily forgotten.

But what was the meaning of that singular expression? Astonishment undoubtedly. But the flushed face and the truculent grey eyes suggested emotions other than surprise. There was no denying that the woman's expression and manner had been definitely hostile. She was an unmistakably angry woman.

The incident, with its uncomfortable implications, supplied him with matter for thought until he reached his lodgings. And when he had unpacked the suitcase and went forth for a walk on the Heath, it continued to intrude itself as an added complication to the difficulties of his other problems.

But as he turned into the High Street on his way home, his attention was brought back to the main issues by the voice of a paper-boy announcing the contents of the late evening paper. As the boy came nearer, the generalized howl resolved itself into the words:

"Ribble's Cross Murder: Inquest."

In an instant the woman was forgotten, blotted out by the picture of the lonely road, the car with its two occupants, and the figures of the flying bandits. With a thrill of mingled curiosity and terror, Andrew stopped the boy, bought a copy of the paper, and, having folded it and stowed it in an inner pocket, stole into his lodgings to read it in secret.

The report was complete to the inevitable verdict, for the inquest had been held in the morning and the proceedings had been comparatively brief. The deceased was a Mr Oliver Hudson, the publisher of a technical journal, and the woman who was with him was his secretary, Miss Kate Booth. She, naturally, was the principal witness, and her evidence was taken first, and was to the following effect.

In the evening of Monday, the 27th of August, she was driving Mr Hudson from his office to his home at Lenham. She was accustomed to drive him daily to and from his office and knew the road well. On the night of the murder, as they were approaching Ribble's Cross, she saw a closed car drawn up at the corner with its head pointing towards the side road. She thought she saw a man standing by it, but was not certain, as, owing to the speed at which she was driving – about forty miles an hour – she had to keep her attention fixed on the road. But someone must have made a signal of some kind for her car to stop, though she did not see it, for deceased exclaimed: "Confound them! Pull up and see what they want."

She put on the brakes and stopped the car. A man came to the window and deceased said: "Well, what is it?" and put his hand into the pocket in which he carried his revolver. The man said: "Put 'em up, both of you," and pointed a revolver at deceased, who, almost at the same moment, drew his revolver from his pocket.

She had only a rather confused recollection of what followed. Both revolvers seemed to go off almost at the same moment, and the bullet from one – it must have been Mr Hudson's – made a hole through the windscreen. Deceased uttered a cry and lurched up against her. When the revolvers were fired, she instinctively put down the accelerator pedal and the car jumped forward. She did not look back through the rear window as she had accelerated to over fifty miles an hour and she had to keep her eyes on the road.

At Padsworth, four miles farther on, she halted at the Welbeck Hotel and sent for a doctor and the police; but deceased was already dead. A police patrol came in a few minutes and she told him what had happened.

"Can you describe the man whom you saw at the window?" the coroner asked.

"Yes," she replied, "I saw him very distinctly, because, as he appeared at the window, deceased threw the light of a torch full on his face, and it was a most extraordinary face – one that I could never forget. His nose appeared to have been broken; at any rate, it had no bridge. It was perfectly flat excepting at the tip, which was of the ordinary length and stuck out from his face like a bird's beak. He had grey eyes and I should say he was about thirty years of age."

"Could you see how he was dressed?"

"No; at least, I didn't notice anything about his clothing excepting that he had no hat on."

"Was he the only person present, or were there others?"

"I had an impression that there was someone behind him, but I did not actually see anyone. My eyes were fixed on the face that was lighted up by the torch."

"Are you quite sure that the man whom you have described is the man who fired the shot?"

"Yes, quite sure. There was no one else that I could see. And I saw the revolver pushed in over the edge of the window."

"Do you think you would recognize this man if you were to see him again?"

"I am certain that I should. It was a face that you could never forget."

"Did deceased usually carry a revolver?"

"Only, I think, when he was motoring at night. Then he always did; and he declared that he meant to use it if he was stopped by an armed robber."

"Do you know of any reason for this attack? Had you anything of value in the car?"

"No; there was nothing of any value in the car beyond the money in our pockets."

"Did you notice if any cars overtook and passed you on the road?"

"Yes; several cars overtook us and passed ahead near London. I always drive at a very moderate speed until I am clear of the town and let the faster cars go by."

"Do you remember any car in particular?"

"Yes, there was one which passed us at great speed just as we were approaching the open country road. Mr Hudson remarked upon it as it flew past."

That was the sum of the secretary's evidence. It was followed by that of the medical witness; who deposed that death was due to a gunshot wound penetrating the heart, and must have been practically instantaneous. Then came the patrol officer, who had not much to tell, and finally a detective-inspector with a remarkable gift for keeping his own counsel. But if somewhat elusive in regard to matters of fact, he was prepared to offer certain rather guarded opinions. Thus, when asked by the coroner if the circumstances of the attack were not very unusual and surprising, he agreed, and continued in explanation:

"The police are inclined to believe that the whole affair was a mistake. There is reason for suspecting that it was a carefully planned robbery concerned with certain very valuable property which was being conveyed in a car along this road at about this time; but, at the last moment, the thieves got flurried and attacked the wrong car. It is a pity," the inspector added, "that deceased produced his revolver, because that probably flurried them still more, and led to the disaster."

The coroner discreetly refrained from further questions on this subject, but, turning to another, asked:

"With regard to the man who has been stated to have fired the fatal shot; is there any clue to his identity?"

Here, the inspector became once more distinctly elusive, but he was of opinion that, having regard to the man's very unusual and distinctive appearance, there ought not to be much difficulty in finding him; and, once found, the witness, Miss Booth, would be able to identify him beyond any reasonable doubt.

This completed the evidence. If the police knew any more about the case, they were reserving their knowledge, and the coroner was wise enough to ask no questions that were not strictly relevant to the inquiry. There was no doubt as to how deceased had met his death, and the verdict of wilful murder by a person unknown was a foregone conclusion.

The reading of this report had no other effect upon Andrew than to confirm him in his resolve to abandon for ever his original personality. The guarded tone of the inspector's evidence left him in little doubt that "the man with the deformed nose" had already been identified as Mr Andrew Barton, and that the police were in hot pursuit. What would have happened if they had been able to run him to earth? The woman, Booth, was evidently prepared to swear that she saw him fire the fatal shot; and to this, the clear testimony of a competent eye-witness, there appeared to him no possible answer. Of course he was wrong; and in his peculiar state of mind, he was ignoring the strength of his defence. But even if he was mistaken as to his position if he were brought to trial, who can say that he was wrong in his choice of action? Who would accept the chances of a trial for murder – and an atrocious murder at that – when he could, by lying perdu, avoid even the accusation. In the character of Ronald Barton he lay under no suspicion whatever. His security was complete. If there were any incidental disadvantages, he had yet to discover them.

When he had finished the report, he turned over the leaves of the paper in search of some notice of the discovery of Ronald's body. He found it near the bottom of the page, headed, "A mystery of the Sea", and the brief account read as follows:

"Yesterday afternoon, a party of fishermen, sailing along the coast near Crompton, made a strange and gruesome discovery. Looking shorewards, they saw what appeared to be a pair of nude human legs protruding from under a heap of chalk which seemed to have fallen recently from the cliff. On this, they ran their boat inshore and landed to investigate, when they found the nude body of a man buried under a mass of chalk fragments. The largest of the fragments, a mass weighing fully a hundredweight, had fallen on his head and crushed it so completely as to render the face unrecognizable. The man had apparently been bathing, as a complete set of clothes was under the body, and from articles found in the pockets, it is inferred that the remains are those of Mr Andrew Barton, of Fairfield near Bunsford. The inquest is to be held at Crompton tomorrow."

He laid the newspaper aside and fell into a train of deep but uneasy thought. And once again, the sense of unreality, of illusion, which had never quite left him since Professor Booley had waved the magician's wand to such amazing purpose, came over him with renewed intensity. He repeated the statement to himself: "The inquest is to be held tomorrow." The inquest! The inquiry into his own death! And he, the deceased, would read the report of the proceedings! It was an incredible situation; and the more he thought of it, the more impossible and unbelievable did it appear.

Yet he knew that it was a reality; and presently, as his thoughts settled down into a more orderly train, he began to be aware of certain possibilities which might affect his future and influence his conduct most profoundly. At present the position was that the body of Mr Andrew Barton had been found on the shore. The identification by the clothing was not legally conclusive; but it would have occurred to nobody to doubt whose body it was. And the suggestion which had influenced others would doubtless take effect also on Molly. Her husband was missing; and here was a dead man − unrecognizable, but of similar age, size and general appearance − who had been wearing her husband's clothes. Would the idea that this might possibly be another man even enter her head? It was practically certain that it would not. She, like the others, would take the appearances at their obvious face value; unless −

He sat up with suddenly sharpened attention to consider the position more critically. Yes, undoubtedly there were counter possibilities that had to be reckoned with. A single item of positive evidence would shatter the whole illusion. It need be but the merest trifle; a mole, a wart, a scar, a tattoo mark; any permanent characteristic on that body, which was not on the body of Andrew Barton, would be enough to destroy the suggestion effect of the clothing. And when once the question of identity was raised, all the mysterious and abnormal circumstances would combine to confirm the suspicion of a substitution.

And how would that affect him? On the whole, favourably; for it would simplify his task when he sought to convince Molly of his changed identity. True, it would set the police once more searching for the man with the deformed nose. But that need cause him no concern. That man was dead. If he had not died at the foot of the cliffs, he had at least died in Professor Booley's "beauty parlour". And, mercifully, the Professor would be on the high seas before the inquest opened.

But when the report of the inquest appeared, it raised questions of a somewhat different kind from those which Andrew had anticipated. The evening paper of Thursday contained only the opening of the proceedings; but the *Daily Telegraph* of the following morning had a full report, given in considerable detail, and this Andrew studied with the closest attention.

The first witness was Samuel Sharpin, the skipper of the fishing lugger, who deposed as follows:

"On Tuesday, the 28th of August, I was aboard my boat, the *Sunflower*. We was beating up for Meregate Cove, where we berths. About four o'clock in the afternoon we was opposite Hunstone Gap when I noticed that some of the cliff had fallen down and I remarked to my mate that it was a good job that no one was underneath when it came down. Then the apprentice, Joe Todd, said he thought someone had been underneath, because he seemed to see what looked like a pair of legs sticking out from under the heap of chalk. So I got my glass and looked; and then I saw a pair of naked legs sticking out. So we put the boat about and turned her head inshore; and, when we was near enough in, we dropped the anchor and pulled ashore in the dinghy. Then we saw a man lying under a heap of chalk with his legs sticking out. It wasn't a big fall. But one large lump of chalk, nearly half the size of a fish trunk, had come right down on the man's head; and there it sat, resting on his face, with the blood and stuff oozing out at the sides.

"My mate, who is a pretty hefty lad, hove the block of chalk off the man's face, though it must have weighed well over a hundredweight, and then we could see that his head was smashed as flat as a turbot and his face hadn't got no more features than a skate. It was an awful sight. Gave us all a reg'lar turn.

"We took up the body and carried it to the dinghy – it wasn't far to go, for the tide was up and beginning to wash round the corpse when we came ashore. Then we carefully collected the clothes and put them in the boat; and then we just had a look round before we went back aboard."

The coroner: "You had a look round. What were you looking for?"

Witness: "We wanted to see if the man had come to the place by himself. Because, as he was naked, and seemed to have been bathing and sitting on his clothes to dry himself, it seemed funny that he should have come there all by himself. So we had a look round."

"And what did you find?"

74

"We found that he hadn't. There was only a small strip of clear sand left opposite the Gap, but we could see quite plainly that there were two sets of foot marks coming down to the shore from the cart-track that leads down to the Gap, but there was only one set going up. So he must have come there with someone else."

Coroner: "This is very remarkable and very important. Are you quite sure about the two sets of footprints? I mean, are you sure that they were the footprints of two persons walking together and not merely the footprints of two persons who had come to the place separately?"

Witness: "No; they looked like the footprints of two persons who were walking together. So far as we could see them, they went on side by side, keeping at the same distance – about two foot apart.

"Well, when we had got the body on board, we up anchor and beat up for Meregate Cove. When we got there, we brought up at our berth and I sent Joe Todd up to Meregate Farm and told him to ask Farmer Blewitt for the loan of a seaweed cart to take the body into Crompton. So Mr Blewitt he sends a man down with a cart and we brought the body into Crompton and handed it and the clothes over to the police."

The coroner thanked the witness for the clear way in which he had given his evidence and was about to dismiss him when Mrs Barton, the wife of the deceased (if the identification is correct) asked to be allowed to put a question to him.

Coroner: "Certainly you may. What is it that you wish to ask?"

Mrs Barton: "He has said that he saw two sets of footprints going down to the shore. I want to ask him if either of those two sets were the footprints of the – the deceased."

The coroner looked interrogatively at the witness, who replied:

"Well, ma'am, I really can't say. How would I know whether they were his footprints or no?"

Mrs Barton: "You found the shoes with the body. Did you not compare those shoes with the footprints?"

Witness: "No, ma'am, I never thought of it, like a dam' fool – begging your pardon."

Coroner: "What makes you ask that question? Is there anything special in your mind?"

Mrs Barton: "Yes. I find it impossible to believe that my husband came there of his own free will."

Coroner: "We must consider that question presently. I think there is nothing more that we need ask this witness."

The next witnesses were the rest of the crew of the *Sunflower* who, however, had nothing fresh to tell. They merely confirmed the evidence of the skipper. They were followed by Mrs Barton, the dead man's wife. As she took her place, the coroner expressed his sympathy and that of the jury, and his regret at having to subject her to the distress of giving evidence on so painful an occasion. He then proceeded with his examination.

"You have seen the body of deceased. Do you recognize it as the body of your husband, Andrew Barton?"

"No. It might be his body, but the dreadful injuries make it impossible for me to recognize it."

"Have you any doubt that it is the body of your husband?"

Here the witness was somewhat overcome but, after a pause, she replied: "No, I am afraid not. The clothes are his, and the things from the pockets are his; and the body might be his. There is nothing to suggest that it is not. But it is all very mysterious."

"In what way mysterious?"

"That he should be there at all, in that strange place. He left home in the morning to go to London on definite business, taking with him an attaché case containing some of his paintings; and he is found here, miles away from home and from London, apparently behaving in a way in which I don't believe he would have behaved – I mean bathing without bathing-clothes or towels – and accompanied by at least one unknown person. And the attaché case seems to be missing. I think there is something very suspicious about the whole affair."

"When you say 'suspicious', do you mean to suggest that your husband met with foul play?"

"That is what it looks like to me."

"But do you think that the mode of death is compatible with such a suspicion?"

"I don't know what to think. It is all so strange and unnatural."

"We can quite understand your feeling about it. The circumstances are, in fact, very remarkable. But now, to pass on to another matter, can you give us a description of your husband?"

"He was just under thirty years of age, about five feet eleven in height, of medium complexion with grey eyes and darkish brown hair. His nose had been struck by a cricket-ball which broke the bridge and caused some little disfigurement."

"I am sorry to have to refer to a subject that will be painful, but which is relevant to this inquiry. Are you aware that a man answering to the description of your husband has been accused of complicity in an attack on a motorcar when a Mr Hudson was killed?"

"Yes. A police officer called on me to make inquiries and I told him all I knew about the affair. Of course, it is a mistake. The thing is ridiculous. My husband was a gentleman of reputation and of substantial means. He happened to be present when the attack was made. He told me all about it when he came home that night; and I repeated what he told me to the police officer."

"When he came home that night, did he seem at all agitated?"

"Not in the least. Of course, he was rather excited, though, at that time, he did not know that anyone had been killed."

"And in the morning when he left home?"

"He was in his usual spirits. I understood that he proposed to call at the police station to report what he had seen."

"And do you connect his disappearance with the circumstances of that crime?"

"Certainly not. There was no reason why he should run away. He had nothing to fear."

"Is there anything more that you can tell us that would help the jury in arriving at their verdict?"

"No; I have told you all I know."

"Then I think we need not trouble you any further. We thank you for the very clear way in which you have given your evidence in circumstances which must have been very painful to you, and we should wish once more to offer you our most sincere sympathy."

The rest of the evidence was of little significance. The medical witness gave a brief description of the injuries and stated that death must have been practically instantaneous. The police superintendent described the reception of the body and the articles found in the pockets, by which the remains were identified in the first place, and mentioned as a curious coincidence that a bill containing the description of the deceased was posted up outside the station when the body was brought in. He was the last witness; and, when he had given his evidence, the coroner proceeded to sum up the case for the jury to the following effect:

"This inquiry is in some respects perfectly simple and in others rather obscure. Death was obviously caused by the fall of a heavy mass of chalk on the head of deceased; and it is difficult to see how the fall of that mass could be other than accidental. On the other hand, an element of obscurity is introduced into the case by the fact that deceased was apparently accompanied to the shore by some other person; that that person never reported the accident and has not come forward to give any information. There is no denying that the behaviour of that person to some extent justifies the suspicion that has been expressed by the wife of the deceased. If the cause of death were such as to admit of the idea of homicide, the conduct of that person would expose him to the gravest suspicion. As no such idea appears possible, his behaviour is quite incomprehensible.

"With regard to the strange conduct of deceased, the circumstances connected with the murder of Mr Hudson may offer some explanation. The superintendent has told us that at the very moment when the body was brought to the station, there was a bill posted outside giving a description of deceased and stating that he was wanted for the murder. Such bills must have been posted outside all other police stations, and it may easily have happened that deceased had seen one. Then, even though he were innocent, he might have become seized by panic and fled to hide himself. It is rather an alarming thing to see one's description outside a police station and to learn that one is wanted for murder.

"That, however, is only a surmise. What we have to decide is when, where and by what means deceased met his death. You have heard the evidence, and on that you must form your decision."

The jury eventually returned an open verdict. They were not entirely satisfied, the foreman said, that it was a case of death by misadventure. The presence of an unknown person, who had absconded and made no sign, suggested that there might be more in the case than met the eye. And to this, after some demur, the coroner assented.

# CHAPTER SEVEN

## *Molly*

Andrew had read the report of the inquest on his own supposed remains with profound interest but with rather mixed feelings. The possibilities which he had envisaged had not been realized, and certain facts which he had overlooked had come into view. The double set of footprints, for instance, introducing an undoubted element of suspicion, came to him as a something quite unexpected. His attention had been so completely focused on the question of identity that he was unprepared for the new issues that had been raised.

Another matter of surprise to him was the shrewdness and strength of character displayed by his wife. It dawned on him that he had considerably underrated her intelligence. In spite of the agitation that she must have suffered from the terrible circumstances in which she was suddenly placed, she had not only kept her wits unclouded but had shown a quick perception of the significance of the facts which had transpired. She had, indeed, accepted the identity of the corpse – no reason had been shown for doubting it – but, with her ready common sense, she had instantly detected the abnormal character of the whole set of circumstances, and refused to take them at their face value.

The conclusions, then, which emerged were these. First, Molly had no doubt that her husband was dead. Second, that she utterly refused to regard that death as due to a mere accident. She was clearly convinced that some unknown person or persons were implicated in it. In short, that there had been some sort of foul play. Incidentally, it was clear that she did not take the murder charge seriously. To her, it appeared simply as a ridiculous mistake which would be instantly disposed of when suitable explanations were given. That he could have taken fright at the accusation and gone into hiding would appear to her incredible.

These were the data which he had to consider in forming his decision as to what line of action he should adopt. Hitherto he had responded passively to the pressure of events. He had simply gone whither he had been driven. But he could drift passively no longer. He had got to make up his mind as to what course he would steer through the amazing complications with which he was encompassed. So, for the first time, he set himself fairly to face the realities and decide what it was possible to do.

But to all his cogitations, as he tramped along the secluded paths of the Heath where he could think uninterrupted, and turned over one plan after another, there was a permanent background. The tremendous shock that he had sustained from the police bill at Crompton had established in his mind an abiding horror – a sort of "gallows-phobia". And not, perhaps, quite unreasonably. Innocent men have been hanged on worse evidence than that which Miss Booth was prepared confidently to swear to. The man whom she had described had been identified as the artist, Andrew Barton; and since Andrew Barton was conveniently dead, dead he had got to remain. That was the undeniable postulate on which all his plans were based. There could be no resurrection of Andrew; for the instant he appeared, the police would pounce on him. But that postulate seemed to block every avenue of escape.

Thus, the idea of going home and taking up the old life was obviously unthinkable; for Molly's husband was dead, and he was a visibly different person. The explanation which would have made it possible could not be given; for that would bring Andrew to life – and death. Some other plan would have to be thought of – when he had made things clear to Molly. And the question was, how was that to be done?

His first idea was to write her a long letter telling her all that had happened, signing his own name and announcing his intention to come home. She would recognize his handwriting, and that would make the story credible enough to prepare her for his changed appearance. But would she recognize his handwriting? It was not so very characteristic, and there was an awkward complication. It often happens that a similarity of handwriting runs in families; and his was a case in point. Ronald's handwriting had borne a distinct resemblance to his. Molly had noticed it and remarked on it. Then the handwriting would not be conclusive, and the fantastic story would have to rest on its merits. Then there was the complication of Ronald's character. Molly had admired Ronald, and had been indulgent in regard to his faults. Perhaps she liked him; but she had no delusions as to his character. She knew him to be a slippery rascal whose word was of no value whatever. She might – and probably would – reject the letter as an impudent imposture; an attempt on Ronald's part to personate her dead husband. And when he appeared, miraculously transformed into the outward semblance of Ronald, her suspicions would be instantly confirmed, and she would probably refuse to let him enter the house or to listen to anything that he might wish to say.

But that was not the worst. Molly had expressed her suspicion that there had been foul play of some kind. Now, if he wrote such a letter, he would have to admit that he had been on the shore at the time of the catastrophe; in short, that one of the sets of footprints had been his. What more likely than that she should suspect him (in the character of Ronald) of having made away with her husband? And, once the suspicion of foul play was aroused, the letter, itself, would seem to supply the motive for the crime. It would suggest to her that Ronald, relying on his resemblance to her husband, had made away with Andrew with the deliberate purpose of stepping into Andrew's shoes.

Then what would she do? There was very little doubt. Molly had certain very pronounced feminine characteristics; she was quick to decide, confident when she had decided, and quick to act on her decision. If she disbelieved the wildly improbable story and wrote the letter down as a fraudulent attempt on Ronald's part to personate her husband, she would, without waiting for him to appear in person, at once communicate her suspicions to the police and show them the letter.

And what then? In spite of his anxieties, Andrew smiled grimly at the thought of the dilemma which would be created. He would stand to be accused of having murdered himself; and his only defence would be to prove his real identity – that of a person who was already accused of having murdered someone else.

Evidently, the letter would not do; nor would an unannounced visit, with verbal explanations, be much safer. The story that he had to tell was so preposterous that she would probably dismiss it off-hand as an imposture; and then there would be the same trouble as in the case of the letter.

So, once again, Andrew found himself shepherded by inexorable circumstance in the direction in which he did not want to go. For, in the end, he had to fall back on a compromise, and not a very good one at that. He decided, instead of committing himself either by letter or word of mouth, to feel his way cautiously and see if any opportunity offered. He would write to Molly, signing himself "Ronald", and proposing to call on her. When he met her, he would be better able to judge what was possible. Perhaps it might be easier than it looked. It was actually possible that she might recognize him in spite of the disguise. He had examined himself repeatedly in the mirror and had thought he had detected some small differences between himself and Ronald. Perhaps, after all, they were not so much alike as he had thought; and there might be some little peculiarities in his own face and person of which he was not aware, but which might be familiar to her. At any rate, he would see what happened; and if he failed the first time, at least he would not be landed in the net of the police.

But he would not write for a day or two. He would give her time to settle down after the inquest. And then, of course, there was the funeral. The funeral! He had not thought of that before. Now the idea came upon him with devastating effect, imparting a horrible reality to the whole hideous farce. It was an appalling thing to think of his beloved wife standing in tears beside the grave of what was in effect a dummy corpse. It was an obscene outrage. But even in his anger, he realized how that dreadful farce seemed to set the seal of finality on his changed condition; what a formidable obstacle it raised to his attempts to dispel the illusion.

A couple of days later he dispatched the momentous letter; quite a short one, suggesting a call about teatime on the following Wednesday; which elicited a still briefer reply agreeing to the date and time. Brief and rather colourless as it was, Andrew read it again and again. For it was Molly's own writing; and though it was addressed to a fictitious person, yet it seemed to bring him, for the first time since the transformation, into some sort of touch with real life – his own real life.

The days passed in a fever of impatience mingled with anxiety; of longing to stand once more within his own house and to see and talk with the woman who had become to him the centre and focus of life; of anxiety lest he should, after all, fail to break the spell that circumstance had cast over him. And when at last the day of the visit came, he set forth on his adventure thrilling with the strangest mixture of emotions; with love and yearning for the woman who was at once his wife and his lover, with hope and apprehension and even a queer, irrational tinge of jealousy. For it was Ronald, and not he, who was going to meet and talk with Molly. Any tokens of kindliness or affection that she might bestow would be for Ronald, not for him. And thus his thoughts, swaying back and forth to the contending pull of two opposing sets of emotions, oscillated continually between the intense yearning to give expression to the love that was welling up in his heart and a jealous fear lest the rival whom he was impersonating should be received with undue warmth.

At Bunsford, he changed on to the branch line, and, alighting presently at the little wayside station of Fairfield, set forth to walk the familiar road that led to his home. It was a strange experience, that walk from the station. He had the feeling of a traveller, returning after a long absence, treading the well-remembered ways and looking on the familiar scenes of long ago. It seemed as if years had passed since he last turned into the lane. He found it unbelievable that it was but a week and a day since he had kissed Molly at the door and waved his hand to her from the gate. Once more the sense of illusion and enchantment came over him; and, as he approached the cottage and his eyes were greeted by the fresh gashes that his hastily wielded shears had made in the privet hedge, the conflict between his inner sensations and the visible and undeniable facts became positively bewildering.

Like a man in a dream, he opened the gate, stole unsteadily up the path, and plied the little knocker with a shaking hand. And all the while, he was trying confusedly to think what he should say to her, while in the background of his consciousness there lurked a dim hope that she might recognize him despite the transformation.

A few seconds passed. Then a light footstep in the hall, at the sound of which his heart seemed to stand still. The door opened and there she stood, his dearest Molly, his own beloved wife, garbed in a simple black dress, and looking pale and tired, but sweeter and more lovely than ever. At the sight of her, a flood of passionate love surged through him; a wild impulse to take her in his arms and kiss the roses back into her cheeks. It was but a momentary impulse, instantly checked, not only by reason but by something in the way in which she looked at him. She greeted him cordially enough, but yet there was in her manner something new to him; a quiet self-possession with, perhaps, just a shade of chilliness.

He took the proffered hand with a deep sense of anticlimax. She had not recognized him. Of course she had not. How could he have expected it? But the initial failure left him with all his difficulties before him. He could do no more than wait and see if any opening offered.

"Go and sit down, Ronald, while I make the tea," she said in a friendly, matter-of-fact tone, still with that faint suggestion of coolness. "I won't be a minute. You know the way. No, you don't, though. You have never been in this house before. It's in here."

She threw open the door of the dining-room and bustled away towards the kitchen, leaving him to enter alone. He stepped in through the open doorway and stood for a few seconds at the threshold, looking, with a lump in his throat, at the familiar room – his own room, where he had passed so many delightful hours, and where he now stood, a mere visitor, almost a stranger.

He ran his eye over the table, fondly taking in all the little, trivial details; the foolish little flower vases, the cake basket, the biscuit box, the jam jars; all set out in correct array just as he, himself, had set them out on that *dies iræ* in the irrevocable past when Fate, in the garb of a postman, had delivered his summons. And yet Fate had not been unkindly. For its messenger had forestalled another kind of summons, uttered in the King's name to the jingling of handcuffs. The reflection came to him as an opportune reminder just as Molly entered with the teapot and hot-water jug on the little tray.

She took her seat at the head of the table and he drew up his chair; but as he did so, he noted that it was not his own particular chair, in which he had always been used to sit. That was drawn back against the wall. And the place that was "laid" for him was not his customary place, but was on the opposite side of the table. It was a small matter but it defined his position as a visitor.

"It is nice of you to come and see me, Ronald," she said, as she poured out the tea. "I couldn't write to you because I didn't know your address. I suppose you saw it in the papers?"

"Yes," he replied. "It was a dreadful shock, even to me. I can't bear to think of what it must have been to you."

She made no comment on this, and he continued: "I would have written sooner but I thought it better to wait until the – er – the – "

"Yes," she replied quietly, "I understand. It was on Saturday. In Fairfield churchyard. I brought him from Crompton. Everybody was awfully kind, especially the police."

She finished a little unsteadily with a catch in her voice, and Andrew, deeply moved, stole a furtive glance at her, marvelling admiringly at her quiet dignity and self-restraint. She made no parade of grief nor showed any outward sign other than the pale, weary face, the set composure of which smote him to the heart.

For some time neither of them spoke. She sipped her tea mechanically, seeming to be wrapped in thought while he searched his mind frantically for some suitable words but could think of none. At length she asked:

"When did you see him last?"

He started, and his gorge rose at the lie that he would have to tell. But he made it as near the truth as he could.

"I think," he faltered, "it was about two years ago, when I met him by chance in London."

"I remember," said she. "He told me he had met you. But I thought you might have seen him recently. I noticed that he had drawn a cheque for you – I am his executrix, you know – so I thought you might have met. He never mentioned the cheque to me."

"No," stammered Andrew, "I suppose he would not. It was a – a loan, you know, to enable me to – a – to pay a deposit. But I must refund it as soon as I can."

"You needn't worry, Ronald," she replied. "I don't suppose he intended you to repay it. At any rate, there is nothing to show that it was a loan, and if there were, I, as executrix, can use my own discretion in regard to debts. And I shall do what he would have wished me to do."

"That is very good of you, Molly," he said. "But things are different now. I ought to repay that loan when I am able to – though," he added, with a sudden realization of his present plight, "I don't know when that will be."

"As to that, Ronald," she said, in the same curiously quiet, level tone, "you know there is something to come to you when the will has been proved; or had you forgotten?"

He did know, of course; but he had completely forgotten until this moment. Now he gazed at her in dismay as she went on, without raising her eyes from her teacup:

"There is a legacy of five hundred pounds. It was a separate insurance that he made in your favour in case he should die before you. He knew that his death would rob you of a faithful and generous friend, and this was to compensate you."

Andrew was thunderstruck. Here was an appalling complication! This money would presently be paid to him. He could not refuse it without disclosing the whole deception. Yet to accept it was to commit a blatant fraud on the Insurance Society; a fraud for which, if it were discovered, he could be sent to penal servitude. And that was not all. There was the principal insurance, which would be paid to Molly with his connivance. The whole affair was plainly and grossly fraudulent.

He was so overwhelmed by this new complication that he could only mumble incoherent acknowledgments and then once more subside into silence. Molly, having given the explanation, let the subject drop; and, since he sat in dumb confusion, she made shift to keep up some sort of conversation, with long intervals of silence, avoiding, as far as possible, any references to the tragedy or her own immediate affairs. She spoke just in the colourless way in which she might have spoken to some chance stranger who had come to make a ceremonial call.

Meanwhile Andrew, returning such banal answers as fitted the indifferent, semi-formal character of the conversation, was inwardly fermenting with suppressed emotion; with surprise, bewilderment and exasperation. The position was preposterous. The woman who was making polite conversation and so obviously, though tactfully, holding him at arm's length, was his wife! His own wife, whom he loved passionately and who loved him with answering passion! He was starving for her love, filled with a devouring desire to fold her in his arms, to cover her pale face with kisses and murmur into her ear those soft endearments that had always evoked such sweetly frank response. If only he could shake off this bewitchment, how gladly and with what lavish affection would she fall into his arms! He knew it; and yet he could only sit like a fool, talking commonplace drawing-room stuff and even doing that badly.

But he could see no way out. The opening for which he had hoped had failed to present itself. Not only had there been no glimmer of recognition, but, what was worse, she had accepted him as Ronald without a sign of doubt or hesitation. And civil and even kindly as was her bearing towards him, she was evidently on her guard. He could see clearly that she did not trust cousin Ronald: and he realized that she had understood that gentleman's character better than he had supposed.

But this wariness on her part was a complete bar to the revelation that he wanted to make. At the first word her suspicion would light up, and, as the preposterous tale unfolded, she would listen – if she listened at all – with angry impatience to what would seem like a mere crude, silly imposture. It was useless to think of making the attempt, for failure seemed inevitable; and the probable consequences of failure were too appalling to contemplate.

Nevertheless, he tried to pull himself together and at least find something to say. From time to time, as they had been talking, he had caught her looking at him with a rather curious expression; an expression of faint surprise, as if she were "sizing him up" and found something in his manner a little puzzling. This he put down to, his deplorably bad acting, for assuredly the real Ronald – the voluble, ready talker, suave, genial and self-possessed – would not have sat mumchance at the table opposite his pretty cousin. He must rouse himself, and, if he could not be Andrew, then he must be a reasonably convincing Ronald.

"I suppose," he ventured, "you will shut up the studio now?"

"No," she answered, "I have taken it as my sitting-room."

He was slightly surprised. She had always left him in undisputed possession of the studio as a place that was entirely outside her province.

"I have never seen this studio," said he (reconciling the blatant untruth to his conscience by the fiction that he was speaking in the character of Ronald). "Would you let me have a look at it presently? Andrew's pictures were always a great delight to me."

"Were they?" she exclaimed, in evident surprise. "I didn't know that you took any interest in them at all. Certainly, I will show you the studio. We will go down there as soon as we have finished tea. Can I give you another cup?"

"No, thank you," he replied. "I have finished."

"Then," said she, rising, "we may as well go now; and I shall be able to show you one or two of his later works."

As they made their way to the back door and down the garden path, Andrew was impressed by a distinct change in her manner. She was still grave and a trifle prim, but, ever since his reference to the pictures, a new note of cordiality had come into her voice. At the studio door, she produced her little key-wallet, and, taking from it the well-remembered Yale key, inserted it, turned it, and pushed the door open.

"You see," she said, as they entered, glancing at him for a moment with a wan smile, "I am keeping the nest warm."

He looked round the place, choking with emotion. Everything in it hailed him in a familiar voice and called to him to come back. Nothing was changed – with one exception. Formerly, the walls had borne only a few sketches given him by brother artists, and one or two of their paintings which he had bought from Montagu. Now these had been removed, and every available space was occupied by his own work. Every finished picture of his that they possessed had been collected from the house – excepting those which he, himself, had hung in the drawing-room – and put on the wall; and a number of sketches from his portfolio had been affixed to the match-boarding with drawing-pins – carefully placed at the edges to avoid making holes in the paper – and he noted with surprise the judgement with which they had been selected. His workshop had become a one-man exhibition.

Otherwise the place was just as he had left it. The half-finished picture stood on the easel, protected by its paper dust-cover; the "models" that he had been using – an old wooden-faced clock, the dismembered remains of another clock and a number of tools and implements – were on a side table, together with the studies that he had made for the details of the picture. His big folding palette lay on the table beside the painting-chair with the brushes set out tidily on the rough wooden rack that he had made. Even the water dipper, he noticed, was full of clean water.

"This is the picture he was at work on when he went away," said Molly, carefully turning back the dust-cover. "I think it was to be called 'The Clock-Jobber'. I don't know where he did the sketch for the interior, but the old man is our village cobbler. It is quite a good likeness, too."

Andrew looked at the picture with profound interest, trying vainly to realize that he had actually been working at it but little more than a week ago. The figure and part of the detail were nearly finished, but the background, the general lighting and colour scheme were only indicated. The most interesting part of the work was waiting to be done – waiting for him, who had the completed picture in his mind's eye. Would it wait for ever?

He made a few appreciative but critical comments on the picture, to which she listened respectfully, and then (still in the character of Ronald) said:

"I suppose his pictures have always been a great interest and pleasure to you."

"No," she replied. "That is what I now look back on with astonishment and bitter self-reproach. I never interested myself in his work, though it meant so much to him. Somehow, I let it become a thing apart, outside my own life and personal interests. I used to let him go off to this studio to do his day's work, just as if he were going off to a bank or an office. I was satisfied to hear what he had done and to see the pictures when they were finished; and I feel that I didn't understand them or appreciate them a bit. They were just our livelihood; and I used to see them packed up to go to Mr Montagu – the dealer, you know – without a pang of regret. It seems very strange now when I think of it. It was a great opportunity. I might have been his good comrade in what he cared for most. And I let it go."

As she concluded, her voice sank almost to a whisper and her eyes filled with tears. He looked at her with adoring sympathy, and a flood of affectionate yearning surged through him. The impulse to take her in his arms and kiss away her tears was almost irresistible. He could hardly restrain himself. And yet his reason held him back. He realized that this was no opportunity; that her very preoccupation with her lost husband would make her poof against the grotesque story that he had to tell.

But what an exasperating absurdity it was! She was his own wife, his sweet Molly, sweeter than ever and still more dear; and he was her loved husband for whom her poor heart was hungering. And here they stood, held apart by this preposterous make-believe! The thing was monstrous!

"I suppose," she resumed, reflectively, "it was because he was so interesting in himself and so sympathetic; because he entered so keenly into all my little feminine pleasures and interests as if they were his own, that I never realized that he might want some sympathy from me in the work that he loved. And he never obtruded his own personal affairs on me. There was not a grain of egotism in his nature. And, oh! Ronald! he was such a perfect husband, such a dear companion! In all the years of our married life, never an unkind word passed between us."

"No," Andrew said, huskily, "I know how fond he was of you and how happy you made him. He would like to think of you living here with his pictures to keep you company."

"Yes," she said, "that is just what they do. When I look round at them, I feel that he isn't quite lost to me. Because each of them is, in a way, a part of himself. The little figures in them were his friends, his children. They are acting his thoughts, just as he used to express them in words. And the places – the rooms and gardens and inn parlours – are places that he knew, because he built them up out of his own imaginings. They, too, are really part of him."

"Yes," said Andrew, "that is quite true. A picture is, in a way, a detached piece of the painter's personality, just as a book is a sort of spiritual bud or outgrowth from the mind of the man who wrote it. And I think you will find the pictures grow more friendly and intimate the longer you live with them."

"But I do!" she exclaimed. "Already, I am beginning to see them with a new eye. At first it was the little stories that they tell that impressed me most. But now I begin to see that the story was only the subject, the peg, as it were, on which the real picture was hung. And I try to see how he did them and what he was thinking about and aiming at as he worked."

"Yes," said Andrew, "that is the way to look at pictures. Try to see what the artist had in his mind, what he wanted to do and what he wanted you to see; especially the composition, the pattern of form and colour and light and shade – the effect of the picture as a whole."

"That is what I am trying to do," said she, "and I think I am getting on." She glanced fondly round at the walls and murmured: "The dear things! They grow on me from day to day."

When they had examined the unfinished painting, she brought out the portfolio and they looked through the collection of sketches and studies, one or two of which he picked out to replace some of those on the wall. She adopted his suggestions readily and listened attentively to his comments and criticisms.

"I didn't realize, Ronald," she said, "that you knew so much about painting. I never heard you talk about it to Andrew."

From the subject of pictures the conversation turned to her own domestic affairs, directed thereto by Andrew. But she was not very expansive and, somehow, her newborn cordiality of manner seemed to fade somewhat, especially when he ventured to proffer his assistance in setting her affairs in order. And, indeed, he was conscious of the incongruity of such a suggestion coming from the feckless, unthrifty Ronald.

"I really don't need any help," she said. "Andrew had made such complete provision for me and left his affairs in such perfect order that there is hardly anything for me to do."

"Well," he said, "if I can't give you any help in that way, I hope you will let me look you up from time to time. I think we ought to see more of each other in the future than we have in the past."

She did not reply immediately, but he could see that the suggestion was not received enthusiastically, and that she was rather carefully considering her answer. At length in an earnestly apologetic tone, she replied: "Later, perhaps, Ronald, but not just at present. It was kind of you to come and I am glad you came. But it has been a painful experience. You are so dreadfully like Andrew. I had no idea you were so much alike. I suppose when I saw you together I only noticed the differences, but now everything about you reminds me of him, and I feel I can hardly bear it."

"But," he urged, "don't you like to be reminded of him?"

"In some ways," she replied. "In his pictures, for instance. But they are really himself. But this resemblance is different. There is something awful and uncanny about it, something ghostly and unreal. You've no idea, Ronald, how strangely like him you are. Even your face is his face."

"I should have thought we were quite unlike in that respect," he said.

"You are thinking of that dent on his nose," said she, "that troubled him so much, poor boy. But he exaggerated the disfigurement. It was only an accidental mark. It really didn't make any difference, at least to me. I was sorry that he let it worry him so much – principally on my account, I am afraid. And now, as I look at you, I see how little difference it did make. But you are like him in every way. You move like him, you write like him – your handwriting is his handwriting, and your voice! When you speak, I could shut my eyes and believe it was Andrew speaking."

His heart leapt. She had recognized him, after all! True, she thought she had only recognized his ghost. She was deluded by the false circumstances. But he could explain them away. His opportunity had come. And as she continued, he tried to think how he should approach the revelation.

"You mustn't misunderstand me, Ronald. It is not that I am not your friend as I always was. Try to put yourself in my place. Remember what Andrew was to me – my dear husband, my faithful and loving friend, the very centre and focus of my life – and think what it must be to me to be in the presence of a counterfeit of him – now that he has gone for ever – mimicking his looks, his movements, the very tones of his dear voice. Don't you understand how it wrings my heart?"

He listened, entranced and yet bewildered, still fumbling for the words which would enable him to open his revelation without setting up an immediate barrier of suspicion.

"It is hard enough to bear," she went on, "to know that I shall never see him again, without having it driven home by a presence which mocks at my grief – a presence which seems to be his and yet is not his. Forgive me if I am unreasonable, but I am a broken woman. I have been robbed of all that I cared for and I cannot endure it patiently. My soul is in revolt. I ask myself: Can there be a God of Justice if such horrible wickedness is permitted?"

Her sudden change of mood disconcerted him.

"You mean," he stammered feebly, "that dreadful, most deplorable accident?"

"Accident!" she repeated; and her voice, ringing out like a pistol-shot, made him start as if he had been struck. "No! I mean that crime. You don't suppose it was an accident, do you?"

"That was what I understood," he murmured uncomfortably. "I thought a block of chalk fell on him."

"A block of chalk was found resting on his poor battered head, and they assumed that it fell on him by chance. But did it? I don't believe it for a moment. A man – a good, kind fisherman – was able to lift it off by himself. Then another man could have lifted it on – to cover up the marks of murder. That is what happened. I am convinced of it."

"Why are you?" he asked.

"Why!" she repeated. "Because everything about the horrible affair shouts of murder. You know he was not alone. The footprints prove that – two sets going to the place and only one coming away. Some-body was with him. Who was it? Who was that secret wretch who sneaked away and hid himself like Cain? Nobody knows. But he shall be found. I will never rest, or let the police rest, until he is found. And when we find him, he shall pay his debt. He shall pay it to the uttermost farthing!"

Andrew looked at her in astonishment and dismay. This was a new Molly who confronted him with blazing eyes and hard-set mouth as she poured out her fierce denunciations. Never before had he seen her even ruffled; and he found it hard to realize that this stern-faced, resolute woman was his soft, gentle, girlish wife. But, as he gazed at her, all his new-born confidence and optimism melted away like snow before the sunshine. For he saw clearly that his opportunity – if there had ever been one – was gone. How, after what he had heard – could he tell her that *he* had been there? That those retreating footprints were *his* footprints? He dared not. As to the rest of his fantastic story, if she listened to it at all – which she probably would not – she would dismiss it with angry contempt, and denounce him to the police.

There was nothing more to say or do. His mission had failed; and, since he had received more than a hint that his presence was not acceptable, there was no reason for prolonging his visit. Silently and gloomily he followed his unconscious wife up the garden to the house and, without re-entering the dining-room, prepared to take his leave.

"If I mustn't come and see you, Molly," he said, as he took up his hat and stick, "I hope you will let me write to you sometimes. I hate the idea of dropping out of your life."

"Oh, I didn't mean that, Ronald," she replied. "Don't think I want to cut you. Perhaps, later, when I have got more used to – to my new condition, I shall be able to see and talk with you without having this awful ghostly feeling. At any rate, there is no reason why you should not send me a letter now and again. I should like to hear how you are getting on."

With this she opened the outer door and, apparently with some not unnatural feeling of compunction, shook his hand quite cordially, though her eyes remained averted from his face. He held her hand for a second or two, gazing, with a bursting heart, into the pale, sweet face that he was forbidden henceforth to look upon. Then, with a huskily murmured "Goodbye!" he turned away and plunged down the flagged path, pausing, by habit, at the gate to look back and wave his hand in the old familiar way.

It was a grievous journey to the station. All the well-remembered objects that had greeted his arrival, now seemed, as he passed them and left them behind, to give him a sad and solemn farewell; and, when he turned out of the homely little lane into the road, it was with something of the feeling of our earliest ancestors when they passed out through the gates of Paradise.

# CHAPTER EIGHT

## The Deserted Wife

It was in a mood of the deepest depression, combined with a sort of angry bewilderment, that Andrew reviewed his affairs as the train bore him back to London. To a permanent separation from Molly his mind refused assent as a thing to be seriously considered. He could not, and did not, for a moment entertain the idea of giving her up. Yet what could he do? For the time being, the barrier that she had placed between them seemed insurmountable. One plan only seemed possible; and for a few moments he was actually disposed to adopt it – the plan of going boldly to the police, proclaiming his identity, and taking the chances of his trial for the murder of Mr Hudson.

But a very brief reflection convinced him of the futility of any such proceeding. For he was still obsessed with the infallibility of an eye-witness. There, at his trial, would be Miss Booth, who would swear that she actually saw him commit the murder. What answer could he give to that but a bare denial? And what weight would that denial have? It would have none. He would be found guilty and most certainly hanged.

No. There was no escape that way. He would have to put up with his false identity, even for Molly's sake. For she was, at least, better off as the widow of a man who had possibly been murdered than as the widow of one who had certainly been hanged. So he must wait and hope that some other way of escape from his intolerable dilemma might present itself.

But it was a maddening situation. Apart from the hideous illusion which cut him off from his wife, were other incidental and subordinate perplexities. There was, for instance, the life insurance. If he allowed the money to be paid, he would be not merely a party but the principal in a most blatant fraud. Yet he could not prevent the payment without disclosing his identity. Again, there was the probate of the will. It must be a criminal offence to connive at the probate of the will of a living man.

It was all very bewildering. Little did Professor Booley foresee the intricate train of consequences that the stroke of his syringe had set in motion! Nor was it possible for Andrew, himself, to foresee what further links in this extraordinary chain of causation might presently come into view; and as he realized this, he was disposed to speculate very uncomfortably on the possible surprises that might yet be awaiting him in the incalculable future.

But at least one good result followed from his disappointing visit. The sight of his studio and his pictures had set his thoughts moving along the old, familiar channels. The artist in him had awakened. Once more, he was aware of the impulse to paint. And the impulse was not only artistic. He would have to earn his living somehow, and he knew that he could earn it by his brush. The painting would come, not only as a relief but as the necessary means of livelihood. Before he had reached the end of his journey, he had decided to set to work without delay.

Thus deeply preoccupied with his present difficulties and his plans for the future, he walked unguardedly into the first ambush that Fate had prepared for him. From Cannon Street he took his way through the fast-emptying streets to the terminus of the North London Railway, where he bought a first-class ticket for Hampstead Heath. Still wrapped in profound thought, he ascended the stairs to the platform and, worming his way through the throng of passengers, sought an empty compartment in the waiting train.

The guard was slamming the doors in preparation for departure as he reached the forward part of the train. Selecting one of several vacant compartments, he entered it and shut himself in. As he sat down, by a natural train of association, his thoughts reverted to the curious incident that had occurred on the last occasion when he had travelled on this line. He was even tempted to rise and look out of the window to see if that strange woman was by any chance on the platform.

But there was no need. At the very moment when the shrill screech of the guard's whistle rang out and the train began to move, a woman darted at the door, wrenched it open, bounced into the carriage and slammed the door after her. Then she sat down in the seat opposite his and fixed her eyes on him with an unwinking, truculent stare.

He had recognized her in the first, instantaneous glance, and immediately averted his gaze to look out of the window. Not that he expected that manœuvre to be of any avail. And it was not. There she sat, facing him with a stare as immovable as that of a waxwork figure. He avoided looking at her; but he was fully conscious of that basilisk stare, and it seemed to stir the very marrow of his bones. As the train gathered speed, he waited in fearful expectation for the next development.

It came after some three minutes of appalling silence.

"Well. Haven't you anything to say to me?"

The voice was not unmusical, but it had a peculiar suppressed, menacing quality, as if the speaker were restraining herself with difficulty from shouting. Andrew turned his head and met the gaze of the pale, truculent, wide-open eyes.

"I think, madam," he replied, fully conscious of the futility of his answer, "that you must be mistaking me for some other person. I have no recollection of having had the honour of meeting you before."

The effect was very much what he had expected. She gave a shrill yelp of extremely mirthless laughter and then exclaimed:

"Well, I'm damned! I really am, Tony! I knew you had the cheek of the devil, but this is a record performance, even for you. So you have no recollection of having had the honour of meeting your lawful wife before! Haven't you, indeed? Don't happen to remember meeting her at the prison gate at Wormwood Scrubs on Easter

Sunday three years ago, when she wasn't too thin-skinned to ask for Mr Septimus Neville, the swindler, then due for discharge? Eh? You recognized her quickly enough then, didn't you, when she took you home and gave you your first square meal? But now your memory has given out. You are looking pretty prosperous. Perhaps you have got another wife, with a bit of money. Hey? Have you?"

As she ran off this string of questions, Andrew looked at her with very mixed feelings. For himself, he was frankly terrified; but he would have given a great deal to be able to speak some comforting words to her. For, in spite of her harsh tones and fierce manner, there was a faint undertone of tenderness in her voice and a suggestion of wistfulness in the way she looked in his eyes. He was profoundly sorry for her, and it was with real regret that he repeated – unavoidably – his futile disclaimer.

"I assure you, most solemnly, Mrs Neville – if that is your name – '

"Oh, drop it, Tony!" she interrupted impatiently. "Don't be a fool! What's the use of this play-acting? There's nobody here but ourselves. Now, listen to me. If I had any sense, I should be only too glad to be quit of you. But I'm not. Women are fools, and I'm one of the biggest of them. You've been a regular bad egg. You had all my money and spent it – and you know how that money was got; you've given me the slip over and over again and left me to get my own living as best I could; you've gone off philandering with other women, and you may have one or two other wives for all I know. I ought to hate you but, as I said, I am a fool. I am ready now to forget it all if you will only come back to me."

As she paused, Andrew gazed at her helplessly, utterly at a loss what to say. He was deeply moved and would have offered consolation, but that, he realized, would only have enraged her. But his silence and the sympathy and pity that his looks expressed led only to further misunderstanding. The fierceness died out of her face and her eyes filled.

"Come back to me, Tony," she urged in soft, coaxing tones, "and we will let bygones be bygones. I won't reproach you with what is past. You used to be fond of me, and I've never ceased to be fond of you. Come back and let us be as we were in the old days. I've got quite a decent job in the City, and I've made a nice little home out Brondesbury way. Come back to me, Tony, and I'll promise to make you as happy as you used to be. What do you say, Tony dear?"

The pitiful appeal in her swimming eyes and in the soft, wheedling tones of her voice wrung his heart. But he had to say something; and what could he say? It was a dreadful situation. At length, he stammered:

"My dear lady, pray try to believe me when I assure you that there is some strange mistake, due no doubt, to an extraordinary resemblance. On my honour, you are a complete stranger to me."

The result was inevitable and clearly foreseen. In a moment all the softness faded out of her eyes; the blood rushed to her face and she drew herself up, formidable and menacing.

"Now, listen," she commanded in a stern voice. "I give you one more chance, and it is the last. Drop this foolery instantly and do as I said. The door is still open. But go on with this mumming for another instant and the door will slam. And, by God, it is not the only door that will slam. You know what I mean; and you know me well enough to be aware that when I start to fight, the gloves are off. Now, what do you say?"

"I can only say what I said before," he replied miserably. "If you would only try to believe – "

"That will do!" she interrupted furiously. "I've given you fair warning; and now it's a fight to a finish."

She flung herself back on her seat and for the short remainder of the journey sat silent, crimson-faced and scowling, perfectly still, but with a stillness suggestive of violence repressed to bursting-point. Andrew felt as if he were travelling with a Mills bomb.

As the train approached his destination, he watched her with furtive anxiety. His expectation was that when he got out, she would follow him to ascertain where he lived. But, to his surprise and relief, she did not. When the train stopped at Hampstead Heath station and he rose to alight, she made no move; and when he opened the door and wished her a civil "good evening," she gave him one quick glance of concentrated anger and hatred and then averted her face.

Nevertheless, he walked very slowly along the platform, lingering at the farther end to see the train start; and it was not until it was well on the move that he turned towards the exit. And, even then, he waited at the foot of the stairs to see her carriage pass, and caught a fleeting glimpse of her face at the window, now glaring out at him like the face of some avenging Fury.

He drew a deep breath when the guard's van passed out and left the station empty. At least she was fairly out of his neighbourhood – for the present – and he was at liberty to consider precautions to avoid any future meetings. But so deep was the impression that she had made on him that, on leaving the station, instead of making his way directly to the town, he took the footpath that leads past the ponds and made a wide detour of the Heath, approaching the town – or "village" – eventually from the Vale of Health. And as he strode across the open expanse of the Heath, with an occasional nervous glance behind him, and sneaked back towards his lodgings, he turned over in his mind the possible significance, as to the past and the future, of this ominous encounter; so ominous as, for the moment, to oust from his thoughts all his other difficulties and embarrassments.

Who was this woman? – this Mrs Septimus Neville, if that was her name? He could have little doubt. She was Ronald's wife; and, therefore, in the existing circumstances, his wife. It was a very awkward situation. As he reflected on the grim farce, he could not but be struck by the malignant perversity of Fate. From what insignificant causes do the most portentous consequences ensue! When Professor Booley had consulted him as to the type of nose that was to be created, he had hardly taken the question seriously. He had expected no more than a more or less shapeless lump; and all that he had desired in that moment of panic was to be made as unlike Andrew Barton, the missing murderer, as might be. And so he had asked for a curved nose – and had straightway been transformed into the likeness of his cousin Ronald. It had turned out to be a fatal decision. If he had only asked for a straight nose, all would have been well. He would have ceased to be the murderer and yet he would have been no one else; merely a person with a good deal of resemblance to the late Andrew Barton. Then he would probably have had no difficulty with Molly; and with her help he could have lived, under an assumed name, in peace and security.

However, the deed was done and could not be undone. In slipping out of his own personality, he had slipped into that of another person; and thereby had taken over the reversion of that other person's crop of wild oats. And it seemed that those wild oats were now ripe for the harvest. This woman certainly meant mischief; very naturally, as Andrew felt. And she was no contemptible antagonist. She was a fine woman, picturesque and rather handsome in a way, and obviously strong, energetic and resolute. Obviously too, a woman of strong passions.

What was she planning to do? In his ignorance of her past – and his own, in his new character – he found her threats somewhat obscure. She had hinted darkly at some unlawful acts on his part, and had referred to the slamming of doors. What doors? The most probable answer was not a pleasant one.

His instinctive caution was not relaxed even when he approached his lodgings. On entering the little close, instead of going straight to the house in which he lived, he walked on to the extreme end that he might look back at the entrance and make sure that he had not been followed. And here he made a very welcome discovery. He had supposed that the close was a cul-de-sac with only one entrance. Now, he found at what he had thought to be the blind end, an arched opening like a doorway, giving entrance to a narrow alley. Following this, he emerged into a quiet by-street which presently brought him to Well Walk and so out on to the Heath. Having explored thus far, he retraced his steps; greatly encouraged; for here was almost complete security from the possibility of being followed, and tracked to his abode. He decided henceforth to adopt this approach to his lodgings and avoid the danger of entering the close from the High Street.

In the peace and security of his pleasant sitting-room he spent the evening in considering his position and making plans to meet the new complications that had arisen. Prudence suggested that he would be wise to migrate from Hampstead to some safer locality. But he was unwilling to move. His present quarters suited him perfectly. His landlady, Mrs Pendlewick, was a delightful old woman with whom he was already on terms that were almost affectionate; and, in view of his intention to resume his painting, the little old house was quite a valuable asset. The old-world room in which he sat, with its picturesque bay window and antique furniture, gave him an ideal cottage interior which would supply the backgrounds for a dozen pictures. So he decided to stay where he was, at least for the present, and avoid, as far as possible, exposing himself to view in frequented places; and having reached this decision, he spent the rest of the evening in making out a list of the things which he would need to enable him to get to work.

On the following morning, with the list in his pocket, he set forth (after a cautious inspection of the close from his bay window) by way of the back exit and the alley and along the open Heath to the tram terminus; walking warily, like a Red Indian upon the warpath, with an alert and suspicious eye on every human being who came into sight, especially on those of the feminine gender. Arrived at the terminus, he took up a sheltered and retired position to watch the waiting tram and observe the passengers as they took their places; and only when it was on the point of starting did he enter and select a seat near the door, whence he could escape easily if the need should arise.

It was all very irksome and disturbing to the mind, this furtiveness and incessant watchfulness. As he sat in his corner with the feeling of a fugitive from justice, while the tram rumbled on its way southward, Andrew reflected almost incredulously that but a fortnight ago he had been a reputable gentleman, living an ordered, peaceful life without a single enemy in the world. However, as the journey passed without incident, his mind became gradually more at ease, and he alighted in the Hampstead Road opposite the premises of the artist's colourman ready to give his attention to the business of the moment.

The outfit of a watercolour painter is a good deal more portable than that of a painter in oil, but as Andrew's purchases amounted to the entire stock-in-trade, including a substantial folding easel, a stool, drawing-boards, palette, brushes, tubes of colour, a supply of paper and various other items, they resulted in two bulky and heavy parcels; burdened with which he went forth (having regretfully declined the salesman's offer to send them, as that would have involved disclosing his address) and waited in some anxiety for the tram. The chances that his pursuer – as he assumed her to be – would happen to be on that tram were infinitesimal to the point of absurdity. Nevertheless, when the vehicle drew up in response to his hail, he scanned the faces of the female passengers nervously as he stepped up to the footboard.

Similarly, but with more reason, he looked about him apprehensively as he alighted at the terminus; and disregarding the weight of his burden, struck out across the Heath with elaborate precaution and an occasional glance to the rear, before making the final turn into Well Walk. At the mouth of the alley he paused for a moment to make sure that the close contained no enemy and that no one was looking in from the High Street; and when, at length, he let himself in with his latchkey and closed the door, he experienced a sense of relief which he himself recognized as slightly ridiculous.

Having deposited his parcels in his sitting-room, he walked through to the back room, half-kitchen and half-parlour, to report his return and exchange a few words with his landlady. And here he had a genuine stroke of luck. At intervals, amidst his distractions, he had been trying to think of a subject to fit into the background of his own room. Now, as he opened the door, after a perfunctory tap with his knuckles, behold a subject almost ready made. By the low, small-paned window sat Mrs Pendlewick in a Windsor armchair with a little gate-leg table by her side and a lace pillow on her lap.

She looked up with a smile of welcome, viewing him over the tops of her spectacles as he stood in the doorway regarding her with delighted surprise. She made a charming picture. Figure, lighting and accessories made up just such an ensemble as the old "genre" painters would have loved; and Andrew, being a belated survivor of that school, felt a like enthusiasm. For a while he stood, taking in the effect of the group – the old-world figure with its silky-white hair and antique cap, the black pillow with its covering of lace and rows of bobbins, the simple, elegant chair and the ancient table – until the old lady became quite puzzled.

"I am taking the liberty of admiring you, Mrs Pendlewick," he said at length.

"Law!" she exclaimed, "I thought I had got beyond that."

"But this is a new accomplishment," said he. "I didn't know you were a lace-maker."

"New!" she chuckled. "I was a lace-maker before I was eight year old. Had my own pillow and bobbins and used to play at making lace. All the girls did down at my home; began it as child's play, and that's how we learnt. Down where I come from – I'm a Buckinghamshire woman, born and brought up at Wendover – down there you wouldn't meet a woman, no, nor a girl over ten, that couldn't make bone lace. They usually began to learn when they were about four or five."

"Why do you call it bone lace?" he asked.

"It's on account of these," she explained, indicating the bewildering multitude of little bobbins that dangled by their threads from the edge of the work. "They were mostly made of bone, though sometimes they used horn or hard wood. But bone was the regular thing because it was easy to come by. The lads used to make 'em for their sweethearts; carved 'em out with their pocket knives, they did, and some of them were uncommonly pretty bits of work. There's one that my grandfather made when he was courting my grandmother more than a hundred years ago; and it's as good as new now."

She picked out the historic bobbin – a little bone stick elaborately decorated with shallow carving – and held it up proudly for his inspection; and as he examined it she babbled on:

"Yes, we're all of a piece, me and my belongings. We are all getting on. This chair that I'm sitting in was made by my Uncle James. He was a chair-maker at High Wycombe, and they used to work out in the open beech-woods. And this little table was made by my grandfather – him that made that bobbin. He was a wheelwright, but he used to make furniture in the winter when the wagons was laid up and work was slack."

So she rambled on, but not to the hindrance of her work; for, as she talked, her fingers were busy with their task, the right hand managing the pins while the left manipulated the bobbins, and all with an effortless dexterity that was delightful to watch. Nor were her babblings of the old country life in the Vale of Aylesbury without interest; and Andrew, looking on and listening, found himself gathering the sentiment and atmosphere that he hoped presently to express in his picture.

After a spell of somewhat one-sided conversation, he ventured cautiously to approach the subject of that picture. But his caution was unnecessary, for Mrs Pendlewick was all agog to "have her likeness drawn", as she expressed it.

"Not but what I should have thought," she remarked, "that you might have found someone better worth drawing. Who wants to look at the likeness of an old woman like me?"

"You are too modest, Mrs Pendlewick," he replied. "You don't appreciate your own beauty. Wait until you see my picture; you'll be surprised to find how handsome you are."

With this he retired – leaving her chuckling over her work – to unpack his parcels and to spend what was left of the morning in straining a sheet of paper on one of the boards and making one or two preliminary sketches to settle the composition and arrangement of the projected picture. Then, after the simple midday meal, he set up his easel in the kitchen, arranged the accessories, and, while Mrs Pendlewick went about her household activities, he drew in the background – the interior of the room, the window and the furniture; finishing with a short sitting until it was time for the model to lay the pillow on the table, spread a handkerchief over her face, and compose herself for her afternoon nap.

The painting of that picture did Andrew a world of good. It kept him indoors during the daylight hours and enabled him partly to forget the Avenger who was on his track; and, as a normal and customary occupation, it brought him back out of the nightmare world in which he had been living, into the region of sane and ordinary human life. He worked with intense enjoyment. Painting was at all times the passion of his life; but now, to the pleasure that he always found in his work, was added a certain feeling of novelty, due to the nightmare interregnum. And, as the work progressed and he perceived with some surprise that he was painting "at the top of his form", the discovery engendered a sense of power which was very pleasant in contrast to the sense of feebleness and futility by which he had been oppressed.

He worked steadily for four days, by which time the background was well advanced and the figure practically finished; and a most excellent portrait of the old lady it turned out, though he had not specially aimed at a likeness. They had been happy days, days of blessed relief from his troubles and distractions. But now, as the finishing work could be done at his own time without the model's assistance, his thoughts turned to an outdoor subject or a study which would serve as the background for a studio composition. By this time his terror of the mysterious woman had subsided to a great extent. After all, what was the risk of her shadowing him? She lived at Brondesbury and she had a job in the City. It was hardly possible that she could be haunting the neighbourhood of Hampstead.

Thus reassuring himself, and tempted out by a brilliant autumn morning, he set forth with his sketching kit to look for a subject. Sneaking out with his usual caution by the back way, he made for Well Walk and then struck out across the Heath to the Vale of Health. Here, on the high ground above the pond, he paused to look about him and consider which direction he should take, laying down his easel and stool the more conveniently to fill his pipe. But as he felt for his pouch, its lean and deflated condition reminded him that his stock of tobacco had run out.

It was very annoying, for his tobacconist's shop was at the lower end of High Street, a locality which he preferred to avoid by daylight. However, his stock would have to be replenished, and, as he habitually smoked as he worked, he decided to brave the terrors of the High Street rather than go on with an empty pouch. Accordingly he picked up his easel, and, turning his face westward, re-entered the village by way of Heath Street, walking quickly down that thoroughfare and the High Street and keeping a bright lookout for any suspicious figures of the feminine gender.

Having arrived safely at the tobacconist's and made his purchase, he began once more to turn over in his mind the most likely spots in which to look for a subject; and as the High Street and its northward continuations would, if he followed them, eventually bring him to the West Heath, he decided to explore that locality and particularly the neighbourhood of the Leg of Mutton Pond, in spite of the fact that this route involved the passage of close upon a mile of fairly frequented streets and roads. But the acute alarm which had affected him on the day following the encounter in the train had to a great extent subsided; notwithstanding which, as he strode along, pipe in mouth, he kept a wary eye ahead and around and even paused from time to time to look back and scrutinize such wayfarers as happened to be coming in the same direction. It was only when he had at length emerged from the village on to the rustic road known as Rotten Row, with the open Heath on all sides of him, that he was able to dismiss from his mind the idea of a possible "shadower" and give his attention to the search for a subject.

The search did not, in fact, take up very much time. He knew the place pretty well and was able to make his way almost at once to a suitable spot, which he found within a short distance from the pond. Here he spent a quarter of an hour circling round and trying various points of view with the aid of a little cardboard viewfinder; and having, at length, decided on the most satisfactory composition, he set up his easel and stool, refilled his pipe and set to work with his open satchel hitched to the foot of the easel so that his materials were all conveniently within reach.

For upwards of an hour he worked away in uninterrupted peace, becoming more and more absorbed in his occupation as he proceeded from the preliminary drawing to the stage of colour. From time to time, solitary wayfarers had passed along the road below him and once a horseman had gone by at a canter. But although they all looked up at him as they passed, they had made no nearer approach. His pitch might have been in some remote country district rather than in a populous London suburb.

But his peace was not to remain entirely undisturbed. Pausing in his work to squeeze out on to his palette a fresh supply of colour from a tube, he became aware of a phenomenon familiar to outdoor painters and designated in the slang of the craft a "snooper". The peculiarity of this type of onlooker is in his mode of approach. The simple rustic spectator regards the artist frankly as a public entertainer. He approaches boldly, takes up his position with an air of permanence and stares with undissembled wonder, sometimes at the painting but more usually at the painter. Not so the snooper. His approach is devious and unpredictable as to direction – excepting that it will inevitably bring him within a yard or so of the easel. He maintains an ostentatious unawareness of the painter's existence until, by some unforeseen chance, his sinuous advance (at a gradually diminishing speed) has brought him abreast of the easel; when he takes one long, hungry, sidelong look and passes on.

As he squeezed out the little blob of pigment, Andrew observed a man approaching from the high ground above him, and, by the manner of his advance was able to make a provisional diagnosis. Not that he minded in the least. He had no prejudice against the snooper; who, after all, is actuated only by a reasonable curiosity tempered by good manners. It is only the unseasoned amateur who quails at the snooper's approach.

The man drew nearer by degrees, meandering down the slope, and still profoundly unconscious of Andrew's existence, until he had reached the inevitable spot a yard or two from the artist's pitch; when he suddenly "unsnooped" (if I may use the expression) and became a normal spectator.

"Mind my having a look?" he asked civilly, with his eye on the painting.

"Not at all," Andrew replied; "but there isn't much to look at. I have only just begun."

With this permission, the man stepped forward and took up a position close beside the artist, making a show of examining the painting, though, in fact, he seemed more interested in the painter, judging by the frequent and somewhat furtive glances that he stole at Andrew's profile.

"A lovely scene!" he remarked. "Don't you think so?"

"Well," replied Andrew, "I would rather say 'pleasant'. It is not romantically beautiful."

"No," the other agreed; "not romantic, but, as you say, very pleasant; extremely so. You are making a pretty big sketch, aren't you?"

"It isn't a sketch," Andrew explained; "it is going to be a rather detailed study, so it has to be a good size."

"I see. But there will be a lot of work in it, won't there? If you are going to paint all the detail?"

"Yes," Andrew replied, "there will be plenty to do. But I rather like a subject with a fair amount of matter in it."

"But won't it take a deuce of a time to do? I should think there will be a week's work in it, at least."

"No," said Andrew, "not as much as that. I shall probably get it finished in three or four sittings."

"Will you, indeed? Three or four sittings? And how long do you generally work at a sitting?"

"As long as the light will let me," Andrew replied. "Three hours, at the outside. It doesn't do to go on too long, or you get the light and shade all wrong.

Here Andrew paused rather definitely. He was a naturally polite and civil man, but he disliked interruptions of his work and he felt that the conversation had gone on long enough. Apparently, he had managed to convey a hint to this effect, for the man stepped back a pace and remarked apologetically:

"I am afraid I am hindering you, and that won't do. Perhaps I shall be passing this way again before you have finished your study. I should like to see the completed work. In the meantime I will wish you 'Good morning' and many thanks for letting me see it in its early stage."

With this he turned away and walked off towards the road; and Andrew, glancing at his retreating figure, was struck by the contrast between the brisk, purposive manner of his retirement and his aimless, sauntering approach. Apparently he was making up for the time that he had spent in the conversation; and Andrew, turning once more to his painting, proceeded to do likewise.

But in spite of his growing interest in his work as the picture progressed, the incident had left a slightly disagreeable impression. Perhaps it was natural that the disturbing and insecure circumstances in which he was living should cause him to view with a critical and suspicious eye any chance contacts with strangers. So he persuaded himself and tried to dismiss the matter from his thoughts. Nevertheless, he could not quite get rid of the impression. Little details of the incident tended obstinately to recur. He recalled the elaborate, leisurely, snooperesque manoeuvres by which the man had managed to establish the contact, and then the quick, definite way in which he had departed, with the air of having accomplished some specific object. Again there was the rather futile conversation. Obviously, the man neither knew nor cared anything about painting. Yet he had made a very evident pretext to open the conversation.

Then there was the appearance of the man. Once or twice as they were talking Andrew had looked in his face; and his artist's eye had been quick to note certain slight anomalies. The hair was sleek and black and had somewhat the appearance of a wig; and the eyebrows were black and heavy, like little moustaches. But the eyes were pale blue and the skin was fair and slightly freckled. Now, the black-haired blond is a recognized type, and is not so very rare. Still, there was an anomaly; and to a man in Andrew's circumstances, it tended to attract uneasy notice. Oddly enough, the one really significant point in the incident escaped him entirely. It was only by the light of subsequent events that he was able to perceive the relevancy of that apparently futile conversation.

He worked on for nearly an hour beyond his allotted time in order to get the painting well started; and, by degrees, as he became more and more engrossed in his task, the incident faded into the background of his mind. But the impression tended to revive when, the day's work finished, he packed up his kit and started on his way home; manifesting itself in a long detour, punctuated by searching glances around, before the final plunge into Well Walk.

# CHAPTER NINE

## The Axe Falls

Andrew's forecast was so far correct that, by the end of the third sitting, his picture was virtually finished. Another short sitting to "pull it together" would see the work complete. He leaned back on his stool and viewed the painting critically and not without satisfaction. For the work of one who was not a professed landscape painter, it was quite a creditable performance; and, as the material for future studio subjects, it should be of some value.

He had sat thus for a minute or two, inspecting his work and comparing it with the landscape before him when he became conscious of someone standing behind him. Assuming that it was some stranger who had crept up to have a look at the painting, he took no notice and remained still, in the hope that the spectator would presently depart without attempting to open a conversation. But as the time ran on and the onlooker remained immovable, he began unostentatiously to put his kit together; for he had finished work, and certain internal sensations associated themselves pleasantly with the lamb cutlets which he happened to know would be awaiting him at his lodgings.

He disposed of his colours, put the brushes away tidily in their case, emptied the dipper and put it into its special pocket, and still the person behind him made no move. Finally, he took the pin-frame board, on which the painting was stretched, off the easel and slipped it into its compartment in the satchel. Then he stood up and turned round to face the spectator; and, instantly, he realized that some kind of mischief was brewing. There was not one spectator, but three; two tall, massive men and one shorter; and though the latter had close-cropped reddish hair and no eyebrows to speak of, Andrew had no difficulty in recognizing the "snooper" of two days ago.

The shorter man looked at him insolently and asked:

"Well, have you quite finished?"

"I have finished work for today," Andrew answered.

"Good!" the other rejoined. "Now we can get to business. I don't think you spotted me a couple of days ago."

"I did not," Andrew replied, "and I don't spot you now. Who are you?"

The man laughed, contemptuously. "Well, I'm damned, Tony!" he exclaimed. "Lizzie's right. You've got the cheek of the devil. Pretending to my face that you don't know who I am!"

"It is no pretence at all," said Andrew. "You are a complete stranger to me."

The man laughed again, more savagely, and was about to make some further rejoinder when one of the tall men interposed.

"There's no use in wasting time on talk," said he. "Is this the man?"

"Yes," was the reply. "This is the man." Thereupon the tall man took a pace forward, and, touching Andrew lightly on the arm, said:

"I am a police officer, and I arrest you, Anthony Kempster, on a charge of fraud and personation."

"But," protested Andrew, "my name is not Anthony Kempster."

"That may be," replied the officer, "but my information is that you are Anthony Kempster and I hold a warrant for your arrest. You can see it if you like."

"There is no need," said Andrew. "I am not disputing your authority to arrest Anthony Kempster. My point is that I am not Anthony Kempster. This gentleman has made a mistake."

"Well, you know," the officer replied, not uncivilly, "we can't go into that here. You must come with me to the station. Then the Inspector will read the charge over to you and you can say anything that you want to say. I can't listen to any statements. My duty is simply to arrest you and hand you over to the proper authorities. And you had better not say anything until you get to the station. May I take it that you are coming along quietly?"

Andrew smiled sourly. "It doesn't seem as if I had much choice," said he. "I'm certainly not going to make a scene, and I hope you are not going to."

"No," replied the officer, "you will not be subjected to any unnecessary indignities if you don't give any trouble. We've got a car waiting down the road. We shan't have to walk you through the streets. Are you ready?"

"I shall be when I have strapped my easel and stool together," Andrew replied.

"Very well," the officer agreed. "Be as quick as you can."

Andrew folded up the easel and the stool and strapped them together. Then, grasping the handle of the strap, and slinging the satchel over his shoulder, he turned to the officer.

"I am at your service now," said he; whereupon the two officers placed themselves one on either side, and, as the informer walked on ahead down the slope, they followed in his wake. Looking forward in the direction which the red-headed man was taking, Andrew now saw, on the road below, just at the entrance to Rotten Row, a large car, and, a few yards ahead of it, a taxicab. As they bore down on the car, Andrew observed that the driver, who wore some kind of official uniform, had emerged from his place by the wheel and was standing by the door, which he was holding open; and, glancing at the taxicab, he could see, though not very distinctly, the face of some person peering out through the rear window. But he had not much time for observation, for when they reached the car one of the officers immediately stepped in and directed him to follow, which he did. Then the other officer entered and was shut in by the driver, who now walked round to the front and took his place at the wheel; and Andrew, glancing out through the front window, saw the red-headed man getting into the taxi, which started as he slammed the door. After a few seconds the car – the engine of which was already running –

started forward and the mysterious and not very promising journey had commenced.

It was not in any sense an agreeable journey. Sitting jammed in between the two rather bulky officers, Andrew's bodily discomfort was swallowed up by his mental distress. For he could not view the immediate future without the gravest forebodings. He had disclaimed all knowledge of the red-headed man, but, as he recalled his features and his colouring, he was conscious of a distinct reminiscence of the woman who had threatened him with retribution. With those threats he naturally associated the present proceedings; and although the whole affair was founded on a mistake, he had grave misgivings as to the possibility of rectifying that mistake.

"I take it," said he, "that that man who was with you is not a police officer?"

"No," was the reply, "he is a civilian. Name of Blake. Said you knew him."

"I don't know either the name or the man," said Andrew.

"Well," the officer rejoined, "he knew you – unless, as you say, he has made a mistake. However, we'd better not discuss that now; and if you take my advice you won't do any talking until we get to the station because whatever you may say will be taken down in writing and used in evidence, and then, perhaps, you will wish you hadn't spoken."

Andrew thanked the officer for his advice, and in pursuance of it relapsed into silence. He had plenty to think about; but, oddly enough, his thoughts tended principally to concern themselves with Mrs Pendlewick. At this moment she was probably laying aside her lace pillow and considering, with an eye on the old wooden-faced clock, whether it was yet time to commence operations on the lamb cutlets. His direct, physical interest in those cutlets had suddenly become extinct; but his thoughts turned wistfully to the peaceful little room, the table with its snowy cloth and immaculate china and the picturesque little brown jug which gave the beer an added flavour. He could see it all vividly in his mind's eye, and already he began to wonder gloomily when he should look on it again in the flesh.

But his chief concern was for Mrs Pendlewick. He thought of her with all her preparations made for his entertainment, awaiting him, at first impatiently, then anxiously, and then, as the time ran on, and it became evident that something out of the ordinary had happened, in real alarm. He was very troubled about her and wondered vaguely what she would do when night came and still he did not return. Would she set inquiries on foot? And if so, how would she go about it? Perhaps she would apply to the police. He hoped not; because it was his intention, at present, not to disclose the whereabouts of his abode. He didn't want the police to get access to his rooms to rummage among his possessions and possibly establish a connection between Molly and the alleged Anthony Kempster. That would be intolerable in any case; but, if he should be unable to dispel the illusion as to his identity, it would be absolutely disastrous.

So his thoughts rambled on until the slowing down of the car in a rather narrow street recalled him suddenly to his present business. He had taken no note of the route that the car had followed and had no idea as to his present whereabouts; but when the car stopped opposite a building with a large doorway and a constable in the uniform of the City Police came forward to open the door, he realized that he must be somewhere in the City of London.

The senior officer stepped out and halted to wait for him, and he followed immediately with the other officer close on his heels. They entered through the wide doorway and passed into a large, bare room furnished with some benches and a few plain Windsor chairs. On two of the latter were seated the only occupants of the room; the red-headed man and the woman whom he had met in the train. The former greeted him with an insolent stare and a half-suppressed grin; the latter – to whom he bowed stiffly, raising his hat – gave him one swift glance and averted her face. It was evident to him that she was greatly distressed and agitated, for not only were there traces of tears on her pale and drawn face, but her hands, resting on her lap, trembled visibly. It was easy to see that already she was being torn by pangs of remorse.

The senior officer had gone out of the room immediately on their arrival. He now returned and took charge of Andrew, beckoning to the woman to follow.

"Not you," he added, as the red-headed man rose from his chair. "You stay where you are. I'll send for you if I want you."

With this, he conducted Andrew out of the room, along a passage and into a large, barely furnished office where an inspector sat at a desk with a number of papers before him; a grave, scholarly looking man with a bald head and a pair of round-eyed, horn-rimmed spectacles. As they entered, he motioned the woman to a chair and cast an inquisitive glance at Andrew.

"Is this Kempster?" he asked.

"Yes, sir," was the reply.

"Has he made any statement?"

"No, sir, excepting that he denies that he is Anthony Kempster."

The inspector nodded, and, pulling out a drawer of the desk, selected a paper from a number of other documents and turned to Andrew.

"You will want to know exactly what you are charged with. I will read out the charge and then hear if you have anything to say. It is that you, Anthony Kempster, did, on the 20th of April, 1919, and on divers other occasions, falsely personate one Francis Redwood deceased, for the purpose of effecting a fraudulent life insurance. That is the charge. Now, is there anything that you wish to say? You are not bound to say anything, but if you do, I have to caution you that anything that you may say will be taken down in writing and used in evidence."

"All that I have to say," said Andrew, "is that I am not Anthony Kempster."

The inspector looked round at the woman and asked:

"What do you say to that, Mrs Kempster? Is this man your husband or is he not?"

"I say that he is," she replied in a low voice.

The inspector turned to Andrew. "Now," said he, "what do *you* say to *that*? Do you say that this lady is making a false statement?"

"No, not at all," Andrew replied earnestly. "I have not the least doubt that she is speaking in perfect good faith. But she is mistaken. She is, indeed. I can only suppose that I bear a remarkable resemblance to her husband, but I assure you that I never met her until a few days ago when she spoke to me in the train. I beg you, madam, to look at me again and see if you are not mistaken."

As he spoke, he looked appealingly in the woman's face; and as he did so, he saw that it had taken on a very curious expression – an expression of which he could make nothing. Whether it denoted doubt or hope or relief or merely bewilderment he was unable to judge. But it was a very singular expression: so singular that the inspector noticed it, for he remarked:

"I suppose there isn't any mistake? I don't see how there could be, but still, we want to be sure. *Are* you sure, Mrs Kempster?"

She hesitated for a few moments and then replied, doggedly:

"Yes. He is Anthony Kempster."

The inspector turned once more to Andrew and said in a patient, persuasive tone:

"You hear that. What do you say now?"

"I say again that this lady is mistaken."

"Very well," said the inspector, in the same quiet, persuasive tone, "let us suppose that she is. Then, you see, if you are not Anthony Kempster, you must be someone else. You see that, don't you?"

Andrew had to admit that the inspector's logic was unimpeachable.

"Then," the inspector pursued, "all that you have got to do is to prove that you are someone else and we shall know that you can't be Anthony Kempster. Come, now. Tell us who you are."

Andrew was, naturally, not unprepared for this question, and had already decided on his reply.

"I think," he said, "that, under the present circumstances, I would rather not give my real name."

"Very well," said the inspector, without the slightest trace of irritation, "then, for the present, we will call you Anthony Kempster. Any objection to telling us where you live?"

"I would rather not give any address, at present," Andrew replied.

"Quite so," said the inspector. "Not a very communicative gentleman. But if you won't tell us anything about yourself, we shall have to find out as best we can. Perhaps you have got something in your pockets that will help us."

He glanced significantly at the officer who was standing by; who immediately stepped forward and laid an expert hand on Andrew's coat in the region of the right breast.

"What's this?" said he. "Feels like a pocketbook."

He slipped his hand into the pocket and adroitly fished out a wallet, which he handed to the inspector; and, as Andrew saw it transferred, his heart sank. For it was Ronald's wallet; the one which he had found in the pocket of the coat on that fatal day at Crompton. He had used it ever since, but merely as a receptacle for notes; and exactly what else it now contained he had no clear idea. There were one or two closed compartments, which he had opened and glanced into in case one of them should contain his own or any other letter which might have to be burned. But there were no letters; and the few scraps of crumpled paper that were in them he had carelessly left there unexamined. It was a singularly foolish thing to have done, as he now realized; and he watched the inspector's proceedings with growing alarm.

"Four pound notes," the latter remarked, laying them out on the desk. "Clean ones. Look as if they had come from a bank." He looked into the open compartments, and, seeing that they were empty, went on to the two closed ones. Opening one, he apparently drew a blank, for he reclosed it and passed on to the other. From this he extracted three crumpled pieces of thin paper, one of which he smoothed out carefully and studied with evident interest. Turning to Mrs Kempster, he asked:

"Do you know the names, Bailey and Warman?"

"Yes," she replied. "They are wine merchants at Ipswich."

"Did you ever live at Ipswich? And if so, at what address?"

"I lived at Ipswich with my husband at Number 23, Beckton Street."

The inspector nodded. Then, taking up the piece of paper, he held it out towards Andrew for his inspection.

"Just take a glance at that," said he.

Andrew took a glance at it; and instantly realized that he was lost. It was a tradesman's bill ("account rendered"), and it set forth that A Kempster, Esq., 23, Beckton Street, was a debtor to Bailey and Warman, Wine and Spirit Merchants, Ipswich, in the sum of four pounds.

"Well," said the inspector, "that seems to dispose of the mistaken identity racket. I presume you agree with me?"

"I agree with you that it seems to," Andrew replied. "But I still maintain that I am not Anthony Kempster."

The inspector smiled sardonically. "You certainly know your own mind," said he; "but you have got to explain how you come to have a bill in your pocket addressed to A Kempster, Esq. Can you explain that?"

"I am afraid I can't," Andrew had to admit.

"No," said the inspector. "I don't suppose you can. And that, I think, completes our business for the present. You will remember, Mrs Kempster, that you are bound over to give evidence. You had better come back here about three o'clock. We shall take Kempster before the magistrate as soon as possible. Say a quarter to three."

While these directions were being given Andrew looked at his alleged wife. Her expression had changed and was more inscrutable to him than ever. There was nothing in it in the least suggestive of elation or triumph. Rather did it suggest disappointment and the most profound dejection. As the inspector finished speaking, she rose, and, without a glance at Andrew, turned away and walked slowly towards the door. Suddenly she snatched out her handkerchief and held it to her face; and there came to his ear the sound of muffled sobs.

The inspector followed her with an impassive, but not unkindly eye, and, as she disappeared, he proceeded to moralize.

"Women," he remarked, "are kittle cattle. She started the ball, all agog to get it moving; and now she'd like to stop it. And she can't. She doesn't know her own mind as well as you do, Kempster."

He smoothed out the other pieces of paper, and, having glanced at them, attached them to certain other documents which he put away in a tray. Then he copied on a slip of paper the numbers of the notes, and, having put this slip with the other papers, replaced the notes in the wallet and handed the latter back to Andrew.

"You may as well keep that for the present," he remarked. "You will be detained here until we are able to bring you before the magistrate, which we shall do this afternoon."

With this, he drew his chair up to the desk and resumed the studious pursuits in which he had been "discovered", as the playwrights express it, and Andrew reverted to the custody of the attendant officer, who proceeded to pilot him out of the room, and presently to transfer him to the care of a uniformed constable; who conducted him to a passage in which were a couple of rows of black-painted doors, each distinguished by a number. One of these doors the constable unlocked and opened; and, having thrust in his head and sniffed, shut it again and passed on to the next. Here, the result being apparently satisfactory, he threw the door wide open and invited Andrew to enter.

"I may as well relieve you of your kit," he remarked, assisting his charge to remove the satchel from his shoulder and taking possession of the easel and stool. "The things will be taken care of and given back to you at the proper time. And I must just see what you have got in your pockets. It is only a formality; but there are certain things that you are not allowed to have about you while you are in custody. Just put them out on the table and let me look through them."

Andrew emptied his pockets, laying the various objects on the little fixed table. These the constable glanced through, and, having satisfied himself that the pockets had been really emptied, selected from the collection a pocket knife and a small bundle of string.

"You can put the rest back for the present," said he, "and I hope you'll be able to keep them and have the others back. And now, what about grub? When did you have your last meal?"

"About eight o'clock this morning," Andrew replied. "But I don't really feel as if I could manage any food."

The constable shook his head. "That won't do," said he. "Mustn't give way. You'll be going before the magistrate presently, and you'd better not go on an empty stomach. Take my advice and get a square meal while you can. You'll feel better after it. You have got some money, and you can have anything in reason that you want. Better let me send out for something."

Andrew accepted the well-meant and obviously sensible advice, handing over the modest sum that his custodian suggested as sufficient. Then the constable retired, locking the door and leaving him to his own reflections. Those reflections were, naturally, not of the most agreeable kind and were singularly confused. The attitude of the constable impressed him with mild surprise. He might have been a nurse or attendant in some Erewhonian convalescent home for moral invalids, so solicitous did he seem for the welfare of his charge. And even the dry, impersonal civility of the other officers was not what he would have expected.

But, once more, his thoughts reverted to Mrs Pendlewick. By this time, the lamb cutlets were ruined beyond redemption, but she would not have given him up. He pictured her sitting, working automatically at her lace, looking up from time to time at the clock and painfully aware of the aroma of the half-cremated cutlets.

His meditations were interrupted by the arrival of his meal; and, acting on the further exhortations of the constable, he made a determined and moderately successful effort to dispose of it, with the result foreseen by that experienced officer. He felt better in a bodily sense. The physical depression left him, and even his mental state seemed to be improved.

But his mind was still in a state of utter confusion. Presently he would be brought before a magistrate and charged with a crime that he knew nothing about. What was he to say? Of course, he would declare his innocence, and he would continue to deny that he was the person charged. That he must do, since it was the actual truth. But he realized the utter futility of it. The wine merchant's bill had labelled him Anthony Kempster, and to that "attribution" he had no answer. It was even doubtful whether he would not further prejudice his case by saying anything at all.

At any rate, there was nothing that he could do. When the time came, he would have to stand passively and watch this tragedy of errors working itself out to its illogical conclusion. He felt like a swimmer in some swift stream, borne along by the irresistible force of the torrent. Ahead of him the rapids were roaring; but he could do no more than drift passively to his destruction.

# CHAPTER TEN

## *Gaol*

---

As Andrew took his place in the dock at the police court, he looked around him with a sort of dull, impersonal curiosity. He had never been in a police court before and had but a vague idea as to the nature of the proceedings that were conducted in such places. First, he noted the persons present. Of those whom he knew, the one who instantly caught his eye was his accuser, Mrs Kempster; and as he looked commiseratingly at her pale, haggard face and the restless hands that were incessantly clasping and unclasping themselves, he realized the truth of the inspector's remarks. It was easy to see that she would have given a good deal to be able to undo the knot that she had tied.

Sitting beside her on the same bench was the red-headed man; and, now that he saw them together, the likeness between them which he had detected at the morning's meeting was still more noticeable. From them his eyes wandered to the inspector and the two officers who had arrested him and, passing quickly over the background of mostly squalid strangers who had loafed in to look on, he looked lastly at the magistrate, a wooden-faced elderly man of a pronounced legal type.

The proceedings were opened by a senior police officer, apparently a superintendent. He began by intimating that he was proposing only to produce evidence of arrest and identification and that he would ask for a remand to enable the necessary evidence to be obtained and the witnesses notified. Then he went on to give a general outline of the case; to which Andrew listened with profound interest, having, up to this time, only the most obscure notion as to what he was accused of.

"This," said the superintendent, "is a prosecution under the False Personation Act. The prosecutors are the Griffin Insurance Society, but it has not been possible for them to be represented on this occasion. The facts of the case are, in broad outline, as follows:

"In February, 1919, the accused, Anthony Kempster, came to live as a boarder with Mr and Mrs Francis Redwood at Colchester. Francis Redwood was a retired builder who had given up his business on account of bad health. He was more or less an invalid, and, in addition, he suffered from an aneurism, from which it appeared certain that he would die in the course of a year or two. He had saved a little money, on which he lived, but his means were very small and he took a boarder to eke them out. In view of his bad health, and especially of the aneurism, he had some time previously made a will, leaving the little property that he had to his wife and making her sole executrix.

"When the accused had been living with them about a month, he began to urge Mrs Redwood to insure her husband's life, pointing out how very little provision there was for her under the will. But, of course, Redwood was uninsurable by reason of his aneurism, as she explained to him, the question of insurance having been already considered. Then Kempster suggested to her that he thought he could manage the insurance if she left the business to him, but stipulated that nothing should be said about the matter to her husband. She did not at all clearly understand what it was that he proposed to do, but, as he assured her that he would take the whole responsibility, she agreed and promised to keep the affair secret from her husband.

"Then Kempster left Colchester for a time and went to live at Dartford under the name of Francis Redwood. There he consulted a Dr Croft about his health – which was quite good – and mentioned that he was thinking of insuring his life. Now, Dr Croft was the local examiner for the Griffin Insurance Society, and he naturally recommended his office and, at Kempster's request, gave him a proposal form. This Kempster filled up – in the name of Francis Redwood – giving the name of Dr Croft as his ordinary medical attendant. Then he went up to the London office for the medical examination and in the end managed to effect an insurance in the sum of two thousand pounds.

"As soon as the business was concluded, he went back to Colchester and took up residence with the Redwoods. After a month or two, he notified the Insurance Company of his change of address, still in the name of Francis Redwood, although he had by now resumed his own name of Anthony Kempster, imitating Redwood's signature as he had done on the proposal form.

"In April, 1921, shortly after the second premium had been paid, Francis Redwood died. But he did not die of the aneurism. He died of pneumonia following influenza, and a death certificate was given to that effect. Accordingly, as there was nothing unusual in the circumstances of the death, no inquiries were made but when the will was proved, the two thousand pounds were paid to the executrix in the ordinary way.

"About six months after the death of Francis Redwood, Kempster proposed marriage to the widow, Elizabeth Redwood, and was accepted. They were married at Ipswich and went to live there, having sold the Colchester house. After the marriage, Kempster managed to persuade his wife to allow him to put all their money into his bank with a view to making some investments. But those investments were never made. What became of the money, Mrs Kempster never knew. In some way it disappeared; and then Kempster himself disappeared; and from that time until a week or two ago she never set eyes on him again.

"Then one day she got a passing glimpse of him getting into a train and was subsequently able, with the assistance of her brother, Joseph Blake, to locate him as living in the neighbourhood of Hampstead. There he was arrested this morning by Detective Sergeant Morton. On his arrest, he stated that his name was not Anthony Kempster and that he had never heard of such a person. At the police station he was confronted with Mrs Kempster, who identified him as her husband, Anthony Kempster, but he still denied that that was his name and insisted that she was mistaking him for someone else."

"Apart from the identification by Mrs Kempster," said the magistrate, "is there any evidence that he is Anthony Kempster?"

"Yes, your worship," replied the superintendent. "As he refused to give any name or address or any sort of account of himself, it was necessary to search him. Then there was found in his pocket a bill addressed to A Kempster; but he still denied that that was his name. That is a summary of the case, your worship, and I shall now call the witnesses to prove the arrest and the identity."

The first witness was Detective Sergeant Roger Morton who deposed that, acting on information received, he had that morning proceeded to Hampstead Heath where he had arrested the accused, who was then engaged in making a sketch of the Heath, in execution of a warrant. He had administered the usual caution and the accused had made no statement beyond a flat denial that he was the person named in the warrant. Accused had not, however, resisted arrest.

The next witness was Inspector Frank Butt. He deposed that the accused had been brought to the station by the last witness at 1.45 p.m. He (the inspector) had read the charge to him and administered the usual caution. The accused was then confronted with Elizabeth Kempster, who identified him as her husband, Anthony Kempster. The accused declared that she was mistaken and that he was not Kempster, but he would not say who he was or give any address or any account of himself whatever. He was then searched and there was found in his pocket a wine merchant's bill (produced and handed to the magistrate), addressed to A Kempster. He could not account for his having this bill in his pocket, but he still maintained that the charge was a mistake and that he was not Kempster.

When the inspector had retired, the superintendent intimated that that was all the evidence that he was producing on this occasion; that he was asking for a remand to enable him to produce the other evidence and summon the witnesses, and that, as the accused refused to give any account of himself and his place of abode was unknown, he opposed bail.

The magistrate looked curiously at Andrew for a few moments and then said:

"You have heard the evidence that has been given. Do you wish to say anything? You are not bound to. But – " and here followed the inevitable caution.

"I don't wish to say anything at present," Andrew replied, "excepting that my name is not Anthony Kempster and that Mrs Kempster is mistaken in believing me to be her husband."

"What do you say that your name is?" the magistrate asked.

"I prefer not to give my name, at present," Andrew answered.

"Nor your address or occupation?"

"No, your worship."

"Then," said the magistrate, in the calm, impersonal tones to which Andrew was becoming accustomed, "you will have to be remanded in custody. You are remanded for seven days."

Thereupon Andrew was taken in custody by two constables and removed from the court. But he was not taken back to the police cells. Instead, he was conducted out of the building by a side passage and, on emerging into the street, found a prison van drawn up at the kerb. Passing – like a wedding guest, but with certain differences – between two rows of spectators, he was conducted to the van and assisted up the back steps into the dim and rather malodorous interior.

He had often wondered what the inside of a prison van was like. Now his curiosity was satisfied. It consisted of a dark and narrow passage with a row of doors on either side. Each door was furnished with a keyhole and a small grated window like the inspection trap in a convent gate. When one of the doors was opened, it disclosed a narrow compartment suggesting something between a sentry box and an extremely ascetic sedan chair, with a fixed seat, polished by friction with the persons of dynasties of disreputable occupants, and a small space in front of it to accommodate the feet of the sitter. On this uncommodious seat Andrew sat down gingerly, not without some uncomfortable speculations as to the characteristics and personal habits of the last occupant; and so soon as he was seated, the door was closed and locked.

It was a strange experience and far from an agreeable one. On the closing of the door, he seemed to be plunged into almost total darkness, excepting a faint glimmer from a ventilator over his head and the little square of twilight before him which indicated the position of the tiny grated window. For the back door of this criminal omnibus, when it was closed, admitted no more light than what was able to struggle through a very moderate-sized grated opening, and even this was largely obscured by the person of the "conductor".

But any deficiency in the matter of light was more than made up in smell. The whole vehicle was pervaded by the peculiar and distinctive odour of unwashed humanity; and, as the van proceeded on its round, picking up from time to time fresh consignments (which were fresh only in a limited sense), the flavour of the "imperfect ablutioner" became ever more pronounced. Yet these halts were not altogether unwelcome; for then, for a few moments, the back door was flung open and the depressing darkness was relieved by a flood of light, by which Andrew, peering out through the little grating, could get a glimpse of the new arrivals and could observe that the few other gratings which were within the range of his vision were each occupied by an eye similarly engaged in inspecting the new tenants.

But even the round of a prison van comes at last to an end. The termination of this journey was indicated to Andrew by a slowing down of the vehicle, a sudden increase of darkness, and then, as the van stopped, a clang from the rear as of the shutting of a heavy gate. After a brief interval there came a sound from the front like the opening of another gate; the van moved on, the light reappeared, the gate – now behind – clanged to and its closure was immediately followed by the click of a large lock. Finally, the van stopped once more, the back door was opened, the doors of the respective cells were unlocked, and the process of unloading began.

As he took his place in the queue that filed in at the prison gate, Andrew glanced curiously at his fellow sufferers. Assuming with more probability than charity that they were mostly criminals, their appearance was no advertisement for crime as a profession. Nor did it suggest that the profession was favoured by the élite of mankind. Manifest poverty and physical uncleanness were the distinguishing characteristics of the immense majority and, taken as a random sample of the population, even this small group was noticeably below the average both in physique and in the outward signs of intelligence. It looked as if crime were not a "paying proposition", though, to be sure, it might be argued that the present assembly represented only the unsuccessful practitioners.

Meditating this question as he followed the shuffling crowd, Andrew was yet again impressed by the civil and tolerant attitude of the officials. In the reception ward, the officer who presided over the ceremonies instructed him quite kindly in the necessary preparations; and the doctor who examined him might have been the medical referee of an insurance office. Nevertheless, the general atmosphere of the place was unspeakably grim and forbidding. Never for a moment was the inmate allowed to forget that he was a prisoner in the custody of the law. As he followed the warder from "Receptions" to his final resting-place in a faraway gallery, every one of the innumerable light iron gates which they passed had to be unlocked to admit them and was immediately locked behind them; and when, tramping along the iron-floored gallery, they came to a door bearing a number corresponding to that on the label which had been attached to his coat, that door had to be unlocked to admit him to his cell, though being furnished with a spring lock, it fastened him in without the aid of a key. But before it was closed the warder, having gathered that he was a "green hand", lingered to give him a few general instructions, to explain the use of the bell by which an attendant could be summoned and to caution him against the improper use of this important appliance. Then he retired from the cell; the heavy door slammed, the spring lock snapped audibly, and the sounds from the galleries without suddenly became muffled and remote.

When Andrew was left alone he proceeded to do what every man probably does when he finds himself in prison for the first time; he made a tour of inspection of his apartment and examined its furniture and appointments. There was little of the picturesque dungeon in the appearance of the cell. It was just a small, bare room with whitewashed walls and a fair-sized iron-framed window with very small panes. The furniture consisted of a small fixed table, a solid stool and a plank bed, with the bedding – mattress, pillow, blanket, sheets, rug and pillow-slip – neatly rolled up into a cylindrical bundle, not without regard to the decorative possibilities of the variously-coloured items. There was a tin jug, filled with water, a drinking vessel (officially known as a "pint"), a tin plate, a salt cellar and a wooden spoon. Other conveniences included a tin basin, a comb and brush, a dust pan, a queer little sweeping brush like a tiny besom without a handle, and a slate with a stump of pencil attached by a length of string. A bell push communicated with the warder's room and actuated a sort of semaphore arm outside the cell; and, lastly, the massive door was furnished with a tiny round window of thick glass covered by a sliding shutter – but the shutter was outside and beyond the prisoner's control.

Having made his inspection, he looked round for other objects of interest. The slate did not attract him. As a writing or drawing medium it was a poor substitute for the excellent paper to which he was accustomed; and the stump of pencil was worn to a shapeless end which repelled him. He would have liked to sharpen it, but his knife had been taken from him. Then he transferred his attention to the walls of the cell. In one respect they conformed to the traditional ideas of a dungeon, for they were covered with the comments and lamentations inscribed by former tenants; and, as these were written in lead pencil, it was obvious that they were the work of "remands" like himself. He wandered round idly reading them and filled with an ever-increasing wonder at their amazing puerility and the almost incredibly low intelligence that they suggested. He was surprised, too, to notice the almost complete absence of any tendency to obscenity in them. They seemed to be just the harmless outpourings of perfectly vacant minds. Most of them might have been the work of backward children of eight or nine.

Some were mere pathetic expressions of self-pity, such as "Poor old Blower", repeated more than a dozen times on different parts of the walls. Others gave bald particulars of their offences with rough estimates of their expectations. Thus, "Joe Viney from Wood Green expects a stretch for stabbing"; "Moley from Upper Rathbone Place,

Oxford St. W. Committed for trial North London Sessions for a Byke"; "Nobbie in for a bust"; "Jim Brads from Rathbone Place fullied for a bust"; "T. Savage from Chapel St. expects 6 wks"; "J. Williams expects 3 years"; and so on. Others made complaints or accusations; as "Charles Kemp was put away for deserting by Mr Goldstein of Hackney road", or "Jackson is the one. Hurry up and catch HIM. Jackson you have ruined me. Jackson will get 300 years"; while yet others merely recorded names, as "Mikey from the Boro.", written in reverse in six places with several unfinished attempts, and "Hymey from Brick Lane and Ginger Jim".

Andrew studied these curious memorials gravely and with deep interest. They were certainly quaint, and to some they might have been amusing. But not to Andrew. To him their significance was too sinister. They labelled their writers the refuse, the "throw-outs", of humanity. And what was he but one of them? He drew the stool up against the wall to provide a back, and, seating himself, fell into a train of vague reflection on the dismal prospects that were opening out before him. His feeling was one of utter helplessness. He was the victim of a whole complex of illusions, and he did not in the least see how those illusions could be dispelled. Perhaps some ideas might come to him later. There was plenty of time to think over matters – seven days before he had to make his next appearance before the magistrate. And so his mind rambled off to other subjects, to thoughts of Molly and especially to Mrs Pendlewick.

His reflections were interrupted by the arrival of his supper; a hunk of brown bread and a mug of cocoa, both excellent and very welcome. Refreshed by his meal, he took a little exercise pacing up and down his cell. Finally, having laid his mattress and made his bed, he took off his shoes and some of his clothes and laid himself down on his not very resilient couch.

Naturally, in the early part of the night, he slept little if at all. The day's excitements and the unusual surroundings tended to keep him awake, as did the lack of the customary darkness; for, when the daylight faded, the cell was lighted by a square of ground glass illuminated by a lamp outside the cell, which threw in its unwelcome rays throughout the night. And then there was the "Judas" – the little round spy-hole in the door. To Andrew that was the most disturbing influence of all. He found himself continually watching it with expectant nervousness and straining his ears to catch the footfalls of the warder on his rounds and to be ready to see it open. Later he learned that the night warders wear shoes with list soles, which explained why, on each occasion, the uncanny, secret "blink" of the Judas – like the opening and closing of a bird's eye – startled him by occurring silently and without warning. And each time it left him more nervous and more profoundly humiliated.

But even a prisoner's night is not endless. He heard midnight strike on some clock in the world of freedom without, and then he knew no more until he was roused to clean up his cell and get ready for breakfast. And so began a day which was like all the succeeding days. He washed himself in the tin basin and even brushed his hair gingerly with the official brush. When he was summoned out for exercise, he tidied himself up as well as he could, and, having taken his number label, or badge, down from the hook on which it hung when he was "in residence", he attached it to his coat in the prescribed manner and was ready to take his place in the ranks of the other occupants of the gallery and be marched off to the prison yard.

The process of taking exercise was doubtless beneficial, but it was not exhilarating. The surroundings of the exercise ground of a local prison are hardly romantic. Still, to Andrew, on his first morning, the experience had the charm of novelty. He found himself embedded in a long and squalid procession trailing interminably at a quick, mechanical stride along narrow, sinuous paved paths just wide enough to accommodate the single file that moved along them; supervised by a number of warders, each of whom stood, statue-like, on a low stone pedestal, from which he could look over the heads of the exercisers. Nominally, the march was conducted in absolute silence. Actually, there was a more or less continuous hum of conversation of a very curious ventriloquial quality due to the fact that the "old hand" can talk without moving his face. From time to time a warder would call out sternly to the conversationalists to "stop that talking"; but still the mumble went on. Even the most experienced officer is baffled by a talker who stares straight before him and preserves a face of wood.

The experiences of this first day included two that were not repeated. The first was connected with the prison photographer; who, having looked him over critically, proceeded to execute a couple of portraits of him, one full face and one in profile. The other brought him within the province of the officer who took the fingerprints of His Majesty's guests and entered their descriptions and other "particulars" on the prescribed form for deposit at the Criminal Record Office; to all of which procedure Andrew submitted without demur, although, as an unconvicted, and therefore nominally innocent man, he was entitled to object. But he saw no reason for objecting; indeed, he was fast settling down into a state of dull fatalism, apprehensive of the future but hopeless of any means of controlling it.

This fatalistic attitude was viewed with deep disapproval by the fatherly middle-aged officer who looked after him by day. Andrew, as we have said, was a naturally polite man, instinctively suave and courteous in manner, with the obvious appearance and habits of a gentleman, circumstances which commended him to Officer Bolton, who had been in the army and had something of the old soldier's social exclusiveness. Moreover, Andrew gave no trouble. He obeyed the rules, accepted the discipline, made no complaints as to his food or otherwise, and was in all respects a model prisoner, and, as such, was duly appreciated by the staff who had to deal with him.

But his passive attitude, apparently taking no measures for his defence, caused the good-natured warder great concern; and, in the course of his official visitations, he took the opportunity to offer advice and admonitions which became more urgent as the days passed.

"Look here, Kempster," he said, "you ought to have legal assistance. Get a decent solicitor, tell him all about it and let him make out the best case he can."

"I don't see what he could do for me," replied Andrew, "as I don't choose to give my real name."

"I can understand that," said Bolton (who, to Andrew's astonishment, seemed quite prepared to entertain his innocence). "But it's no use being thin-skinned. The name is bound to come out, sooner or later, if you get sent to prison. You know, you are not taking this affair seriously enough. You are charged with personation. Now, that's a felony; and the magistrate can't deal with it. He will commit you for trial at the Old Bailey if you can't make a proper defence, and you may get a nasty sentence. Don't wait for that. Get a solicitor and tell him the whole truth. Don't you see, my lad, it's no use your going into court and telling them that you didn't commit the crime and they've arrested the wrong man. That's what every accused man says, and nobody takes any notice. You've got to get someone who knows the ropes to manage your little business. And you've got to look sharp about it. Time's running on. In three days more the remand expires, and then you'll be up before the magistrate for the second hearing; and, if you haven't got something definite to say, you'll be fullied as the crooks call it – committed for trial. Now, you think over what I've said, and don't take too long thinking over it."

Accordingly, Andrew did think over it; but his thinking brought him no more forward. Once more he considered the advisability of boldly proclaiming his real identity. But the plan did not commend itself for two reasons. First, it would be useless. No one would believe him. There was Elizabeth Kempster, ready to swear to him as her husband and probably there would be other witnesses who would swear to his identity as Anthony Kempster. And what evidence could he produce in support of his statement that he was the late Andrew Barton? To call Molly would be obviously useless. Her manner towards him when he had visited her had shown evident mistrust. She would certainly scout his claim to be her dead husband as a transparent and impudent fraud. The only witness who would be of any use – Professor Booley – was on the high seas or in some inaccessible part of the United States.

But even if he were able to prove his real identity; how would that help him? He would merely prove that, instead of Anthony Kempster, charged with personation, he was Andrew Barton, charged with murder. It was the old dilemma; and, so far as he could see, there was no way out.

So, once more, he was thrown back on his original position. Fate had him fast in its clutches. He had no choice but to accept whatever might befall. And in this frame of mind he waited in dull expectation for the second hearing; waited to see what Fate really had in store for him.

The second hearing impressed him as something compounded of a nightmare and a chapter from *The Arabian Nights*. In spite of Bolton's exhortations, he was unrepresented by a lawyer. As he did not mean to disclose his identity, he had nothing to tell the solicitor, and he could make his bald denial without legal aid.

But it was a strange and bewildering experience. Standing in the dock, he listened to the evidence with a feeling of stupefaction. He heard a gentleman from the insurance office read out the proposal form for the insurance of Francis Redwood and give the particulars of the transaction, including the payment of £2,000. He heard the doctor from Dartford identify him as the man whom he had treated under the name of Francis Redwood, to whom he had given a proposal form made out in the same name; whom he had examined in connection with the said proposal form and whom he had, in the character of the proposer's usual medical attendant, certified as a first class life, still under the name of Francis Redwood. He heard a person of the name of Baines, who appeared to be Redwood's successor in the business, describe the late Francis Redwood, whom he had known long and intimately, as a feeble, sickly man, extremely unlike the accused, and further declare most positively that the accused was certainly not Francis Redwood but was one Anthony Kempster, well known to him as a man who had lodged in Redwood's house.

And so on. It was a most conclusive and convincing mass of evidence, and the mere fact that it was all totally untrue was known to Andrew alone, and could not be communicated by him to anyone else excepting in the unconvincing form of a comprehensive denial. But it was all rolled out with exhaustive and tedious thoroughness. Each deposition was taken down verbatim by the clerk, read over to

R AUSTIN FREEMAN

the witness and signed by him as well as by the magistrate. And even that was not the end of it; for when the whole of the evidence had been given, the depositions of all the witnesses were solemnly read over again for Andrew's special benefit. Then the magistrate addressed him in the usual formal terms.

"Having heard the evidence, do you wish to say anything in answer to the charge? You are not obliged to say anything unless you desire to do so; but whatever you say will be taken down in writing and may be given in evidence upon your trial. And you are also clearly to understand that you have nothing to hope from any promise of favour, and nothing to fear from any threat which may have been holden out to you to induce you to make any admission or confession of your guilt; but whatever you now say may be given in evidence against you upon your trial, notwithstanding such promise or threat."

"All I wish to say," replied Andrew, with a perfect recognition of the fatuousness of his reply, "is that I am not Anthony Kempster, and that the evidence which has been given does not apply to me."

The magistrate wrote this down and then asked:

"Do you wish to say who you are?"

"Not on this occasion," Andrew answered.

"Nor to give any account of yourself?"

"No," was the hopeless reply; on which the magistrate, having written down the answers and signed them, informed the accused that he stood committed for trial at the Central Criminal Court, and he was forthwith removed from the dock and taken back "to the place from whence he had come".

140

# CHAPTER ELEVEN

## The Last Straw

As Andrew sat in his cell, recalling again and again the incredible proceedings of the police court, he was conscious of the first stirrings of revolt against the malignity of Fate. The wild absurdity of the whole affair tended to dispel his apathy and rouse a spirit of resistance.

After all, the final blow had not fallen. He was not condemned; he was only committed for trial. There was still time for him to set up a defence; and Bolton's indelicately broad hints as to what he might expect from the judge if he made no reasonable defence spurred him on to reconsider his tactics. It was no question, the worthy officer pointed out, of a few months in prison. The crime of false personation is a felony and may carry a substantial term of penal servitude. That was an appalling prospect. It meant several years cut out of the best part of his life, to say nothing of the misery of those years; and at the end of it he would be no better off. For he would come out of prison with the label of Anthony Kempster affixed to him immovably and for ever.

Something would have to be done. But the question was, what? Perhaps there was something in Bolton's idea after all. To a reputable solicitor he could safely tell his story, for a lawyer is entitled to hold sacred the secrets of his client. But when he had told his story, what then? His lawyer would be involved in the old dilemma. His client was either Anthony Kempster or Andrew Barton. If he was Kempster, he was guilty of personation; if he was Barton, he was guilty of the

141

murder of Oliver Hudson. It was a hopeless position, and he did not see how any amount of legal acumen could steer a course between the two impossible alternatives.

So, ineffectively, he struggled to find a way out of the labyrinth of perplexities in which he had become involved. How long he would have continued to struggle and what he would eventually have done, it is impossible to say. For the problem of Anthony Kempster suddenly receded into the background. Fate had another little selection from its repertoire to offer for his consideration and a new problem to submit for solution.

It was the second day after the police court hearing, early in the afternoon, when the door of his cell was thrown open, disclosing his usual custodian and a couple of gentlemen standing in the gallery outside, one of whom he recognized as Inspector Butt and the other as Superintendent Barnes, the officer who had opened the case against him at the first hearing. The two men entered the cell and the warder retired into the gallery, leaving the door ajar. It was the superintendent who addressed him.

"We have come here," said he, "to discharge a disagreeable duty; to convey to you the information that you are charged with murder."

"With murder!" Andrew exclaimed, gazing at the officer in amazement. He could hardly believe his ears. It seemed incredible that even the police should have penetrated his disguise. This was the very last thing that he had expected or been prepared for.

"The charge is," the officer continued, "that on the 28th of August, 1928, at a place called Hunstone Gap, you, Ronald Barton, alias Anthony Kempster, alias Walter Green, feloniously did kill and murder one Andrew Barton. That is the charge. I don't know whether you wish to say anything, but it is my duty to caution you that anything you may say will be taken down in writing and used in evidence at your trial."

As the superintendent read out the charge, Andrew's feelings underwent a curious revulsion. Somehow, he experienced a sense of relief, almost of amusement. For the thing was so utterly preposterous. He was actually accused of having murdered himself!

"May I ask," he said, "what reasons there are for supposing that I murdered Andrew Barton?"

"A summary of the evidence against you," the superintendent replied, "will be supplied for your use or that of your lawyers, if you obtain legal assistance, as I suppose you will, and as you certainly ought to; but I will give you the main facts that are in the possession of the police.

"First, on the day of Andrew Barton's death, you were seen in his company, and you appear to have been the last person who saw him alive, as you were seen walking with him in the direction of Hunstone Gap.

"Second, there was found in your possession, in your lodgings at Hampstead, an attaché case containing ninety pounds in money and certain valuable property. This case, and the property in it, has been identified as the property of the deceased Andrew Barton, which he had with him on the day of his death. It has also been ascertained that this case was seen in your possession, in your lodgings at Crompton on the evening of that same day.

"Third, it is known that, on the day following the death of deceased, you cashed a cheque at deceased's London bank, which cheque was either in the case or on the person of deceased when he left home. Those are the principal points in the evidence at present available; and I now ask you if you wish to make any statement, bearing in mind the caution that I have just given you."

Andrew reflected rapidly. He was not disposed to make any statement until he had given some thought to the new developments. But there was one thing which instantly struck him. The case must have been identified by Molly; and, if that were so, she would be called to give evidence as to its identity at his trial. But the idea was so repugnant to him that he was prepared to compromise himself to some extent if by so doing he could prevent her from being called.

"May I ask who identified the case?" he inquired.

"Mrs Barton, the wife of the deceased," was the reply; "and she is prepared to swear that the case was in deceased's possession when he left home on the morning of his death."

"Yes," said Andrew. "It will be very disagreeable for her to appear as a witness. Would it simplify matters if I were to admit that the case is the property of Andrew Barton? Would, that render it unnecessary for her to be called?"

"It might," the superintendent replied, "but I can give no promise or make any kind of conditions. Do I understand that you admit that the case that was found in your lodgings at Hampstead was the property of the late Andrew Barton?"

Again Andrew reflected, with a new mental alertness. He could not accept the superintendent's wording but yet he did not wish to alter it conspicuously until he had considered his course of action. Eventually he said:

"I admit that the case which you found in my rooms at Hampstead is the case which Andrew Barton was carrying when he left home on the morning of the 28th of August. Will you write that down?"

The superintendent, with a look of obvious surprise, wrote the statement down in his notebook and then asked:

"Do you wish to state how the case came into your possession?"

"No," Andrew replied, "I do not wish to make any further statement."

"Very well," said the superintendent, "then I will ask you to read the statement and, if you find it correct, to sign your name underneath."

He handed the book and his fountain pen to Andrew, who read the statement and, finding it faithfully set down in his own words, affixed his signature and returned the book to its owner, who, having added his own signature, as a witness, pocketed it.

"I think that is all there is to say at present," said the superintendent. "You will be given all necessary facilities for preparing your defence if you apply to the Governor of the prison, and you will be brought before the magistrate as soon as possible. You are sure you don't want to make any further statement?"

"Quite sure," Andrew replied; whereupon the two officers retired, and Bolton, with a wistful look into the cell, slammed the door and left the prisoner to his own thoughts.

The immediate effect of this bolt which had fallen, not, indeed, out of the blue, but out of an uncommonly stormy sky, was to bring Andrew abruptly to his senses. Curiously enough, he was not particularly alarmed by this new charge. He was still under the influence of Miss Booth's accusation and was more afraid of being charged with the murder of Mr Hudson than with that of Andrew Barton. Nevertheless, he realized that this was a charge of murder and that, if he made no effective answer to it, he stood to be hanged. And to being hanged he had as great an objection as ever. To a term of imprisonment he might have resigned himself if there had been no way of avoiding it. But to the rope he could not resign himself at all. Some effective defence he would have to set up, though at the moment he could think of none, seeing that the evidence that the superintendent had recited was all true in fact; but already he was beginning dimly to recognize that he was receiving yet another shove from circumstance; that Miss Booth's accusation notwithstanding, he would be forced to make an effort to recover his own identity.

Indeed, the more he reflected on the matter the more did the motor crime tend to recede into a second place. A bird in the hand is worth two in the bush. The murder of Andrew Barton was a criminal charge that was very much in the hand, whereas the Hudson murder was still in the bush, even though that bush was uncomfortably near. Moreover, as he compared the two cases, he began to see that the new charge was the more formidable of the two. For the first time, he realized that Miss Booth's accusation was opposed to all reasonable probabilities and that he really had something weighty and material to offer in reply. In fact, with the clarity of vision that the new danger had produced, he began to suspect that he might have exaggerated the former danger.

On the other hand, the more he considered the new charge, the more did its formidable character tend to make itself felt. For here all the probabilities were against him. The absurdity of the charge was beside the mark; indeed, it was an added element of danger when the incredible nature of his own story was taken into consideration. Now that it had been ascertained that he had been present at Hunstone Gap when the death occurred and that he had "sneaked away like Cain", as Molly had expressed it, he could see that his subsequent conduct in keeping out of sight and offering no word of explanation was in the highest degree suspicious.

These cogitations led him to the inevitable conclusion. He would have to proclaim his real identity and he would have to tell the whole of his preposterous story. He would tell it to a lawyer and trust to his capacity to present it to the court in as plausible and credible a form as was possible. But the difficulty was that the lawyer would, at least in his own mind, reject it as a mere silly fable. It was even possible that a reputable lawyer might refuse to undertake a defence which was based on such a mass of absurdities, while the type of lawyer who would be ready to undertake any kind of case, good or bad, would probably have neither the skill nor the personal credit which would be necessary to give so unconvincing a case a fair chance. And there was the further difficulty that he knew no lawyers excepting his family solicitor, Mr Wakefield; a respectable provincial practitioner who had no experience of criminal practice and who would pretty certainly flatly refuse to have anything to do with a man whom he would regard as his late client's murderer.

Eventually, he decided, as a preliminary measure, to discuss the position with Bolton. But it presently appeared that that kindly and conscientious officer, in his anxieties at the new position, had made representations in higher quarters. The fact transpired when the Medical Officer made one of his periodical visits to inspect his charge and inquire if there were "any complaints". When he had finished his professional business, instead of bustling away in his usual fashion, he lingered with a somewhat hesitating air and a thoughtful eye on his patient, and at length opened the subject that was in his mind.

"I don't want to meddle in your affairs, Barton – your name is Barton, isn't it?"

"Yes," Andrew replied, "my name is Barton."

"Well," said the doctor, "as I said, I don't want to meddle, but your day officer, Bolton, is rather concerned about you, and he has spoken to me, suggesting that I might have a few words with you. He thinks that you have not given yourself a chance, so far; that you have had no legal assistance and taken no measures for your defence. Now, if that is so, it is a serious matter. Judges and magistrates will do all they can to see that you get fair play, but they can't conduct your defence. You have got to help them by giving them the facts on your side; facts which are known only to you. But perhaps you would rather that I did not interfere."

"On the contrary," Andrew replied, earnestly, "I am most grateful to you, and would thankfully accept your advice if you are not compromising yourself officially by giving it."

"Good Lord!" exclaimed the doctor, "of course I am not. Everyone wants you to have a fair trial. Even the police don't want a conviction against an innocent man; and as to me, it is perfectly correct for me, or any other prison official, to advise a prisoner if he wants advice."

"I am glad of that," said Andrew, "because I want advice very badly. I realize that I ought to have legal assistance, but appearances are so hopelessly against me that I doubt if a lawyer could help me."

"But," the doctor protested, "the more appearances are against you, the more do you need the help of a lawyer. I take it that you are not going to plead guilty?"

"Certainly not. I am absolutely innocent of both of the charges against me."

"Then," said the doctor, "if you are innocent, there must be facts producible which would form an answer to the charges."

"There are," said Andrew, "but they are known only to me; and they are so extraordinary and incredible that no one would believe them. That is my difficulty. I have a perfectly complete and consistent story; but if I should tell that story to a lawyer, he would think I was merely romancing."

"Your lawyer isn't going to try you," the doctor remarked, adding with a queer, one-sided smile, "and you mustn't misunderstand his position. The function of an advocate is not to experience belief in his own person but to be the occasion of belief in others."

"Still," Andrew persisted, "it is rather hopeless to be defended by a lawyer who believes one to be guilty. I should have liked to convince him that, at least, I might possibly be innocent."

"Naturally, and very properly. But why not? The truth of those facts which are known to you must be susceptible of proof or disproof. If they are true, it is for your lawyer to ascertain and demonstrate their truth." He paused for a moment and then, speaking with marked emphasis, said: "Now tell me, Barton, supposing a competent lawyer should undertake your defence, would you be prepared to give him all the facts in your possession – to tell him everything that you know, truthfully and without any reservation whatever?"

"Certainly," Andrew replied. "I would promise to hide nothing from him."

The doctor reflected for a few moments. Then he asked:

"Have you any lawyer in your mind whom you would like to consult?"

"No," Andrew answered. "I know of no lawyer. That is a point on which I was going to ask for your advice. Is there anyone whom you can recommend me to apply to?"

"I think there is," the doctor replied, "but I am not quite sure whether all the circumstances are suitable. When I was a student I had the good fortune to be the pupil of a very great man. His name is Dr John Thorndyke – perhaps you may have heard of him."

"I seem to have heard the name," said Andrew, "but I know nothing about him. I take it that he is a doctor, not a lawyer."

"He is both, and he was our lecturer on Medical Jurisprudence – that is the legal aspect of medicine or the medical aspect of law. He practises as a barrister but he is not an advocate in the sense in which I was speaking just now. His speciality is the examination and analysis of evidence, and it seems to me that your case might interest him. You see, Barton, that I am taking your statement at its face value; I am assuming that you are an innocent man who is the victim of misleading appearances."

"That," said Andrew, "I swear most solemnly is the absolute truth."

"I hope it is, and I accept your statement. Now, would you like me to see Dr Thorndyke and explain your position and find out whether he would be prepared to consider the question of his conducting your defence?"

"I should be profoundly grateful if you would. But do you think he would believe my story?"

The doctor smiled his queer, lopsided smile. "I don't think, Barton. I know. He wouldn't. But neither would he disbelieve it. He would just treat it as material for investigation. He would pick out the alleged facts which were capable of being verified or disproved and he would proceed to verify or disprove them. If he found your statements to be true, he would go on with the case. If he found them untrue, he would decline the brief and pass you on to a counsel who would conduct the defence without prejudice as to his personal convictions."

"That seems to me a very reasonable and proper method," said Andrew. "I ask for nothing more. But I don't see how he is going to find out whether my story is true or false."

"You can leave that to him," the doctor replied. "But," he added, emphatically, "understand once and for all, Barton, I am assuming that your story, whatever it is, is a true story. If it isn't, don't send me on a fool's errand: I assure you that it is impossible to bluff Thorndyke. If he starts on the case, he will have you turned inside out in a twinkling; and if you tell him anything that isn't true, you'll be bowled out first ball. Now, Barton, what do you say? Would you like me to put the case to him?"

"If you would be so very kind," replied Andrew. "It seems to me that Dr Thorndyke is exactly the kind of lawyer that I want."

"I am glad to hear you say that," the doctor rejoined, with obvious satisfaction. "Then I will call on him without delay and use what persuasion I can. But I shall want a written authority from you to offer him the brief. A leaf of my notebook will do to write it on. He won't be unduly critical of the stationery in the special circumstances."

With this and a trace of his quaint smile, he produced his notebook and a fountain pen; and when Andrew had drawn up the stool to the little fixed table and seated himself, he dictated a brief authorization which Andrew wrote and signed "Ronald Barton", enclosing the signature between quotation marks. Then he returned the book and pen to their owner who glanced through the few lines of writing and then looked up sharply.

"Why have you put your signature between inverted commas?" he asked.

"Because I am signing as a prisoner in my prison name, which is not my real name. I am not Ronald Barton."

"Oh, aren't you?" said the doctor, in a tone of surprise and looking at Andrew a little dubiously. "I thought you said your name *was* Barton."

"So it is," replied Andrew, "but not Ronald."

The doctor continued for some seconds to look at him with a puzzled and somewhat dissatisfied expression. At length he said, as he put away the notebook:

"Well, the facts of the case are no concern of mine; but I hope you will be able to make them clear to Dr Thorndyke, if he is willing to listen to them."

With this parting remark, of which the dry and even dubious tone was not lost on Andrew, the doctor pushed open the door, which had (necessarily since there was no inside keyhole) stood ajar during the interview, and, stepping out, closed it behind him.

The clang of the closing door and the snap of the lock suddenly put Andrew back in his place, from which the brief spell of civilized conversation seemed for the time to have liberated him; even as the loop of key-chain that peeped below the hem of the doctor's coat as he retired, served to remind him that this kindly gentleman was, after all, a prison officer, one of whose duties was to hold the captive in secure custody.

# CHAPTER TWELVE

## Dr Thorndyke

The visible results of the doctor's mission appeared early in the afternoon of the following day when the door of Andrew's cell was thrown open and Bolton looked in on his charge.

"Your lawyer is waiting down below," said he. "Just tidy yourself up a bit and come along with me. And look sharp."

There was not much to be done, since razors were forbidden by the regulations. Andrew gave his hair a perfunctory brush, extended the operation to his coat and announced that he was ready.

"You've forgotten your badge," said the officer; and Andrew, with a grim smile, took it down from its hook and fastened it to his coat, remarking that "one might as well look the part". Then they set forth on their journey by innumerable iron staircases and through a long succession of iron gates, each of which had to be unlocked to give them passage and locked again when they had passed. Eventually, they reached their destination, a smallish, very bare room with one door, of which the upper half consisted of a single panel of plate glass through which the warder, posted outside, could keep the prisoner under observation without intruding on the conference. Here, Bolton delivered his charge and shut him in.

There were two persons in the room. One was the doctor and the other was a tall stranger, at whom Andrew looked with deep interest and a certain amount of awe. For this stranger was a very impressive person with a distinctly imposing presence, due not alone to the stature, the upright, dignified carriage and the suggestion of physical strength. In the handsome, intellectual face was a subtle quality that instantly conveyed the impression of power; an impression that was reinforced by a singularly quiet, contained, reposeful and unemotional bearing. His hair was tinged with grey, but the calm, unlined face was almost that of a young man.

"Well, Barton," the Medical Officer said as Andrew entered, "Dr Thorndyke is willing to listen to your story, or as much of it as may be necessary to make clear the nature of the defence; and, as I have done my part by inducing him to come, I will take myself off and leave you to your consultation."

With this he took his departure, carefully shutting the door after him and pausing to say a few words to the warder who was posted outside. Then Dr Thorndyke drew one of the two chairs up to the table, and, indicating the other, said:

"Pray be seated, Mr Barton," (Andrew noted the "Mr" appreciatively), "and draw your chair close to the table so that we need not raise our voices." He opened a case which looked like a small suitcase, and, taking out a block of ruled paper, placed it on the table before him and continued: "Dr Blackford, your Medical Officer, has indicated to me in very general terms the nature of your difficulties, and I understand from him that you have a remarkable and rather incredible story to tell me. We must have that story in detail presently; but before we begin, there is one point which I should like to have cleared up. In this authorization which you gave Dr Blackford," – here he laid it on the table – "you have signed your name, Ronald Barton, between inverted commas; and the doctor quoted you as having explained this on the ground that Ronald Barton is not your name. Is that correct?"

"Quite correct, sir. My name is not Ronald Barton."

"Then," said Dr Thorndyke, "let us start fair with the genuine name."

"My name," replied Andrew, a little hesitatingly and in uncommon trepidation now that the climax was reached, abruptly and all unprepared, "my name is Andrew Barton."

Dr Thorndyke looked slightly surprised.

"Your name, then," said he, "is the same as that of the man whom you are accused of having murdered."

"Not only the same name, sir," said Andrew, with his heart in his mouth. "The same person. I am Andrew Barton. The man who was killed was Ronald Barton."

On receiving this statement, Dr Thorndyke laid down his pen, leaned back in his chair and regarded Andrew with an expression that made his flesh creep.

"I read the report of the inquest at Crompton," he said, in quiet, level tones, "and I filed it. Last night, after seeing Dr Blackford, I read it again with great care. I noted that Andrew Barton was described – by his wife – as a man whose nose had been injured by an accident, with the result that the bridge was broken and rendered completely flat. I need not point out that that description does not apply to you."

"No, it does not," Andrew admitted, "and that is the cause of all the confusion and error."

"Then you still maintain," said Dr Thorndyke, "in spite of the total disagreement between your appearance and the description, that you are Andrew Barton, the husband of the woman who gave that description."

"I do," replied Andrew, "because it is the literal truth."

"And are you proposing to offer a reasonable explanation of this extraordinary discrepancy between the description and the visible facts?"

"Certainly I am," Andrew replied. "It is the essence of my defence. Shall I give you the explanation first, or shall I take it in its proper place in my story?"

"I think," said Thorndyke, "that, as your statement appears to postulate an impossibility, no useful purpose would be served by going into any other matters until this apparent contradiction in facts has been disposed of. Let us begin with the explanation."

Accordingly Andrew launched out into a detailed account of his dealings with Professor Booley, beginning with his panic on reading the description of himself in the police notice and finishing with the shock that he sustained on looking at his reflection in the mirror. To this account Dr Thorndyke listened with the closest attention, jotting down an occasional note on his pad but uttering no word until the whole story was told. Then he put one or two questions, including the exact whereabouts of Professor Booley's premises, and wrote down the answers, finally requesting Andrew to put his finger on the spot at which the Professor had inserted the needle.

"That," said he, "is a very remarkable story. Before we go any further, I should like to make a preliminary examination of your nose. You understand that I am a doctor of medicine as well as a lawyer?"

He opened the case on the table and took from it a small electric lamp, and, by the light of this, and with the aid of a pocket lens, he made a minute examination of the bridge of Andrew's nose, especially in the region in which the entry of the needle had been indicated. Then, laying the edge of his open hand on the bridge of the nose, he brought the lamp close to one side while he scrutinized the other. Finally, he put the lamp on the table and proceeded to explore the nose with the tips of his fingers, winding up by taking the base of the bridge between his finger and thumb (a proceeding that was observed with profound astonishment by the warder on duty outside).

Having made his examination, Dr Thorndyke went back to his chair and made one or two brief notes. Then he looked up; and Andrew, catching his eye, was sensible of a subtle change of expression. And he thought he detected a similarly subtle change of tone when Dr Thorndyke said:

"And now let us have the story."

Andrew hesitated in some slight embarrassment.

"I hardly know where to begin," said he. "It is rather a long story."

"You had better begin," said Thorndyke, "with the first event which had any causal bearing on your present predicament. What took you to Crompton?"

"I went to see my cousin about a letter that he had written to me."

"Then begin with that letter. And never mind the length of the story. We have got to have it all, either now or in instalments. But I want now at least an outline of the whole set of circumstances."

Thus encouraged, Andrew embarked on the strange history of his misadventures from the moment when the fatal letter had been put into his hands. As before, Dr Thorndyke listened without comment or question but making numerous notes – in shorthand, as Andrew subsequently learned. Only twice did he interrupt the narration. The first time was shortly after it had started and was in the nature of a general instruction.

"Don't epitomize, Mr Barton," said he. "Tell the story in detail, and don't be afraid of being prolix. The details may be more significant than they appear to you."

The second interruption occurred when Andrew was recounting the meeting in the train with Elizabeth Kempster.

"She was very angry and indignant," he was saying, "and reproached me for my ingratitude for all that she had done for me – "

It was at this point that Thorndyke held up his hand. "That won't do, Mr Barton," he exclaimed. "I want the conversation verbatim; the very words that were spoken by you and by her – especially by her. You must try to recall them, fully and accurately."

Andrew had little difficulty in doing so, for that terrible interview had burned itself into his memory, though he felt some qualms in retailing to another that unfortunate woman's emotional outpourings. But Dr Thorndyke had no such qualms, for he took down a verbatim report of the entire conversation with a care and minuteness that seemed to Andrew beyond the merits of the matter.

When the narrative came to an end with the narrator's committal for trial, Dr Thorndyke remarked:

"A very strange story, Mr Barton; and I certainly agree with you that it is not one to put to a jury in its raw state. And not such a very long story; but we will now proceed to amplify it a little."

With this he glanced over his notes and then opened a cross-examination, taking the narrative point by point from the beginning. And a very curious cross-examination Andrew thought it. For, to him, it appeared that Dr Thorndyke passed over all the important points and dredged deep for the most exhaustive details of things which did

155

not matter at all. To the murder of Mr Hudson he made no reference whatever, nor did he show any special interest in the tragic events that befell at Hunstone Gap. But his interest in the history and relationships of the Barton family was so profound that, having elicited all that Andrew knew, he not only wrote it down but illustrated it with a sketched pedigree.

Then he was strangely inquisitive as to Andrew's professional career, and especially as to the details of his dealings with Mr Montagu; and his interest in Mrs Pendlewick and her bone lace and the sittings she had given him for his picture filled Andrew with astonishment. What on earth could Mrs Pendlewick have to do with the alleged murder at Hunstone Gap? Nevertheless, he answered the questions with conscientious completeness; and if he was puzzled by their apparent irrelevance to the great issue, he never had a moment's doubt that some good purpose, invisible to him, lay behind them.

When the cross-examination was finished and Thorndyke, having collected his notes, stood up, Andrew plucked up courage to inquire:

"You have now heard my story, sir. May I ask if you find it possible to believe that it is a true story?"

Thorndyke looked at him for a few moments without speaking; and for the first time, his impassive, rather severe face relaxed into a faint smile which seemed to let some inner, unsuspected kindliness show for a moment on the surface.

"I am not going to let you cross-examine me, Mr Barton," said he. "And I am not committing myself to any opinions until I have checked and verified certain facts affirmed in your statement. You have told me a complete and consistent story and I have at present no reason to disbelieve it. But remember that, even if my investigations convince me of its truth, that is only a beginning. The problem will be to transfer my conviction to those who will have to make the decision."

It was a cautious statement, but, somehow, Andrew was not discouraged by its tone of caution. And as to the checking of his alleged facts, since he had told nothing but the truth, they were all in his favour.

"Before I go," said Thorndyke, "I must ask you to sign one or two little documents. I want your written authority to conduct your defence, if I decide to do so, and to make all arrangements to that end at my sole discretion. Then I want your authority to take custody of any of your property at present held by the police, if necessary and if they consent; and I want a similar authority in respect of property of yours in Mrs Pendlewick's possession. The arrangements for the defence will include the selection of a solicitor. In this case it is a mere formality, but the usage in English practice is that a counsel must be instructed by a solicitor. I will arrange with a friend to instruct me, in a technical sense."

He wrote out the three documents and presented them to Andrew for his signature. When he had signed them, Andrew ventured to raise another question.

"We have said nothing about the financial arrangements," said he, and was about to enlarge on the unsatisfactory nature of his resources when Thorndyke interrupted him.

"We had better leave those matters for the present," he suggested. "I shall take it for granted that you will discharge your liabilities if you are in a position to do so. But the costs are really a side issue. And now I must be off. I shall proceed at once with the necessary verification of your statements and when I see you again I shall be able to tell you exactly how we stand."

With this he picked up his case and, being released by the warder, took his departure; and Andrew was, in due course, conducted back to his apartment, where he presently consumed his evening meal of brown bread and cocoa with unwonted relish and thereafter spent the short remainder of the prison day in curious tranquillity of spirit.

This state of mental relief, with a new-born feeling of hope and security, was surprising even to himself. To what was it due? Certainly, he had at last unbosomed himself of his preposterous story and had not been denounced as a liar and an impostor. He had been given a hearing and promised an investigation. That was all to the good. But that did not account for the strange manner in which his fears and his anxieties seemed suddenly to have gone to rest. What was it? And

157

when he asked himself the question, the answer that came to him was – Dr Thorndyke.

And yet it was strange. Nothing could have been more unemotional than the bearing of this calm, quiet, self-contained man. Not a word of sympathy or encouragement had he uttered. By no hair's breadth had he deviated from the most strictly judicial attitude. There he had sat with a face like a mask of stone, listening impassively without sign of belief or disbelief, speaking only to put some searching question or to check some statement. Only one when, for a moment, that faint smile had lighted up his face with a gleam of kindliness, had he manifested any trace of human feeling. And yet, in some mysterious way, some virtue had come out of him and communicated itself to Andrew. Behind that immovable calm, he had had a sense of power, of energy and of incorruptible justice; of justice that would try him impartially in the balance; of power to enforce it, if he was not found wanting.

This restful feeling of having, in a sense, passed on his troubles and responsibilities to another, remained in the days that followed. In the results of Dr Thorndyke's investigations he had perfect confidence, for he knew that they must, of necessity, confirm the truth of his story. So, as the time passed, he waited patiently with sustained courage for the next developments. But it was not until the fifth day that his patience was rewarded by the announcement of Thorndyke's decision.

On entering the room in which the previous interview had taken place, he found Dr Thorndyke in company with another tall and athletic-looking gentleman who was introduced to him as Dr Jervis. Both men shook hands with him and Dr Thorndyke proceeded to state the position.

"I have checked such of your statements as it was possible to check and have been able to confirm them and am now satisfied that the story you told me is a true story. Accordingly, I am prepared to undertake your defence and I have, in fact, made all the necessary arrangements. My friend, Mr Marchmont, a very experienced solicitor, has agreed to act for you and I have asked him to call here and make your acquaintance. So everything is now in order. I suppose you have not thought of anything else that you wish to tell me? No additions to or amplifications of your statement?"

"No," replied Andrew; "I think you squeezed me pretty dry last time."

"Well," said Thorndyke, "I have no questions to ask, but perhaps Mr Marchmont may want some detail filled in. A solicitor sees a case from a slightly different angle and has his own special experiences. And here, I think, he is."

As he spoke, the footsteps of two persons were heard approaching down the corridor, and the warder on guard threw open the glazed door; through which another warder ushered the visitor and then retired after shutting him in.

Mr Marchmont was an elderly gentleman, prim, precise but suave in manner and a lawyer to the fingertips. When the introductions had been effected and a few civilities exchanged, he turned to Thorndyke.

"I have read your summary," said he, "and note that my role is that of a figurehead, as it usually is when I act with you. But there are one or two points on which I want more information. First, as to procedure. I presume that the preliminary investigation will take place before the justices at Crompton and the trial at the Maidstone Assizes. Is that so?"

"No," replied Thorndyke. "The case has been transferred to the Central Criminal Court – "

"By a writ of *certiorari*?"

"No. Under the new procedure provided for in the Criminal Justice Act of 1925."

"Ah!" said Marchmont, "I had overlooked that. Criminal practice is rather out of my province. And as to the preliminary investigation?"

"There isn't going to be any. I am informed that the Director of Public Prosecutions intends to present a voluntary bill to the Grand Jury."

"But that is rather unusual, isn't it?" said Marchmont.

"It will save a great deal of time and trouble and expense," replied Thorndyke, "and I, certainly, shall not complain. It extricates us from quite an awkward dilemma."

"What dilemma?" asked Marchmont.

"My difficulty," Thorndyke replied, "was this: If there had been an investigation before a magistrate, I should have had either to produce all my evidence, which I should not want to do, or to reserve my defence, which I should not have been justified in doing and could not, in fact, have done."

Dr Jervis chuckled softly and, glancing at Marchmont, remarked:

"It is a let-off from Thorndyke's point of view. Can't you imagine how he would have hated letting the cat out of the bag prematurely."

Marchmont laughed in a dry, forensic fashion. "Yes," he agreed, "it wouldn't have suited his tactics; for when once the cat is out, she is out. You can't put her back and repeat the performance. But the effect of this move on the Director's part is that the trial may begin quite soon. However, I shall receive due notice of the date. And now, having made our client's acquaintance and gleaned these particulars, I will take myself off and leave you to your occupations, whatever they may be."

He shook hands with them all round, and as the warder, observing this sign of farewell, opened the door, he bustled out and was taken in tow by the other officer. He had hardly disappeared when yet another official arrived with a message for Thorndyke to the effect that "Dr Blackford sends his compliments and the room is now available."

Andrew looked inquiringly at Thorndyke, who explained briefly:

"The doctor has kindly given us facilities for certain experiments which may help us. You will hear all about them later if their bearing is not apparent at the moment." Then, addressing the officer, he asked: "Do we come with you?"

"If you please, sir," was the reply; and the procession, having formed up, was personally conducted by the officer on a tour of the prison, coming to a halt at last in the neighbourhood of the infirmary where Dr Blackford was awaiting them.

"I have had all your traps put into this room," he said, opening a door as he spoke. "If you should want me, I shall be close at hand."

"Aren't you coming in with us?" asked Jervis. "No," replied the doctor. "I should like to, for I am devoured with curiosity as to what the deuce you are going to be up to. But I am not sure that it would be quite in order. And, besides, it is just as well for me not to know too much about Barton's affairs."

This was evidently Thorndyke's view for, without comment beyond a few words of thanks, he led Andrew into the room and, when Jervis had followed, shut the door.

It was a rather small room, apparently some kind of annexe to the infirmary, to judge by its appointments; which included a plain deal table and a bare, ascetic-looking couch with a distinct suggestion of surgery in its appearance. Looking about him curiously, Andrew noted that the table bore a pile of about a dozen large black envelopes and that at the head of the couch was reared a formidable-looking apparatus of which he could make nothing (scientific knowledge was not his strong point), but which aroused a faint and rather uncomfortable reminiscence of Professor Booley.

He watched, with the rather vague interest of the entirely non-scientific person, while his two friends busied themselves with various preparations and adjustments of the apparatus, speculating a trifle uneasily on the nature of the experiment which was about to be performed and of which it seemed that he was to be the subject. He saw Dr Thorndyke take two of the black paper envelopes from the table and place them carefully on a slab of wood that lay near the head of the couch, and he noted that the envelopes were rigid as if they contained plates of metal or some hard substance. Then he saw him adjust the position of a rather odd-looking electric lamp-bulb, which was fixed on a movable arm, placing it with great care immediately above the black envelopes. At length it appeared that all the preparations were complete, for Thorndyke, stepping back from the couch and taking a last fond look at the apparatus, announced:

"I think we are all ready now, and I suggest that we begin with you, Jervis. What do you say?"

"Yes," replied Jervis. "It is always wise to begin by trying it on the dog. And Barton can watch the procedure."

He took a small rug from the foot of the couch and, folding it, laid it on the black envelopes. Then he lay down on the couch, resting his

161

head on the folded rug. Thorndyke raised the corner of the rug, apparently to ascertain the position of the head on the envelopes, and once more made a slight adjustment of the lamp overhead.

"Ready?" said he, with his hand on a switch, and as Jervis responded, he turned the switch with a snap. Instantly the apparatus emitted a growl which rapidly ran up the scale until it settled into a high-pitched droning like the piping of a giant mosquito. At the same moment the lamp began to glow with a green light at the centre of which appeared a bright spot of red.

"Keep perfectly still, Barton," said Thorndyke, who stood rigid as a statue with his watch in his hand. "It is most important that there should not be the slightest vibration."

Andrew stood, resting with one hand on the table, listening to the curious high-pitched hum of the apparatus, wondering what these mysterious rites and ceremonies might have to do with a charge of murder and sensible of a perverse desire to change his position. At length Thorndyke put away his watch and turned the switch; whereupon the light of the lamp faded out, the whine of the apparatus swept down an octave or two until it died away in a low growl, and Jervis rose from the couch.

"Quite a harmless proceeding, you see, Barton," said he. "Nothing of the Booley touch about us."

He took the two envelopes from the couch and, having written his name with a pencil on each, added his signature and the date and handed them to Thorndyke, who counter-signed them and placed them apart on the table, while Jervis took another two of the envelopes and, having placed them in position on the couch laid the folded rug on them.

"Now, Barton," said Thorndyke, "you saw what Dr Jervis did. Go thou and do likewise. And remember that you have to keep perfectly still; to which end, you must settle yourself comfortably in a position which you can maintain without effort."

Accordingly Andrew laid himself down on the couch in as restful a pose as he could manage; and when Thorndyke had made some slight alteration in the placing of the head, the switch was turned, the apparatus uttered its plaintive whine, the mysterious green light glowed afresh, and the previous proceedings were repeated.

"You heard what we were saying to Mr Marchmont," said Thorndyke, when Andrew had risen from the couch and the envelopes had been signed and put away. "The trial may open quite soon; and in the meanwhile, I would urge you to be very careful to keep your own counsel. Give no information to anybody either as to what we have been doing here or as to anything in any way connected with your case. The special arrangements for presenting the bill of indictment direct to the Grand Jury give us the advantage of going into court without having disclosed the details of the defence. Let us keep that advantage. There may be nothing in it. But it is usually good tactics to let the enemy bring his heavy guns to bear on the place that you don't need to defend. So I say again, don't discuss your case with anybody, no matter how friendly."

Andrew promised to bear this caution in mind, adding:

"I suppose I shall get due notice of the date of the trial."

"Certainly," replied Thorndyke. "You will be kept informed of everything that you ought to know; and if you should want to confer with me or Dr Jervis or Mr Marchmont, you have only to send one of us a line to that effect. Is there anything that you would like to be advised upon now?"

"Yes," Andrew replied, "there is one rather important question that does not seem to have been raised. It is concerned with the Hudson case. When Andrew Barton disappeared, he had been accused of having committed that murder. If he should reappear, it would seem that that accusation will be revived. Isn't that so?"

"No," Thorndyke replied promptly. "You can dismiss the Hudson case from your mind, and you need never have taken the charge seriously. At first, the police, naturally enough, took Miss Booth's statement at its face value. But as soon as they began to make inquiries they realized that she had made a mistake – the common mistake of confusing what she had seen with what she had inferred. She saw a face at the window and she saw a revolver; and she inferred that the revolver and the face appertained to the same person. But when the police ascertained that the face was that of Mr Andrew Barton, and when they had heard his wife's account of the affair, they were satisfied that he was merely a chance spectator of the crime. As a matter of fact, they had some fairly definite information as to who the perpetrators really were. So Andrew Barton's connection with the case will be no more than that of a witness."

Andrew breathed a sigh of relief. "You have lifted a great weight off my mind," said he. "It may have been unreasonable of me, but I think I was more afraid of that accusation than of the charge that has actually been brought against me. It is an immense relief to know that I am free of it."

"I can easily understand that," said Jervis. "One doesn't want to step down from the dock after a triumphant acquittal, to fall into the arms of a detective-sergeant with a fresh warrant. And that isn't going to happen, Barton. When you are acquitted, you will be acquitted completely. Both indictments, murder and personation; for the greater includes the less and our evidence covers both. So keep a good heart and don't be discouraged or alarmed by any signs of preparation, such as identification parades or other movements of the enemy."

"You speak," said Andrew, "as if you were quite confident of an acquittal."

"I am," said Jervis, "and so, I think, is my learned senior. Aren't you, Thorndyke?"

"I certainly expect an acquittal," replied Thorndyke. "The case for the prosecution can't be a strong one, in any event. In fact," he added, with a smile, "my principal anxiety is lest the Grand Jury should throw out the bill."

"That would be rather an anti-climax," said Jervis, "and would crab a most promising defence. But still, it would be, in effect, equivalent to an acquittal."

"Not altogether," Thorndyke dissented, "for it would not cover the personation charge. But you see, Jervis, that a mere acquittal would not be enough for us. We are concerned with something more than the alleged murder. You remember the old schoolboy verses, *Pistor erat quondam*, which were, I think, rendered:

There was a baker heretofore, with labour and great pain,
Did break his neck and break his neck and break his neck again.

"Now that is what Barton has done. He has gone on piling illusions
and false appearances on top of one another until he has got himself
charged with his own murder; and we, like the baker's medical
attendant, have got to deal with the whole series. We have got to
reduce, not only the final fracture but all the others as well. And the
defence to the murder charge will give us the opportunity we want."

"Then," said Jervis, picking up the signed envelopes and bestowing
them tenderly in a suitcase, "let us hope the Grand Jury will not be
too critical in respect of the evidence for the prosecution."

# CHAPTER THIRTEEN

## Prisoner at the Bar

---

The sands of time, which trickle out grudgingly enough within the prison walls alike for the just and the unjust, had run through the glass to the last grain; and it was Jervis' hopes rather than Thorndyke's fears that had been justified by circumstances. For the Grand Jury had returned a true bill, and Andrew Barton stood in the dock at the Central Criminal Court to answer the charge of Wilful Murder.

His state of mind was very peculiar for that of a prisoner arraigned on such a charge. He realized it, himself, and was faintly surprised at it, particularly when he contrasted the abject panic of the terror-stricken wretch who had staggered away from the police bill at Crompton with the serenity of the prisoner at the bar who stood waiting to watch the throw of the dice in the game which was presently to be played between Thorndyke and his accusers; a game of which his life was the stake. The bare possibility that this thing might happen had then paralysed him with horror; and now that the reality was upon him, he seemed to face the terrible chances almost unmoved.

He looked about the court with somewhat of the interest of a spectator. He had never before been in a criminal court and the various objects and persons and the solemn procedure all had the attraction of novelty.

He inspected the scarlet-robed judge approvingly, excepting as to his wig, which he found disappointing. Like most uninformed persons, he had supposed that judges wore full-bottomed wigs when they sat in court. He observed the Clerk of the Court sitting in wig and gown behind his desk below the judge's dais; he counted the jury, who were waiting to be sworn, and noted that two of them were women. Then his eye roamed along the counsels' seats, where Dr Thorndyke sat placidly looking over his brief, and he endeavoured to pick out Sir Oliver Blizzard, who, he had been informed, was to lead for the prosecution; eventually fixing – correctly, as it turned out – upon a clerical-looking gentleman with a monocle firmly jammed in his eye unsecured by any cord or other support.

But all the time he was imperfectly conscious of his actual position. The old feeling of unreality still possessed him; the sense of being in a dream or under some sort of spell, which had first come on him when he looked into Professor Booley's mirror and saw the face of his cousin Ronald looking out at him. Only at intervals, by some special occurrence – as, for instance, when a woman juror asked to be excused from serving, on the grounds that she objected to capital punishment – was he startled out of his curious mental lethargy into a vivid realization of his actual position.

At length his wandering thoughts were interrupted by the Clerk of the Court, who had risen and was addressing him, apparently in the words of a document which lay before him on his desk.

"Ronald Barton, you are charged with the murder of Andrew Barton on the 28th of August, 1928. Are you guilty or not guilty?"

"Not guilty," Andrew replied.

The Clerk noted the answer and then once more addressed him.

"Prisoner at the Bar, if you wish to object to any of the persons whose names I am about to call to form the jury to try you, you must do so as they severally come to the book to be sworn, and before they are sworn, and you will be heard."

There being obviously nothing to say to this, Andrew bowed to the Clerk and resumed his reflections, but in a somewhat more disturbed frame of mind. For there was something deadly realistic in the wording of the charge, and the address which had followed brought home to him vividly that the men and women whose names were now being called out would presently hold his life in the hollow of their hands. They were to be his judges who would decide whether he was or was not guilty of the crime with which he was charged. On their intelligence and capacity to understand evidence, even on their individual temperaments, would depend the decision whether he should go forth a free man or should be haled away to the gallows. It was not a very comfortable thought. As each juror "came to the book", Andrew scanned his or her face anxiously for indications of stupidity, or, still worse, of obstinacy. One man or woman who "knew his or her own mind" might turn the scale against him.

Thus he was reflecting when the process of swearing in came to an end. The jury were then counted and asked by the Clerk of the Court if they were all sworn. When these formalities had been completed, an official of the Court (the Bailiff and Crier) rose and proclaimed in resonant tones and with profound gravity of manner:

"If any one can inform my Lords the King's Justices, or the King's Attorney General, ere this Inquest be taken between our Sovereign Lord the King and the Prisoner at the Bar, of any Treasons, Murders, Felonies, or Misdemeanours, done or committed by the Prisoner at the Bar, let him come forth, and he shall be heard, for the Prisoner now stands at the Bar on his deliverance. And all persons who are bound by recognizance to prosecute or give evidence against the Prisoner at the Bar, let them come forth, prosecute and give evidence, or they shall forfeit their recognizances. God save the King!"

To this proclamation Andrew listened with profound interest tempered with a slightly uncomfortable feeling of awe. For the old-world dignity and solemnity of the phrasing served but to emphasize and intensify the tone of menace than ran through it, and to bring home to "the Prisoner at the Bar" the dreadful reality of his position.

Almost as the tones of the Crier's voice died away, the witnesses filed into the Court and took their places in the seats reserved for them. And at this point he was really startled by the appearance of Molly, who had just entered and was being ushered across to her seat. For some reason, he had assumed that she would avoid being present at his trial, and he had admitted the ownership of the attaché case to the express end that she might not have to be called as a witness; and he now speculated anxiously as to what had brought her there and whether she would have to give evidence against him. Apparently she would, since she had come in with the other witnesses; and, as she walked across the floor of the Court, he followed her wistfully with his eyes. As she sat down, she took one quick glance at him and looked away. But brief as was the moment in which their eyes met, the expression in hers was unmistakable. There was no gleam of pity or compunction. Her pale face was grave and stern and hard as a mask of stone.

He was pondering on her state of mind and how it would be affected by the evidence which he was presently to give when his thoughts were interrupted by the voice of the Clerk of the Court; who had risen, and, turning towards the jury, proceeded to "give the Prisoner in charge" to them.

"Members of the jury, the Prisoner at the Bar is charged with the murder of Andrew Barton on the 28th August, 1928. To this indictment he has pleaded 'Not Guilty' and it is your charge to inquire, having heard the evidence, whether he be guilty or not."

This was the end of the preliminaries. The Clerk sat down behind his desk and the judge, who had inspected the prisoner narrowly from time to time, now turned towards the counsels' bench, and, with a little formal bow, invited the leader for the Crown to open his case. Thereupon, Sir Oliver Blizzard rose, and, having fixed his monocle securely in position, looked steadily across at the jury and began:

"The case, my Lord and members of the jury, which you are about to try has certain unusual features to which I wish to draw your attention before entering into any details. In the majority of cases of murder, the fact of the homicide is obvious and undeniable; and the matter in issue is the connection of the accused person with that homicide. A body is found, or a person is known to have died, and the condition of the body is such that it is obvious that the death was caused by the act of some person; and the question that the jury have to decide is whether the prisoner is, or is not, the person who committed or did that act.

"But in the case which you are going to try, the conditions are exactly the converse of those which I have described. Here, there is no question as to the connection of the prisoner with the death of the deceased Andrew Barton. If Andrew Barton was murdered, there can be no reasonable doubt that he was murdered by the prisoner. The matter in issue, the question on which you have to form a decision, is whether Andrew Barton did, in fact, meet his death by the homicidal act of some person or whether that death was due to what old-fashioned people call 'the act of God', that is, to some natural accident.

"To this question, which is the crucial question in the case, the medical witness can give no decisive answer. He can tell us that Andrew Barton died a violent death; but there is nothing in the appearance of the body that enables him to decide whether the violence was due to human or to natural agencies. Either is equally possible; from which it follows that the question of murder, on the one hand, or a natural accident on the other, will have to be decided by you from a most careful consideration of all the attendant conditions. You will have to examine the strange circumstances in which Andrew Barton met his death; and you will have to consider the conduct of the prisoner at the time of that death and subsequently, and ask yourselves whether such conduct is or is not consistent with his innocence.

"I have put the position before you at the start so that you may realize that your decision is to be formed on all the facts taken together; and I shall now proceed to put you in possession of those facts, first as relating to the deceased Andrew Barton and then as relating to the prisoner. I think it better to take them separately in the first place, as we shall thus get a clearer impression of the sequence of events.

"We begin, then, by following the movements of Andrew Barton on that fatal day at the end of August. And at the very outset, we are confronted by a mystery which we have no means of solving. For on the morning of that day, this unfortunate man set forth from his home on a definite mission and with a specific purpose which he never attempted to accomplish. The object of his journey, as he informed his wife, was to take certain pictures to his dealer in London. But instead of taking the train to London, he took one to Crompton-on-Sea. Why he made this curious change in his plans we shall probably never know. Whether something unforeseen happened after he had left home, or whether he had, for some reason, deliberately misinformed his wife, we can only speculate. But he certainly had the paintings in the attaché case which he carried with him, and his wife will tell you that he was, in general, a most scrupulously truthful man. At any rate, he set out from home carrying an attaché case in which were not only the paintings but, as we now know, a cheque for fifty pounds drawn in favour of his cousin, Ronald Barton, and a bundle of fifty pound notes. The suggestion certainly is that he expected to meet his cousin, but, as I have said, we shall never know; and the point is, in fact, more curious than important.

"His movements on arriving at Crompton are also rather mysterious, for he appears to have made his way direct to the shop of a frame-maker named Cooper, where he made a small purchase and then offered his paintings for Cooper's inspection; which was a very singular proceeding if we remember that a Bond Street dealer was prepared to take the whole of his work and pay high prices for it. But again, this mystery has no direct bearing on the question which you have to decide. The real importance of the incident is that Mr Cooper, having had some conversation with deceased, was able later to identify him and to give a most weighty piece of evidence.

"Our next view of Andrew Barton is at the Excelsior Restaurant, where he lunched in company with the prisoner. The waiter, Albert Wood, who waited on the two men, will describe their appearance to you, and evidence will be given that he picked the prisoner out without hesitation from a row of over twenty. Both he and Mr Cooper noticed the deceased particularly on account of the rather peculiar spectacles that he wore. I may mention in passing that Andrew Barton had suffered an injury to his nose which resulted in considerable disfigurement, concerning which he was rather sensitive, and these spectacles were specially made to cover up the disfigurement by means of an extra broad bridge.

"On leaving the restaurant, the two men, the prisoner and deceased, appear to have gone for a walk in the country, along a road which leads to Hunstone Gap, a place of which you will hear more presently. It is here that Mr Cooper's evidence is of such vital importance. For this gentleman happened to have some business at the outskirts of the town; and just as he came out into the street after finishing his business, he saw the two men passing on the opposite side of the road. He recognized Andrew Barton instantly, and his attention was attracted to the other man by the curious resemblance between the two men, which was noticeable in spite of the spectacles. When they had passed and he got a back view of them, the resemblance was so remarkable that he walked some distance after them the better to observe it. These two men were not only dressed almost exactly alike, and of the same height, colour and figure, but they seemed to him to have precisely the same gait or manner of walking. This similarity in the two men is of no special interest to us, excepting in that it attracted the attention of this witness and caused him to make some further observations which are of the most vital interest. For, following them to observe their gait and gestures, he noted that they took the road which leads out into the country and to Hunstone Gap; and, at the corner of that road, he stood watching them until they disappeared round a bend. And thus, members of the jury, did Andrew Barton pass for ever out of human ken. Thereafter, no eye, save that of the prisoner, looked upon him as a living man. The next eye that looked on him saw, not a young man in the very prime of life, full of vitality and manly strength, but a battered corpse, lying in a dreadful solitude at the foot of a cliff in a remote little bay called Hunstone Gap.

"The discovery was made late in the afternoon by the master of a fishing lugger called the *Sunflower*. Sailing past the Gap, he noticed that there had been a fall of chalk from the cliff; and when he came to examine the place through his glass, he saw a pair of naked legs protruding from under the heap of fragments. Thereupon he steered his craft inshore, and, when she was near enough, he put out the boat and rowed ashore. And there, at the foot of the cliff, he saw the nude body of a man lying on the beach, partly covered with fragments of chalk and with one large block resting on the face. They removed the fragments and then the mate of the lugger, William Cox, lifted the great block off the face, when it was seen that the dead man's head was so horribly battered that it was practically flat. They carried the body to the boat and they then collected the clothing – the dead man had apparently been bathing – and they put the body and the clothes on board the lugger. But before he returned on board, the skipper, Samuel Sharpin by name, and a most intelligent man, had the good sense to examine the beach to see if the dead man had come there alone, or whether he had had any companions. There was only a small space of sand left, for the tide was rising and had already covered the greater part of the beach. But the little patch that was still left uncovered was quite smooth, and on that smooth surface were clearly visible two tracks of human feet. One track consisted of the footprints of two persons, walking side by side and advancing from the sunken road which led down to the beach towards the sea; the other track consisted of the footprints of one person only, and that person was returning across the beach towards the sunken road.

"Now, whose footprints were these? Since there were no others, it is evident that one set of them must have been the footprints of Andrew Barton; and, since he never came away from that fatal place, it is obvious that the returning footprints could not have been his. Two men walked down together into the Gap and one of them returned from the Gap alone. One of those two men was certainly Andrew Barton. Who was the other – the one who came away alone? Can there possibly be a moment's doubt? When Andrew Barton was last seen alive, he was seen walking towards Hunstone Gap in company with the prisoner. I affirm that it is certain, in so far as certainty is possible in human affairs, that the person who walked down into the Gap with Andrew Barton and who afterwards stole away alone, was the prisoner, Ronald Barton.

"We have followed Andrew Barton to the place where he met his death. There is little more to tell. The body was conveyed by these good fishermen to the place where they berthed the lugger and there they put it ashore. Then they borrowed a seaweed cart and in this they carried the corpse into the town and delivered it to the police together with the clothing. And by the police it was deposited in the mortuary.

"And now let us, in the same manner, follow the movements of the prisoner on that fatal day and thereafter. His first appearance in this tragic history is at the Excelsior Restaurant where the waiter, Albert Wood, saw him as I have described, lunching with the deceased. Then we see him again, as described by Mr Cooper, walking with deceased towards Hunstone Gap. After this, there is an interval of several hours, for it is not until late in the evening, about nine o'clock, that we hear of him again. At this time, he was seen by one Frederick Barnard, a waiter at Mason's Restaurant, to enter that establishment and take his seat at a table. Now, however, he was not alone. He was accompanied by an American who was known to Barnard by sight but not by name but who has since been identified as a beauty specialist who described himself as Professor Booley. Unfortunately, this person is not available as a witness as it has been ascertained that he left Crompton on the following morning for Liverpool, where he embarked to return to America.

"The connection of the prisoner with this man Booley is rather mysterious, but there is some suggestion that he may have received some sort of treatment from this charlatan. Barnard observed that the American was the prisoner's guest and that he seemed to take a remarkable interest in the prisoner's appearance, for he watched him almost continuously and with a curious air of satisfaction. Moreover, after the American had left – which he did quite early – Barnard saw the prisoner rise from his chair, walk up to a large mirror and examine himself in it with extraordinary interest and attention.

"However, as I have said, the connection between the prisoner and Booley remains somewhat of a mystery. Presently we shall consider whether it has any bearing on the problem which you have to solve. Of more interest to us are certain other observations made by the observant Barnard. Thus, he noticed instantly when the prisoner entered that he looked ill and distressed and showed evident signs of

174

fatigue; that he hardly spoke a word to his guest; that he improved remarkably in appearance after a substantial meal and a small bottle of wine; and that after dinner, while he was taking his coffee and a liqueur, he seemed to be wrapped in deep and anxious thought.

"The next appearance of the prisoner is most surprising and significant. For it seems that, on leaving the restaurant, he must have made his way directly to the police station. At any rate, there he was seen by no less than four persons and in the most astonishing circumstances. We have seen that the fishermen brought the body of Andrew Barton to the town in a seaweed cart and delivered it to the police. But the skipper, Samuel Sharpin, hurried on in advance to give notice of what had happened and of the approach of the cart with its tragic burden. On receiving this notice, the sergeant procured a stretcher which he and a constable, accompanied by Sharpin, carried out and placed in readiness on the pavement. And there, incredible as it may appear, they found the prisoner, ostensibly reading the notices on the wall, but apparently waiting for the arrival of the cart. For, as the cart turned into the street and the rumble of the wheels became audible, the prisoner turned and looked expectantly up the street; in fact, he walked part of the way as if to meet it, turning about when he met it and walking with it to its halting-place. And there, members of the jury, he stood, placidly watching while the body of his cousin was lifted from the cart and placed on the stretcher; noting the several garments as they were handed out, each of which he must have recognized; and making no sign and speaking no word. Indeed, when the poor remains had been carried away and the carter who stood by the horse approached to speak to him, he turned away and walked up the street.

"The account sounds incredible, but it is true. This secret watcher was seen by four persons, each of whom has since identified him without hesitation. There can be no doubt that this astonishing thing really happened. It is vouched for by the evidence of Sharpin, of Sergeant Steel, of Constable Willis and of the carter, Walter Hood.

"From the police station, the prisoner seems to have gone straight to his lodgings, which were in the same street, and where he was living under the name of Walter Green. And here also some very significant events befell. His landlady, Mrs Baxter, will tell you that at this time, Mr Walter Green was nearly a fortnight in arrear in his rent. She had made several applications for payment, but her lodger was, at the moment, not in a position to pay the very modest sum that he owed. When he came in on this evening, she reminded him of the debt. But now his attitude was entirely different. He seemed to be hard up no longer; for not only was he ready to pay what was owing, but he offered to pay in advance for the remainder of the fortnight; an offer which she discreetly accepted and was duly paid with clean, new Treasury notes.

"Now, this sudden change from penury to comparative affluence would in itself be remarkable. But much more so are the accompanying circumstances. It was on this occasion that Mrs Baxter noticed for the first time an attaché case in the prisoner's possession. She had never seen it before, and when she mentioned the fact to him and asked if it was his, he returned no answer. But the answer to her question can be given to us by Andrew Barton's banker. Those clean, new notes with which Mr Green paid his rent were selections from a bundle of fifty pound notes which had been paid to Andrew Barton by his banker at Bunsford. They were a consecutive series the numbers of which had been noted and their issue to customers recorded; and the police have since been able to trace the four pound notes paid by the prisoner to Mrs Baxter.

"From this witness we also learn that the prisoner suddenly changed his plans. He decided to leave his lodgings on the following morning and go to London; and he was very anxious to catch an early train. That he did catch that train we have other evidence; for, on the following morning, the 29th of August, he presented himself at the London office of Andrew Barton's bank in Cornhill shortly after the doors had been opened. He endorsed and presented an open cheque drawn in favour of Ronald Barton, Esq., for the sum of fifty pounds and signed Andrew Barton; and, having received that sum in Treasury notes, he left the bank.

"From thence he seems to have gone straight to Hampstead, where he engaged lodgings at a house in Vineyard Place occupied by a Mrs Martha Pendlewick; and there he was living up to the time of his arrest. But, before coming to this closing scene, we have to note one more incident which, if it is of no great importance, is of considerable interest. This was his visit to his cousin's widow. He wrote to her from Hampstead proposing to call, and on Wednesday, the 6th of September, he made his appearance at her house.

"We need not go into details of what passed at that visit. But there are two incidents which we may notice. The first is that, when Mrs Barton asked him when he had last seen her husband, he considered for a while and then mentioned a date about two years previously. Thus, in effect, he denied having met him at Crompton. The other incident occurred shortly before he left. He then suggested that he should repeat his visit at an early date, and expressed the hope that they would see more of each other than they had done in the past. To which Mrs Barton replied quite frankly that she would rather that he did not repeat his visit, at least for a considerable time. The reason that she gave for this wish on her part was that his remarkable resemblance to her dead husband made his presence painful to her. That is what she said, and what she still says, and it is quite understandable; but members of the jury may feel, as I confess I do, that there may have been something more subtle in her dislike to having this man in her presence.

"We now come to his arrest; and concerning the circumstances in which that arrest took place it would not be proper for me to say more than that he was arrested when he was engaged calmly in making a sketch on Hampstead Heath. And now, having followed his movements from the moment when he was first seen in company with Andrew Barton, to that when he was taken into custody, we are in a position to take a general view of the whole set of circumstances and consider their significance in relation to the charge which has been brought against him. The prisoner is accused of having murdered his cousin, Andrew Barton, at Hunstone Gap; and the question that you have to decide is: Do all these circumstances, taken together, lead convincingly to the conclusion that he is guilty of that crime, or do they not? If you decide that they do, it will be your duty to return a verdict to that effect. If, on the other hand, you feel any reasonable doubt as to whether he did commit that crime, it will be your duty to give him the benefit of that doubt and pronounce him Not Guilty. Let us now examine these circumstances and see what conclusion emerges from them.

"We have seen that Andrew Barton met his death by violence; but the medical witness cannot tell us with certainty whether that violence was inflicted by natural agencies or by the murderous act of some person. Either is possible, and both are equally consistent with the appearance of the body as observed by the medical examiner. Then, since the most expert examination cannot furnish a decision as to whether death was due to accident or homicide, we must consider what light is thrown on the question from other directions.

"First there is the conduct of the prisoner. Was it that of an innocent or of a guilty man? Remember that when Andrew Barton met his death, the prisoner was present. Of that there can be no doubt. If Andrew Barton's death was due to an accident the prisoner saw that accident happen. If Andrew Barton was murdered, he was murdered by the prisoner. Now I ask: What was the behaviour of the prisoner on that terrible occasion? Was it the behaviour of a man who has witnessed a dreadful accident? Or was it that of a man who has committed a crime?

"How would a man behave in these respective circumstances? Let us take the case of an accident. Supposing that the prisoner had seen that great block of chalk fall with a crash on his cousin's head. What would it have been natural for him to do? Would he not have hurried away in search of help, or at least have given notice of the dreadful thing that had happened? Why should he not? No one would have suspected him of being in any way to blame. Indeed, no suspicion did arise in this case until it was engendered by the prisoner's own conduct. We may say with confidence that if the prisoner had gone at once to the police station and given information, this charge would never have been brought against him.

"But suppose that the prisoner had murdered Andrew Barton. How would he have behaved? Doubtless, if he had been a man of sufficient nerve and sufficient judgement, he would have gone and reported an alleged accident. But that is not usually the way of those who commit crimes. The instinct of the criminal is to keep out of sight; to avoid the appearance of any connection with the crime.

"Now let us observe the prisoner's behaviour. With his cousin's battered corpse lying under the cliff, he steals away secretly and is lost to sight for several hours. He makes no communication to anyone. The tide is rising, and presently the waves will be washing round that corpse. But he takes no measures for its recovery before it shall be borne out to sea. He just steals away alone and hides himself.

"He next comes into view several hours later at Mason's Restaurant; and at once we are impressed by certain remarkable and significant facts. First, his appearance as described by the waiter, Barnard, is that of a man who has been exposed to some unusual strain. He shows signs of fatigue and exhaustion. He looks ill and seems to be suffering from mental distress, but he revives under the influence of food and wine. Then he is accompanied by a stranger who turns out to be what is called a 'beauty doctor'; and Barnard's evidence suggests in the strongest manner that there had been some professional transactions between this man Booley, and the prisoner. Booley appeared to be intensely interested in the prisoner's face. He kept his eyes riveted on it to the neglect of his own food. But it was not the beauty doctor only who was interested in the prisoner's face. When Booley had gone, the prisoner was seen to walk up to the mirror and make a minute inspection of his own countenance.

"Now what can this mean? The suggestion is, as I have said, that Booley had done something to the prisoner's face. But what could he have done? If you will look at the prisoner, you will see that he has no need of the services of a beauty doctor. What, then, could it be that Booley had done to the prisoner's face? Could it be that the tragedy that had been enacted at Hunstone Gap had left its traces on the prisoner's face? That those tell-tale marks had prevented him from giving information of the catastrophe? And that he had invoked the aid of the beauty doctor – skilled in the art of make-up – to paint out, or otherwise obliterate those incriminating marks? That, I submit, is the inference which instantly arises in the mind of any reasonable person. Andrew Barton was a young and strong man and, unless he had been taken completely by surprise, he would assuredly have left some marks of the conflict on his assailant. Admittedly, this is only an inference. But it is a reasonable inference; and the facts seem to admit of no other explanation.

"I pass over the further fact that, after Booley had left, the prisoner remained wrapped in profound thought; for he had matter enough for reflection even if no murder had been committed. Let us proceed to the amazing, the appalling incident described by Sergeant Steel and the others in connection with the arrival of the body in the seaweed cart. I have told you what happened; and no comment seems adequate or necessary. You have to think of this man standing there, a calm and unmoved spectator, while the mutilated corpse of his cousin is lifted from the cart and borne away to the mortuary; looking on with the detached interest of a chance stranger and keeping his knowledge of the dead man's identity locked in his own breast. Think of this amazing callousness and secrecy, and ask yourselves what can be the explanation of it. Is this the conduct of a man who has seen his kinsman killed by a natural accident? Or is it that of one whose guilty knowledge bids him hold his peace? Is it, in short, the conduct of an innocent man? Or is it that of a murderer who is looking on the corpse of his victim?

"When he has seen his cousin's body disposed of, he goes home to his lodgings and forthwith proceeds to take possession of the dead man's property. Andrew Barton's attaché case is already on his table. When or how it came there we do not know; but we do know that, within a few minutes of his return, even while the unburdened seaweed cart was rumbling back up the street, he had possessed himself of some of its contents. For it was with Andrew Barton's money that he paid his debt to the landlady. The cheque we may admit to have been his lawful property; but the cheque had not been cashed. The money with which Mrs Baxter's bill was paid was money that had been stolen from the dead. And again I ask: Is this calm and callous appropriation of the dead man's money the act of an innocent man?

"But the same eager greed is apparent in the actions which followed. As soon as he had paid the landlady, he came to the sudden decision to go to London early on the following morning. For the cheque had to be cashed before the tidings of Andrew Barton's death reached his bank. Otherwise it would have been returned to the payee endorsed 'Drawer deceased'. And, once out of the neighbourhood, he decided to stay out. Regardless of his cousin's corpse, lying in the mortuary, and of the poor wife, waiting for the husband whose voice she was never to hear again, he goes off to Hampstead, there to lie in hiding until things had settled down and all danger might be considered to be over.

"The sordid avidity for money that we have noted on the part of the prisoner leads us to another point. The will of Andrew Barton contains a clause bequeathing to the prisoner the sum of five hundred pounds. The widow, who is the executrix, will tell you that her husband had been in the constant habit of making loans to the prisoner; loans which, it may be remarked, were never repaid and never expected to be repaid. Now, it seems that Andrew Barton, having regard to the fact that, if he should die, these gifts would necessarily cease, decided to make a provision for his cousin. Accordingly, he effected a separate insurance on behalf of his cousin in the sum of five hundred pounds and in his will directed that this sum should be paid to the prisoner. Thus the prisoner, who was aware of the provision, knew that he stood to benefit by the death of Andrew Barton to the extent of five hundred pounds; a fact which, when we consider his avaricious seizure of his dead cousin's money, we cannot but find profoundly significant.

"And now, to sum up in a few words: Taking the prisoner's conduct as a whole, is it that of an innocent man who has nothing on his conscience, or is it that of a man who has a burden of guilt on his conscience and is harbouring in his soul a guilty secret? Did Andrew Barton die by the chance fall on him of a block of chalk? Or was that block used by murderous hands as a terrible weapon to cover the traces, and perhaps complete the work, of some other weapon? The body has no decisive message for us. We must decide from the conduct of the prisoner. And I submit that the prisoner's conduct answers the question conclusively, especially when considered in connection with the substantial sum of money which he stood to gain by his cousin's death. He had a motive – a strong motive to an avaricious man; he was present when the death occurred – he had the opportunity to commit murder; and when the death had occurred, he stole away and instantly laid hands on the dead man's property, thereafter not only hiding himself but denying to his cousin's widow that he had seen that dead man for many months. I repeat, he had a motive to commit the crime, he had the opportunity to commit it, and his subsequent conduct has been, in a striking degree, that of a man who has committed a crime.

"Accordingly, I submit that you can come to no other conclusion but that he did, in fact, commit that crime, and that it will be your duty to return a verdict of 'Guilty'."

# CHAPTER FOURTEEN

## *The Evidence for the Prosecution*

The conclusion of Sir Oliver's opening speech was succeeded by a brief pause before the calling of the witnesses, during which Andrew reflected in a dull, bewildered fashion on what he had heard. It was all surprisingly plausible, even convincing, and the speaker had contrived, in spite of a studied moderation, to convey the feeling that he, himself, was convinced of the prisoner's guilt. Of course, it was all quite unreal; but no one besides himself – and perhaps Thorndyke – knew the real facts. Sir Oliver had in no respect exaggerated or distorted the known facts, and the conclusion that he had suggested as inferable from those facts was a fair, reasonable and logical conclusion.

And now the witnesses would be called; and Andrew knew in advance what they would say. They would fully bear out the counsel's statement; and what they would say would be the truth which no cross-examination would shake. It did not look promising, but yet Dr Thorndyke (who knew all that the prosecution knew) had seemed to be quite confident. But at this point, his reflections were broken in upon by a voice, calling the name of Mary Barton. His eyes had been resting almost continuously on her, and he now saw her rise from her seat and walk resolutely towards the witness-box. He noted that she was pale and haggard and obviously distressed, but her face was set in an expression of hard, stern resolution that he found it difficult to connect with the gentle, kindly Molly whom he had known in the days of his happy and peaceful married life.

Her evidence, as elicited by the "examination in chief", followed the lines of Sir Oliver's opening. There was a brief reference to the Hudson murder and to a visit on the 28th of August of a certain Inspector Sands, who had come to make inquiries as to the personal appearance, habits and occupation of her husband and whom she had referred to her husband's banker in London and to Mr Montagu, his agent and dealer. Then there was the more tragic reference to another visit from the inspector on the following morning, to inform her of the finding of a body believed to be that of her husband, and to request her to go to Crompton to confirm the identification; and her dreadful experiences in the Crompton mortuary when she was confronted with that terrible corpse.

The examination was conducted with the utmost delicacy and consideration that was possible; and Molly rose bravely to the occasion, though now and again there came a break in the clear voice, and her steady answer petered out into something very like a sob. But the counsel passed as quickly as he could over the most distressing incidents, and, when he proceeded to the prisoner's visit to Fairfield, she recovered her self-possession completely.

"When the prisoner came to see you," said Sir Oliver, "did he mention when he had last seen your husband?"

"Yes, I asked him. At first he seemed not to remember, but afterwards he said that he had not seen him for about two years."

"With reference to the benefit which the prisoner receives under your husband's will; was anything said about that?"

"Yes. I reminded him of the special life insurance that my husband had effected on his behalf."

"You say you reminded him. That seems to imply that he knew that the arrangement had been made. Can you say, of your own knowledge, that he was aware of it?"

"Yes. When my husband took out the policy and made his will, he wrote to his cousin, Ronald, and told him exactly what he had done. I saw the letter and read it."

"In that letter, was the amount mentioned?"

"Yes. It was clearly stated that, in the event of my husband dying before Ronald, the latter would receive five hundred pounds free of legacy duty."

"In the course of your interview with the prisoner on this occasion – on the 6th of September – was anything said about future visits?"

"Yes. He said that he should come and see me again soon, and that he thought we ought to see more of each other than we had done in the past."

"And what did you reply to that?"

"I told him that I would rather that he did not come to see me again just at present, as I found that his great resemblance to my husband made his presence painful to me."

"You found it painful to be in his society?"

"Yes. His likeness to my husband got on my nerves. I felt that I could not bear to have him in the house."

"Are you sure that it was the likeness only that caused this feeling of repulsion? Was there nothing else in your mind?"

"I know of nothing else. He seemed unconsciously to be mimicking my husband, and I felt that I could not bear it."

On receiving this reply, Sir Oliver paused to take a glance at his brief. Then he reached down below the bench and produced an attaché case which he handed to an attendant who conveyed it to the witness.

"Can you tell us anything about the case which has just been handed to you?" the counsel asked.

"It belonged to my husband," was the reply. "He was carrying it when he left home on the morning of the 28th of August."

"You have no doubt that it was your husband's case?"

"None whatever. The letters stamped on the lid are his initials, A. B. He stamped them himself with bookbinder's letters. I have the tools here, and you can see that they fit the stamped initials."

She produced from a handbag three brass "handled letters", an A, a B, and a stop, which were taken by the attendant, with the attaché case, and passed round for inspection by the judge and jury.

"Can you tell us," Sir Oliver continued, "what the case contained when your husband left home?"

"I understood that it contained one or two small watercolours, but I did not see them. Of the other contents I know nothing."

The case and the tools made their round, being eventually deposited as "exhibits". Meanwhile, Sir Oliver took another glance at his brief, and finding, apparently, that he had exhausted his matter, sat down; whereupon Dr Thorndyke rose to cross-examine.

"You have told us," he began, "that on the 29th of August, you went to Crompton mortuary for the purpose of inspecting and, if possible, identifying a body which was lying there and which was believed to be the body of your husband, Andrew Barton. I deeply regret the necessity of recalling to your memory what must have been a very terrible experience, but it is essential that we should be quite clear as to the facts. Were you able to identify that body?"

"No," Molly replied, with a visible shudder. "It was quite unrecognizable. But the clothes were my husband's clothes."

"Yes," said Thorndyke. "You identified the clothes as your husband's; but, apart from the clothes, were you able to form any opinion as to whether the body was or was not that of your husband?"

"No," Molly replied. "I was not. I said so."

"So far as you know, was any evidence as to the identity of the body, apart from the clothing, given at the inquest?"

"No. The identity of the body was established by means of the clothing."

"You referred just now to a severe injury to the nose from which your husband had suffered. Did the medical witness at the inquest mention having found any traces of that injury?"

"No. I don't think he knew about it when he made his examination. At any rate, he said nothing about it."

"Did you ever learn what was the exact nature of that injury?"

"Yes. The surgeon at the hospital gave me a certificate for the insurance office. It described the injury as a depressed and comminuted fracture of the nasal bones."

"You have spoken of your alarm when your husband did not come home on the night of the 28th of August. May we take it that he was not in the habit of staying away from home without notice?"

"He never stayed away from home without notice," Molly replied, emphatically. "He hardly ever stayed away at all."

"Did he ever stay away from home, and away from you; for a considerable period; say for more than a month?"

"Never. We used, occasionally, to go away together, but he never went away by himself for longer than a weekend."

"Now, Mrs Barton," Thorndyke said in a persuasive tone, "I want you to try to give me a statement of your husband's whereabouts on a particular date. Can you remember where he was on Good Friday in the year 1925?"

Molly looked at him in evident surprise, but replied, after a few moments' thought:

"I believe he was at home; at any rate, I have no recollection of our having been away at that time."

Thorndyke was manifestly dissatisfied with the reply and pressed for a more precise answer.

"Take a little time to think," he urged, "and see if you cannot recall the circumstances. It is only three years ago, and Good Friday is a very distinctive date. You will surely be able to remember where you spent your Easter."

Again she reflected with knitted brows. Suddenly she exclaimed:

"Oh, yes, I remember. He was at home."

"Something has recalled it to your memory?" he suggested.

"Yes. In that year I undertook to decorate the parish church, and my husband helped me. In fact, he did most of the decoration."

Thorndyke paused to make a note of the answer and then proceeded:

"With reference to the prisoner's visit to you on the 6th of September; you have said that his resemblance to your husband was so close as to cause you great distress. In what respect did he appear to resemble your husband?"

"In every respect," Molly replied, "excepting, of course, that his nose was different. Otherwise, he seemed exactly like my husband; even in the face, in spite of the difference in the shape of the nose. And his figure was the same and he had the same tricks of movement with his hands and the same rather unusual way of picking up his tea-cup without using the handle."

"And what about the voice?"

"That was the worst of all. It was exactly like my husband's. If I had shut my eyes, I could have thought that it was my husband speaking."

"To what extent had you been acquainted with Ronald Barton? Had you previously seen much of him?"

"No. I had met him only twice, when he came to see us. The second occasion was a little over two years ago."

"When you were in his society on that occasion, were you greatly impressed by his resemblance to your husband?"

"Not so much. I could see, of course, they were very much alike, but the resemblance did not strike me as so very extraordinary when I saw them together and could compare them."

"When the prisoner came to see you in September, did his great resemblance to your husband come upon you in any way as a surprise?"

"Yes, very much so. I had no idea that the two men were so much alike. It was quite a shock to me."

"Did it appear to you that he was in any respects different from the Ronald Barton whom you remembered? Did he seem to have changed in any way?"

"Yes, he did seem to have changed in some respects. He was quieter in manner; less boisterous. In fact, he was not boisterous at all, as he used to be. But I put that down to the sad circumstances in which his visit was made. It was only a few days after the funeral."

"Did you notice any other differences from what you remembered of him previously?"

"There was one thing that surprised me. He seemed to know so much more about pictures and painting than I had supposed he did; and he was so much more interested in them. On the previous occasions, he had not seemed to be interested at all in my husband's work or in painting in general."

"Then, taking your impressions as a whole, would it be correct to say that the Ronald Barton who came to see you in September did not seem to be quite the same kind of person as the Ronald Barton whom you remembered having met formerly?"

"Yes, I think that would be correct."

"And would it further be correct to say that such changes as seemed to have occurred, increased his resemblance to your husband?"

"Yes, I think that is so."

On receiving this answer, Thorndyke sat down; and Andrew took a deep breath. He was beginning to understand his counsel's tactics. But he was the only person present who did. Throughout the cross-examination, the judge had listened attentively with an obviously puzzled expression, and Sir Oliver and his junior, Mr Horace Black, had looked frankly bewildered. Even Molly, though she answered readily and with conscientious care, was evidently surprised at the apparent irrelevancy of the questions. There was no re-examination, the two prosecuting counsel being clearly of the opinion that no point had been made and that there was nothing to contest. Accordingly, Molly was released from the witness-box and went back to her seat.

The next witness was Mr Cooper, the carver and gilder, whose evidence repeated in detail the account which had been given by Sir Oliver in his opening address. Having regard to the importance and damaging character of that evidence, it was obviously a matter of surprise to the judge and the prosecuting counsel that Thorndyke allowed the witness to leave the box without any attempt at cross-examination. He was followed by Albert Wood, the waiter at the Excelsior Restaurant, whose evidence was also ignored by Thorndyke. Then the name of Samuel Sharpin was called, and a copper-faced elderly man in a stiff suit of blue cloth, rolled into the witness-box and fixed a seafaring blue eye on Sir Oliver's monocle. In much the same terms as he had used at the inquest, he described the circumstances in which he had observed the body through his glass, had put inshore and salved it and had conveyed it in the seaweed cart to the police station at Crompton. When the narrative was completed, Sir Oliver, having taken out his monocle, wiped it with his handkerchief and refixed it securely, addressed the witness in quiet but impressive tones, pointing his hand towards the dock.

"Look attentively at the prisoner and tell me if you have ever seen him before."

The witness turned slowly and with seeming reluctance and cast a commiserating glance at the prisoner.

"Yes," he said. "I've seen him before."

"Where did you see him?" Sir Oliver demanded, with something of a dramatic flourish.

"I see him," replied Sharpin, "in the prison yard yonder, along of a lot of other fellows in a row. I was told to see if I could pick him out."

"And could you?" asked Sir Oliver, making the best of the slight anticlimax.

"Easily," replied Sharpin. "He was the only decent-looking man there."

"And where and when had you seen him before that?"

"I see him the night we brought the dead man in from Hunstone Gap. He was a-standing on the pavement outside the police station, a-watching of us as we unloaded the dead man out of the cart and set him on the stretcher."

"Are you certain that the prisoner is the man you saw watching you as you took the body out of the cart?"

"Yes," Sharpin replied doggedly. "He's the man."

"Do you swear that he is the man whom you saw there on that night?"

"I ain't much given to swearing," said Sharpin. "Don't hold with it. I've said he is the man, and he is the man."

"Did that man speak to anybody when you were moving the body?"

"Never spoke a word to nobody," was the slightly ambiguous reply.

"Did he seem agitated or upset in any way?"

"He didn't seem to be, but I didn't notice him very much. I was attending to what I was doing."

Having noted this reply, Sir Oliver relinquished his prey and Thorndyke rose.

"When you came ashore and saw the block of chalk resting on the dead man's head, did you look up to see where the block had come from?"

"Yes, I did, in case there might be some more coming down. You could see where the block had broken out. Left a sort of square hole."

"And did you notice whether that hole was straight over the body, or whether it was to one or other side?"

"It was straight overhead; and I kept an eye on the place while we was a-moving of the body."

"You said that your mate, William Cox, lifted the block off the dead man's head. Should you describe Cox as a strong man?"

"Ay. Will Cox is an uncommon beefy lad."

"Should you say that he is an unusually strong man?"

"Yes, strong as a young elephant he is. I gives him all the heavy jobs to do, and he don't never turn a hair and he don't never grumble."

"You seem to be fortunate in your mate," Thorndyke remarked with a smile.

"I am that," agreed Sharpin. "Worth his weight in gold is Will Cox; and he turns the scale at fourteen stun."

This completed Samuel Sharpin's evidence and on his retirement he was succeeded by his much-appreciated mate; a good-looking young giant with a mahogany complexion, bright blue eyes and a mop of curly hair. His skipper's commendations, which he had necessarily overheard, seemed to have covered him with confusion, for he swung shyly into the witness-box and, having taken up a negligent pose, greeted the judge with an embarrassed grin and then fixed an expectant eye on Sir Oliver; being, apparently, like his skipper, fascinated by the learned counsel's "dead-light".

But whatever might have been his worth to his commander, he was of little to the prosecution; and when they observed the way in which Thorndyke pounced on him, they may have regretted the necessity for calling him. His evidence merely confirmed and amplified that of the previous witness; and after a brief and matter-of-fact examination, Sir Oliver resigned him to the defence.

"You have said," Thorndyke began, "that you lifted the block of chalk off the dead man's head. Did you find it easy to lift?"

"No, I did not," replied Cox, with a shake of his curly head. "'Twas most uncommon awkward to lift. Heavy, too, it was."

"You are accustomed, I suppose, to lifting heavy weights? Fish-trunks, for instance?"

"Ay, but, d'ye see, fish-trunks is fitted with rope beckets for to catch hold of. They are easy enough for to hoist. 'Tis only a matter of weight. But this here block of chalk wasn't no sort of shape. There wasn't nothing for to lay hold of or to hook your fingers under."

"What are the usual weights of fish-trunks?"

"They runs five, seven, eight or ten stone."

"And a stone, in your trade, is how many pounds?"

"Fourteen pounds goes to a stone of fish."

"What should you say was the weight of that block of chalk?"

"Somewhere between eight and nine stone, as near as I can judge."

"And how near can you judge a weight of this kind; say a fish-trunk?"

"I can judge the weight of a trunk of fish within two or three pounds."

"You say that you found that block difficult to lift. How high did you lift it from the ground?"

"Only an inch or two. I just hoisted it clear and dropped it alongside."

"Could you have lifted it higher, so far as you could judge? Say two or three feet above the ground?"

"I might have been able to, but I shouldn't have liked to try. Not more than a foot, anyway. He was mighty slippery and difficult to hold, and you don't want eight or nine stone of chalk on your toe."

"Do you find any difficulty in lifting a ten-stone trunk?"

192

"Lord, no sir! Wouldn't be much good in our trade if I did. But, as I was telling you, a trunk has got beckets – rope handles, you know – and if you've got hold of them, the trunk can't slip."

"So you can lift ten stone – a hundred and forty pounds – without difficulty?"

"Yes, and a tidy bit more if need be and if I'd got a proper hand-grip."

Having received and noted this answer, Thorndyke sat down and Sir Oliver rose to re-examine.

"Does it require a specially strong man to lift an ordinary fish-trunk?"

"Not if he's used to it. Them as ain't don't make much of it."

"Take the case of an eight-stone trunk. Do you say that a young man of the prisoner's height and build would have any difficulty in lifting it?"

"No, I suppose he could lift it if he put his back into it. But he'd find it a tidy weight if he wasn't used to hoisting."

Apparently, Sir Oliver judged it wise to let well alone for, having got this qualified assent to his question, he sat down. Then William Cox descended from the witness-box and the name of Frederick Barnard was called.

Frederick Barnard, having been sworn, deposed that he was the senior waiter at Mason's Restaurant, Crompton-on-Sea. He had identified the prisoner among a number of other men at the prison. He recognized him as a man who had come to the restaurant at about half past eight in the evening of the 28th of August. He had noticed him particularly because he looked pale and ill and had a drawn expression as if he were in pain or in some serious trouble. He also looked very tired. Seemed "dead beat". His manner was peculiar. He had a companion with him but hardly spoke a word to him. He improved very much when he had taken some food and wine, but he ate very slowly and carefully, as a man might who had a tender tooth, and he used his napkin as if he was afraid of hurting his mouth.

His companion was an American gentleman whom witness knew well by sight as he had frequently come to the restaurant, sometimes alone and sometimes with a friend. Witness did not, at that time, know the American gentleman's name, but he had since ascertained from the friend who used to come with him that he was a Professor Booley, who described himself as a beauty specialist.

"Do you know what Professor Booley did for a living?"

"I only know what his friend told me; that his work consisted principally in making up ladies' faces; touching up their complexions and eyebrows and covering up any blemishes."

"Did you notice anything peculiar in Booley's behaviour?"

"Yes, his manner was very peculiar. He ate very little, but very fast, and he hardly talked at all. But he sat looking at the prisoner's face as if he couldn't take his eyes off it. It was most singular. Sometimes he would lean back or move his head sideways to get a different view; and sometimes he would look in the big mirror on the wall and then back at the prisoner's face as if he was comparing the reflection in the glass with the original. And he seemed to be extraordinarily pleased with both of them and quite excited about them."

"And did the prisoner show any special interest in his face?"

"Yes. I saw him looking at himself in the glass from time to time and, after Mr Booley had gone – which he did before the prisoner had finished his dinner – he got up from the table and walked up to the mirror and stood there looking at himself for quite a long time."

"And what did he do after that?"

"He sat for close on half an hour over his coffee and a green Chartreuse. He looked quite natural by this time, but he seemed to have something on his mind; at least, he looked as if he was thinking very hard about something."

"Did you see anything about the prisoner's face that might have accounted for the interest that he and Professor Booley seemed to take in it?"

"I didn't then. I just thought that he was a good-looking young man who was rather pleased with himself. I didn't know who Professor Booley was, then. But since I've known what his trade was, I've been disposed to suspect that – "

"Ah!" Sir Oliver interrupted, "but you mustn't tell us what you suspect, though I daresay you may be right. We are dealing with the facts that are known to you. We must not go beyond what you saw or heard."

"Well," said Barnard, slightly crestfallen and even huffy, "I've told you all I saw and heard. I can't remember anything more."

Thereupon Sir Oliver sat down and proceeded thoughtfully to polish his eyeglass. The judge cast an inquiring glance towards Thorndyke, but as the latter made no sign, the witness was released and the name of Thomas Steel was called.

The new witness was a sergeant in the Crompton police force and he gave his evidence with professional readiness and precision. But it did not amount to very much. He had picked the prisoner out of a row of twenty men, and he identified him as the man who had stood outside the police station watching the removal of the body from the seaweed cart. That man had made no sign of recognizing the body and had not spoken to anyone. Did not appear in any way agitated or greatly concerned. Had seemed to be just an ordinary spectator. Witness was quite sure prisoner was the man. Was used to recognizing persons, and prisoner was a rather striking person who would be easy to remember and recognize.

From this incident Sir Oliver turned his attention to Professor Booley, referring to the evidence of Frederick Barnard.

"Do you know anything about this man Booley?"

"I knew him by name and by sight," the sergeant replied, "and I knew his premises in Barleymow Street. He described himself as a beauty specialist and he had a big card in his window setting forth what he could do. I took a photograph of it to keep in case any question of fraud or false pretences should be raised."

"Have you got a copy of that photograph?"

"Yes. I have here an enlarged copy from the small negative."

He produced from an attaché case a whole-plate photograph which was passed across to Sir Oliver, who took out his eyeglass to read it, and then, with an indulgent smile, returned it to the usher who passed it up to the judge. From his Lordship it was conveyed to the jury, who studied it with broad and appreciative grins, and back to the

Counsels' bench, finding its way eventually to the Clerk's table, where it remained.

"Have you any knowledge," Sir Oliver asked, "as to the success of the Professor's methods? Have you, for instance, met anyone who had had a crooked nose straightened out by him?"

The sergeant admitted, amidst a murmur of merriment, that he had not. "But," he added, "I know that he was very clever at painting out black eyes."

"Did you ever see a specimen of his skill?"

"Yes. Our court missionary got a black eye where he was trying to separate two drunken sailors. It was such a bad one that he didn't like to show his face out of doors. But one of our constables took him round to Booley's to have it painted out with grease-paint, and when he came back you couldn't see a trace of the discolouration. It looked perfectly natural."

"So far as you know, did Booley get much work of this kind?"

"I have no personal knowledge beyond this one case. The constable told me that Booley did an extensive trade in painting out black eyes and bruises and pimples and blotches, but I can't verify his statement from my own knowledge."

This concluded the examination in chief. When Sir Oliver sat down, Thorndyke rose to cross-examine.

"You have said that when you came out of the police station with the stretcher, you found the prisoner waiting there and making a show of reading a bill that was affixed to the notice board. Do you recall anything remarkable about that bill?"

"Yes. By a most extraordinary coincidence, that bill contained a description of the man whose body was in the seaweed cart."

"What was the heading of that bill?"

"It was headed, 'Wanted for Murder.' "

"And who was it that was wanted for murder?"

"The dead man; Andrew Barton."

"For the murder of whom was he wanted?"

"For the murder of Mr Hudson at Ribble's Cross."

"Can you remember the exact terms of the description?"

"I cannot remember the exact wording, but I could give you the substance of it."

"I will read you a portion of the bill and you shall tell me whether what I have read is correct. This is the passage:

"'It is believed that more than one man was concerned in the crime, but the only one who was seen was the man who actually fired the shot. He is described as a somewhat fair man with grey eyes, about thirty years of age and easily recognizable by reason of a remarkably deformed nose, which appears to have been broken and is completely flat excepting at the tip, which is rather prominent.'

"Is that a correct quotation from the bill?"

"To the best of my recollection and belief it is quite correct."

"You say that the description in the bill was that of the dead man, Andrew Barton. When did you first learn that the man described in the bill was Andrew Barton?"

"On the following morning, the 29th. A telephone message came through from Bunsford directing us to take down the bill and call in any copies that we had circulated. I took the telephone call."

"Was any reason given for the withdrawal of the bill?"

"Not officially. But I had a few words with the officer at the other end and was informed by him that inquiries had been made and that it appeared that there had been some mistake. It turned out that the man described in the bill was not concerned in the murder at all. I then reported the finding of the body of Andrew Barton of Fairfield, and the officer at Bunsford then informed me that Andrew Barton of Fairfield was the man described in the bill."

"So far as you know, was any public announcement made by the police that the accusation of Andrew Barton was a mistake due to an error in identification?"

"No such announcement ever came to my knowledge; and, as no name had been mentioned, and the man was dead, it would seem to have been unnecessary."

"That," remarked the judge, "seems to be a rather easy-going view to take. There had been a public accusation of a particular person and there ought to have been a public withdrawal of it."

The sergeant agreed that some such announcement ought to have been made, but pointed out that he had merely said that he was not aware of its having been made. It was possible that there had been a public withdrawal which had escaped his notice; and this observation brought his evidence to an end.

The next witness was Mrs Susan Baxter of 16, Barleymow Street, Crompton, who identified the prisoner as her late lodger, Mr Walter Green. She deposed that, on the night of the 28th of August, Mr Green, who had previously been quite impecunious and unable to pay his rent, seemed suddenly to have become flush of money and anxious to discharge his debt. He paid her with four pound notes which were quite clean and new but she had not noticed their numbers and could not identify them. On that occasion she had seen an attaché case on the table in prisoner's room. She had never seen it before and was certain that it had not been in the room until that night. Had asked prisoner if it was his but he had not answered. The case produced and handed to her was like the one she had seen, but she would not swear that it was the same one. Prisoner announced that night that he was going to London the next day and he seemed very anxious to catch an early train. He went away next morning at a little past eight o'clock and she had not seen him since until she picked him out of a row of men at the prison.

When the examination in chief was finished, Thorndyke rose. But he raised only a single point.

"When you were talking to the prisoner on that last night, did you notice anything in his manner that was unusual or different from what you had been accustomed to?"

"Well, yes, I did," Mrs Baxter replied. "He was quieter in his way of speaking, and much more polite and considerate. I noticed it particularly, because he had usually been rather loud-spoken and gave his orders like a lord. And he was a decidedly selfish and inconsiderate lodger."

"Did you notice a great difference in his manner on this occasion?"

"I did. He spoke like a perfect gentleman; most respectful and polite. And he was quite anxious not to put me out by going away so early. I was quite took aback. He seemed like a different gentleman."

Having elicited this answer, Thorndyke sat down; and once more the judge cast a speculative and rather puzzled glance in his direction. Evidently his Lordship was endeavouring to trace through these seeming irrelevancies some intelligible line of defence. To him, as to the prosecuting counsel, these questions of Thorndyke's must have seemed to have no bearing whatever on the issue which was being tried. But experience would have told him that Dr John Thorndyke was not a gentleman who asked irrelevant questions; and a suspicion may have begun to filter into his judicial mind that the defence was going to take the form of a counter-attack – and a flank attack at that. Andrew alone, listening with growing interest and a queer sense of detachment, could recognize the logical structure which his champion was building up, brick by brick.

The evidence of Mrs Baxter was followed by that of the cashier at the London Bank, and, when this had been disposed of, Sir Oliver proceeded to bring up his big gun. And a very big gun it was; and, to tell the truth, the gunner seemed just a shade nervous about "letting it off". For – to drop metaphor – the new witness was no less a person than Sir Artemus Pope, M.D., F.R.S., the eminent pathologist; and the evidence of Sir Artemus Pope was the foundation on which the whole superstructure of the prosecution rested. And the counsel's opening address had made it clear that Sir Artemus was neither an enthusiastic nor a pliable witness. It was certain in advance that he would not budge a hair's-breadth from bald, literal, demonstrable fact.

Sir Oliver approached him cautiously with the introductory questions.

"You have made an examination of the body of the deceased, Andrew Barton, whose death is the subject of the present proceedings. Is that so?"

"Yes," replied Sir Artemus. "On the 6th of November, acting on instructions from the Home Office, I conducted an exhumation at

Fairfield Churchyard of the body of Andrew Barton and made a careful examination of the said body."

"What was the object of the examination?"

"To check the findings of the medical witness at the inquest and to determine, if possible, the cause of death, particularly in connection with the present proceedings."

"Were you given full particulars of the circumstances in which the death occurred?"

"Yes, including the depositions taken at the inquest."

"What were the conditions that your examination revealed?"

"I found extensive multiple fractures of the skull and the bones of the face. Practically all the bones were broken and the head appeared to have been crushed flat. The injuries were of such a kind as would have been produced by an extremely heavy blow from some hard and ponderous object, delivered when the head was lying on the ground, face upwards."

"What conclusions did you reach as to the cause of death?"

"If the man were alive at the moment when the blow took effect, it would certainly have killed him instantly. As there was nothing to suggest that he was not alive at that moment, I concluded that the blow was the cause of death."

"Would the very gross injuries which you have described be sufficient to cover up and obliterate the traces of any lesser injuries which might have been previously inflicted?"

"That would depend on the nature of the previous injuries. If they had been inflicted with a sharp instrument, such as an axe, the incised wounds would be recognizable even after the subsequent smashing. But if they had been inflicted with a blunt implement, all traces of them would probably have been obliterated by the blow which flattened the skull."

"Is it possible that such previous injuries may actually have been inflicted and their traces destroyed by the major injuries?"

"It is possible," Sir Artemus replied, with distinct emphasis on the final word.

"From your examination did you form any opinion as to whether the injuries were due to accident or homicide?"

"The examination informed me only of the nature of the injuries. I have no personal knowledge of the circumstances in which they were inflicted. The information supplied to me set forth that they were produced by a block of chalk, weighing about a hundredweight, which had fallen from the cliff. If it had fallen on to the head of deceased when he was lying face upwards, it would have produced injuries such as those which I found. And in that case, death would be due to accident."

"Precisely," said Sir Oliver. "That is one possibility. Now let us consider another. Suppose that the block had already fallen and was lying on the beach. Suppose that deceased had been killed or rendered insensible by a blow on the head with a heavy stone or some other blunt instrument. Suppose, then, that his assailant picked up the block of chalk and dropped it on his head as he lay. In that case, would the appearances be such as you found?"

"No," replied Sir Artemus. "A man could not lift such a block more than two or three feet, and a fall from that height would not smash the skull into fragments as I found it to be smashed."

"Not with one single blow. But suppose the blow to have been repeated several times?"

"In that case, it is possible that the skull might ultimately have been completely crushed."

"And would it then have presented the appearance which you observed when you examined it?"

"Probably it would, so far as I can judge. But that is merely an opinion. I cannot say definitely that it would."

"Is it possible that the injuries which you found could have been produced by homicidal violence?"

"It is physically possible that they might have been."

"You agree that the appearances which you observed were consistent with the theory that the death of the deceased was due to homicidal violence?"

Sir Artemus did not appear to like the form of the question, but eventually gave a grudging assent; on which Sir Oliver, having got the utmost agreement that he was likely to get, promptly sat down, and Thorndyke rose to cross-examine.

"You have said that the injuries which you found were such as would have been produced if the block of chalk had fallen on the head of deceased when he was lying face upwards. Did you find anything that was in the least degree inconsistent with the belief that death was caused in that way?"

"I did not," Sir Artemus replied, promptly.

"It has been suggested that death or insensibility may have been caused by a blow, or blows, with a blunt instrument. Did you find any traces or any appearances of any kind which led you to believe that such blow, or blows, might have been inflicted?"

"I did not."

"Did you observe anything which suggested to you that the injuries had been produced by human agency rather than by the accidental fall of the block?"

"I did not."

"Did you observe anything, or ascertain any fact, which offered a positive suggestion that death might have been due to homicide?"

"I did not."

"Would it be correct to say that the conditions which you found were entirely consistent with death by accident?"

"It would."

"And that your examination disclosed no positive evidence or any suggestion of any kind that death was due to homicide?"

"Yes. That would be quite correct."

Thorndyke, having squeezed the witness dry (and he had not seemed unwilling to be squeezed), noted the replies and then proceeded:

"Were you supplied with a description of the person of deceased?"

"I was given a copy of the depositions taken at the inquest. They contained a description of the person of deceased."

"Had you any instructions to verify the identity of deceased?"

"No. My instructions were to ascertain the cause of death and consider the possible alternatives of accident or homicide. The question of identity was not raised. The body which I examined was described to me as the body of Andrew Barton, and such I assumed it to be."

"But you had a description of the person of Andrew Barton. Now, when you made your examination, did you find that the body which you were examining corresponded completely with that description?"

The question seemed to put Sir Artemus on the alert, and he gave himself a few seconds to consider it. But he was not the only person who roused at the question. The judge seemed to have found a possible clue to the mystery that had been puzzling him, for he leaned forward with eager interest to catch the reply. The prisoner in the dock, too, perceived a ray of light from an unexpected quarter, and, glancing at Molly, he saw that she had fixed a startled eye on the questioner.

"What do you say, Sir Artemus?" Thorndyke inquired, placidly.

"The deceased," Sir Artemus replied cautiously, "was personally unknown to me, so I was dependent on the description. There did appear to me to be a slight discrepancy between that description and the body which I was examining. The description set forth that deceased had suffered from a severe injury to the nose resulting in complete flattening of the bridge. The conditions which I found were not exactly what I should have expected from that description."

"You have heard the evidence which was given by Mrs Barton that the surgeon's certificate described the injury as a depressed and comminuted fracture of the nasal bones?"

"Yes, I heard that evidence. It agrees with the description that was given to me."

"Did you make a careful examination of the nasal bones of deceased?"

"I did. They were both fractured, but not very extensively. They had been driven bodily into the nasal cavity."

"In a case of comminuted fracture with a depression which remained permanently, what conditions would you expect to find?"

"As the fragments must have united in a false position, I should expect to find the bones distorted in shape and associated with a good deal of callus or new bone."

"What did you actually find?"

"The bones were fractured, as I have said. But when the fragments were put together, they did not appear to be in any way abnormal. I was not able to recognize any callus or traces of repair."

"What conclusions did your observations suggest?"

"I concluded that the original injury could not have been as great as had been supposed; that there must have been some exaggeration, due to error."

"Does that conclusion seem to you to be supported by the evidence which you have heard today?"

"I am hardly prepared to pronounce an opinion on that question. My examination was not concerned with the issue of identity, which you seem to be raising, and I did not give it sufficient attention to enable me to make a perfectly definite statement."

"Are you prepared to admit that, if the description given to you of the person of Andrew Barton was a true and faithfully correct description, the body which you examined could not have been the body of Andrew Barton?"

"That seems rather sweeping," the witness objected. "I don't think I can commit myself to that. But I will admit that, if the description was correct, there were disagreements between that description and the visible facts which I am unable to account for."

As this amounted, in effect, to an affirmative answer to the question, Thorndyke pushed the cross-examination no farther. As he resumed his seat, Sir Oliver rose to re-examine; and as he could evidently make nothing of Thorndyke's later questions, he set himself to mitigate the effects of the earlier ones.

"You have said, Sir Artemus, that you found no positive indications of homicide. Did you find any positive indications that excluded homicide?"

"I did not," was the reply.

"Can you say whether Andrew Barton met his death by accident or by homicide?"

"I cannot. I have said that either is physically possible. I have no means of comparing the probabilities."

Sir Oliver noted the reply. Then, turning towards the judge, he informed the court that "that was his case". Thereupon Thorndyke rose and announced: "I call witnesses," and a few seconds later the name of Ronald Barton was called, and the prisoner was conducted from the dock to the witness-box.

# CHAPTER FIFTEEN

## *The Witnesses for the Defence*

As Andrew made his short journey across the court from the ignominy of the dock to the comparative respectability of the witness-box, he was aware of a curious and unexpected sense of confidence. For now, at last, he was about to make his long-dreaded revelation; to tell, before judge and jury and the crowded court, his preposterous story with all its outrageous improbabilities. And yet, to his surprise, he did not shrink from the ordeal. What had once seemed almost an impossibility had now come within the compass of the possible.

But his surprise was unwarranted, as he himself partially realized. For there is all the difference in the world between making an astounding revelation to an audience that is utterly unprepared for it and making the same revelation to hearers who are already waiting for the solution of a puzzle. And that was his position now. By his skilfully conducted cross-examination, Thorndyke had thoroughly prepared the way for Andrew's statement; ignoring the apparently important issues and building up a fabric of evidence which would immediately drop into its place as soon as Andrew began to tell his story. And when he stood up and faced his witness, it was not the judge alone who leaned forward all agog to hear what the defence really was.

"You are indicted," he began, "in the name of Ronald Barton for the murder of Andrew Barton. Is your name Ronald Barton?"

"No," replied Andrew, "it is not."

"What is your real name?"

"My name is Andrew Barton."

As the answer was given, a startled cry mingled with the universal murmur of astonishment. Glancing quickly at Molly, Andrew could see that she had swung round on her seat and was gazing at him with an expression of the wildest amazement. The judge, after a quick glance towards the interrupter, fixed a look of critical scrutiny on the witness.

"Is this a coincidence in names?" he asked, "or do you mean that you are the Andrew Barton whom you are accused of having murdered?"

"I am that Andrew Barton, my lord," was the reply.

"The same Andrew Barton whose description has been read out to us from the police bill?"

"The same, my lord."

The judge continued to look at him for two or three seconds. Then, with a slight shrug, he bowed to Thorndyke with a manner that seemed to invite him to "get on with it". Meanwhile the jury, suddenly reminded of the police bill, looked first at the prisoner and then at one another, some with frank incredulity and others with undisguised grins. Unperturbed by those grins, Thorndyke proceeded:

"The evidence relating to the alleged crime of which you are accused covers a certain period of time and a certain succession of events. What is the starting-point of that series of events?"

"They began with a letter which I received from my cousin Ronald. It was dated the 21st of August and reached me on the 23rd. Its principal purpose was to ask for a loan of fifty pounds, but it also announced his intention to pay me a visit on the 28th." Andrew then went on, urged by Thorndyke, to give the minutest details, even to the cutting of the privet hedge, of the circumstances connected with the letter and his difficulties in staving off Ronald's visit.

"What was your objection to this visit?"

"From what I knew and suspected of my cousin's mode of life, I did not consider him a suitable person to associate with my wife; and I had also found his manner towards her distinctly objectionable."

"Why did you not tell your wife about this letter?"

"I was afraid that she would misunderstand my motives in objecting to Ronald's visit; that she might feel that I had not complete confidence in her discretion in dealing with him."

"Had you any such fear as to her discretion?"

"Not the least. I had perfect confidence in her. But I thought she did not quite realize what kind of man Ronald was, and might not be completely on her guard if he should try to establish relations of a kind that I considered undesirable."

When the arrangements for the pretended visit to London had been described, Thorndyke proceeded to the incident of the murder of Mr Hudson and led Andrew through it in the closest detail.

"When you went home after the attack, were you at all alarmed or uneasy as to your connection with the affair?"

"Not at all. I did not know that any murder had been committed and, of course, I was only a spectator. I told my wife exactly what had occurred and we discussed what I had better do. I was inclined to go over to Bunsford and give information at once. But my wife thought that, as I could not tell the police anything that they did not know already, I had better wait until some inquiries were made. But I intended to call on the police on the following day and tell them what I knew; and I should have done so had not the train come in sooner than I had expected."

There followed a description of the visit to Crompton in the same minute detail, including the inspection of Professor Booley's window and the remarkable announcements on his advertisement card; of which Andrew was able to remember nearly the whole, and the recital of which was received with murmurs of amusement.

"When you read the list of Professor Booley's accomplishments, did it occur to you to give him a trial and see if you could not dispense with the spectacles which you have described to us?"

"No. I did not take his claims seriously. I thought he was merely an advertising quack."

The account of the day's doings, almost from minute to minute, was continued until the incident of the sea bathing at Hunstone Gap was reached. Then Thorndyke pressed for even more exhaustive details.

"You say that your cousin ran up before you to the place where your clothes were lying and that he took possession of the heap that belonged to you. Is it not remarkable that he should have mistaken your clothes for his own?"

"I don't think so. The outer clothes were almost exactly alike in the two suits. But I don't think that it was really a mistake on his part. I think it was a practical joke. It was just the kind of joke that I should have expected from him."

"What makes you think that it was a joke?"

"I have since remembered that, before sitting down, he turned the clothes over, putting the coat on top. And then he proceeded to wipe himself on my coat."

"Can you account for the circumstance that you did not notice that you were sitting down on the wrong clothes?"

"As I have said, the two suits were almost exactly alike. They were both ordinary grey flannels. But apart from that, I was in a very disturbed state of mind. I was trying to think how I could decently put him off the visit to Fairfield, which he still seemed to be bent on."

The account now approached the tragic incident of the falling block of chalk. The silence in the court was profound; and still Thorndyke insisted on tracing events from moment to moment.

"Did you actually see the block fall?"

"No. I was much agitated by the unpleasant turn the conversation had taken and was avoiding looking at my cousin. I was watching a fishing lugger which was beating up the bay. When the chalk came rattling down, I jumped up and ran away from the cliff. When I stopped and looked round, Ronald was lying in the same place, covered with small lumps of chalk and with the large block resting on his head."

"Was he already dead?"

"He must have been; but his legs were moving slightly with a sort of twitching movement. They continued to move for nearly half a minute."

"Can you explain how it happened that you did not notice that you were putting on the wrong clothes?"

"There was not much to notice. The clothes were almost identical with my own, and they fitted me. But I was so shaken and horrified by what had just happened that I hardly knew what I was doing. As I was dressing, I still had my eyes on the corpse. The only thing that I noticed was the hat, and I did not stop to ask myself how it happened that Ronald was lying on mine."

Andrew then described how he had hurried away from the Gap intending to seek assistance or give information, and how he had missed the road and wandered about in the country, reaching Crompton only after night had fallen, and how he had made his way straight to the police station and had encountered the police notice.

"Did you stop to read the bill?"

"No. I was feeling very confused and shaken and I stopped to think over what I had to tell, and how I should explain my presence in Crompton, and also whether I ought to say anything about the affair of the motor bandits. Then, as I was standing opposite the bill, my eye caught the words, 'Ribble's Cross', and I glanced quickly through the notice to see what had happened. Then I saw the heading, 'Wanted for Murder', and reading down further, I read the description of myself and the statement that I had been seen to fire the shot."

"You read the notice which directly accused you of having committed the murder. Were you particularly alarmed?"

"I was terrified. For the notice not only accused me but stated, on the evidence of an eye-witness, that I had been seen to fire the shot that had killed the man."

"Did you think that you were likely to be convicted of this murder?"

"I thought that I was certain to be. This lady was prepared to swear that she had seen me fire the shot, and I had no answer but a bare denial. I thought that if I was caught I was bound to be condemned."

"And did you think it likely that you would be caught?"

"I considered it a certainty that I should be, as the disfigurement of my nose, which was described on the bill, made me so very easy to recognize. Anyone who had read the bill who should see me would know instantly who I was. And my spectacles, which were the only means of any sort of disguise, were in the pocket of the clothes that had been under the body of my cousin."

The account went on to relate how Andrew had sneaked up the dark street, keeping in the deepest shadow and avoiding the street lamps, and how he had stumbled on the premises of Professor Booley and had then had the sudden idea that the Professor might be able to produce some sort of disguise.

"Had you anything definite in your mind when you decided to apply to Professor Booley?"

"No. I realized that the disfigurement of my nose was the great source of danger as I could not cover it up and anyone would notice it at the first glance. I thought it possible that Professor Booley might be able to do something – even a temporary disguise – which would give me a chance to escape."

"So you decided to see if he could do anything for you. Now tell us exactly what happened."

Andrew proceeded with the description of his interview with the Professor, brought up repeatedly by Thorndyke for the filling in of some apparently trivial detail. He spoke confidently and clearly; and, as he told that strange story, the entire court, judge, jury and spectators alike, listened in breathless silence. He described the Professor's reluctance, changing suddenly into enthusiasm and even eagerness; the consulting room with its chair and instruments and the cake of wax that had been shown to him and the various preparations for the operation, the operation itself, his agonies in the operating-chair, and the climax, when the Professor bade him look in the mirror.

"And when you looked in the mirror, what did you see?"

"I saw the face of my cousin Ronald."

"You mean that your face now resembled the face of your cousin?"

"That, I suppose, is the fact. It must have been. But the resemblance was so complete that it seemed like some magical illusion. What I saw was not my own face but Ronald's. I could hardly believe my eyes."

"Do you now think that the transformation was so very wonderful?"

"No. Since I have had time to think it over, I have realized that it was quite natural. Ronald and I were extraordinarily alike in every respect but our noses. Ronald had a Roman nose and my nose was straight; and after my accident, the difference was much more striking. But Professor Booley, in filling up the notch in my nose, happened to model the patch which he put in so that the repaired bridge was almost exactly the shape of Ronald's. The result was that the only appreciable difference between us was done away with. If Ronald had been alive, he and I would have looked like a pair of twins."

"Professor Booley's magic has had some rather embarrassing effects. What did you do when you recovered from the operation?"

Andrew described the visit to the restaurant and his examination of himself in the mirror, and explained how the complete transformation in his appearance made it impossible for him to go home; how the necessity for recovering his attaché case compelled him to go to Ronald's lodgings, and how, while waiting for an opportunity to enter unobserved, he had halted at the police station to read the bill and had thus been present when the cart arrived bearing his cousin's body. With occasional assistance from Thorndyke in explaining and elucidating the incidents and emphasizing their significance, he continued the narrative, including his life at Hampstead, his visit to Molly, his meeting with Mrs Kempster and so on up to the moment of his arrest and his committal for trial on the charge of fraud and personation.

When the examination in chief had thus brought the story up to his consignment to prison, Thorndyke sat down and Sir Oliver rose to cross-examine; and Andrew realized that the period of plain sailing was over. He had to brace himself up for some difficult questions. The learned counsel discreetly refrained from challenging statements of fact and attacked the evidence from the psychological side.

"Your explanation of the mystery that was made about the visit to Crompton is difficult to follow. What prevented you from giving your wife a straightforward statement of what you intended to do?"

"Nothing but my own stupidity," replied Andrew. "There was not the least necessity for any deception."

"You have described your state of extreme panic on reading the police notice. But what occasion was there for panic? You would surely know that a charge of this kind could not be entertained in the case of a man of good position and known respectability?"

"I did not know it. I supposed that the sworn evidence of a respectable eye-witness would be conclusive. This lady said that she saw me kill Mr Hudson. There seemed no answer to that!"

"Can you explain why, in all this time, you made no attempt to communicate with your wife?"

"Seeing that I was wanted for murder, I did not dare to disclose my identity. I felt sure that, if I told this story to her, she would reject it as an attempt at imposture and communicate with the police; and I could not risk any dealings with them."

"Again, you actually state that you had an interview with your wife and that she did not recognize you, though she noticed your resemblance to her husband. It seems perfectly incredible that she should have failed to recognize her own husband. But allowing that she did, what prevented you from simply telling her who you were?"

"In the first place, she evidently recognized me as Ronald, and she appeared to be distinctly distrustful of Ronald. Then she believed that she had seen the dead body of her husband, and she had attended his funeral only a few days before. Moreover, I found that she was convinced that the person who was with him at Hunstone had murdered him. But I should have had to begin by telling her that I was one of the two persons who were at Hunstone. I thought, and still think, that she would have gone straight out and informed the police."

"There is then the case of the woman, Elizabeth Kempster. You admit that she, having seen and talked with you, was firmly convinced that you were her husband, Anthony Kempster. You admit that there can be no doubt that Anthony Kempster and Ronald Barton are one and the same person. You admit that this woman still believes that you are her husband, Ronald Barton. See, then, what it is that you are asking us to believe. On the one hand, you assert that you had a long

213

interview with your own wife and that she never even suspected that you were her husband. On the other hand, you had an interview of some length with Elizabeth Kempster and she was then convinced, and still remains convinced, that you are her husband. And both these women are convinced that you are Ronald Barton. Do you still maintain and ask the jury to believe that you are not Ronald Barton, which both of these women are convinced that you are, and that you are Andrew Barton, which Andrew Barton's wife is convinced that you are not?"

"I have declared on oath, and I repeat, that I am Andrew Barton."

The learned counsel raised his eyebrows (whereby it became necessary for him to catch his eyeglass as it dropped from his eye; which he did with an expertness born of long practice), and, after a pause to give effect to that gesture of incredulity, continued his cross-examination, skilfully picking out all the improbabilities and apparent contradictions. It was cleverly done and it served, at least, to save the face of the prosecution. But it was all very inconclusive since it left all the evidence on the main questions of fact untouched. Those questions Sir Oliver was too wise to attack. His long experience in the courts would have taught him that technical evidence from Dr John Thorndyke was best left alone. Moreover, he probably suspected that Thorndyke had not played his last card.

And so it turned out when the long cross-examination was ended. For the next witness whose name was called was Dr Christopher Jervis; and it soon appeared that Dr Jervis belonged to the heavy division of the defence's artillery. Having elicited his name and qualifications, Thorndyke began:

"Can you tell us anything about the block of chalk which was found on the body of the dead man who has been described as Andrew Barton?"

"Yes. On the 13th of November I went to Hunstone Gap with the witness, William Cox. He showed me the place where the body was found and the position of the head, which was marked by some splashes of blood which had soaked into the chalk at the foot of the cliff. He also showed me the block of chalk, which was still lying where he had dropped it. Looking up the cliff, I could see the spot from which the block had broken away. It was quite clearly distinguishable as a squarish cavity. I measured, with a sextant, the height of this cavity above the beach and found it to be sixty-three feet. I tested, with a plumb-line, the position of this cavity in relation to the blood-mark at the foot of the cliff and found that they were both exactly in the same vertical line. The head of deceased must, therefore, have been exactly on the spot on to which the block would have fallen. I tested the weight of the block by lifting it. With great difficulty, I was able to lift it a few inches from the ground, but was able to hold it for only a very few seconds owing to the absence of anything for the fingers to grasp."

"Could you have lifted it two or three feet?"

"No, certainly not."

"Are you a fairly strong man?"

"Yes. I am rather above the average of strength for a man of my size. I am just under six feet two inches in height."

"You have heard the suggestions of the prosecution as to the method employed in committing this alleged murder. Do you consider, judging by your experience of the block, that the method suggested is physically practicable?"

"No. I am certain that it would be impossible for even a strong man to lift that block two or three feet from the ground several times in succession."

"Were you present when Sir Artemus Pope made his examination of the body which is alleged to be that of Andrew Barton?"

"Yes; and I was authorized to make any independent examination that I considered necessary."

"What observations did you make?"

"I paid particular attention to the condition of the nasal bones. The description of Andrew Barton made it clear that he had suffered from a severe depressed fracture of the nasal bones, caused by a blow from a cricket-ball. I searched carefully for traces of that fracture and the callus thrown up in the processes of repair. I could find no such traces. The bones were fractured in several places, but these were new

215

fractures. There was not a sign that the bones had ever been fractured before. I carefully separated out the broken pieces and fitted them together on a wax support. I had no authority to bring them away to produce in evidence but I made a plaster cast of the joined fragments on the wax. I produce the cast for inspection; and I have also brought a normal skull for comparison. The cast shows clearly the new fractures in the bones, but it also shows clearly that there are no traces whatever of any old fractures or of any callus or signs of repair. The bones in the cast are perfectly normal, as can be seen by comparing them with the uninjured bones of the skull."

"What do you infer from this?"

"I infer that it is quite impossible that the body which I examined could have been the body of Andrew Barton."

"Are you quite certain that it was not the body of Andrew Barton?"

"I am quite certain that it was not. It is a physical impossibility that his nasal bones could have been perfectly normal in appearance as the bones are seen to be in the cast."

On receiving this answer, Thorndyke paused for a few moments to complete his notes and then proceeded:

"Have you made any examination of the prisoner?"

"Yes. I have examined his nose with the naked eye, with ordinary electric light and with X-rays and also by the sense of touch. To the naked eye it appears to be a completely normal nose of the Roman type with a rather high bridge. To the sense of touch it is hard and smooth in the upper part with some irregular masses at the base. I was unable to feel the lower edges of the nasal bones or the median cartilage. On examination with electric light or sunlight, it is seen that the bridge of the nose is not composed of bone but of some translucent substance which I believe to be paraffin wax."

"What are your reasons for believing it to be paraffin wax?"

"It has all the properties of paraffin wax and no other substance is known to me which could be introduced into that situation and formed into that shape."

"What methods did you use in respect of the X-rays?"

"I took an X-ray photograph of the prisoner and another of myself for comparison as our noses are somewhat alike in shape. I produce those photographs. Each is signed by me and countersigned by John Thorndyke and I swear that they are the photographs of the persons whose names are written on them. On the one of myself it can be seen that the nasal bones are clearly visible occupying the bridge of the nose and corresponding to its outline. In the photograph of the prisoner the outline of the bridge is faintly seen but there are no nasal bones there. At the base is an irregular mass of bone which corresponds to no normal structure. It looks like an old depressed fracture of which the fragments are cemented together with callus, or new bone."

"What conclusions do you draw from these photographs?"

"The photograph of the prisoner shows a condition which exactly agrees with the description of Andrew Barton, plus the shadowy indication of the mass of wax forming the bridge. Disregarding the wax, which is really a foreign body and no part of the prisoner's person, the photograph is that of a man who is identical in appearance with Andrew Barton, according to the various descriptions of him which have been given in evidence, including the surgeon's certificate referred to by Mrs Barton."

This completed the examination in chief. As Thorndyke sat down, Mr Horace Black, Sir Oliver's junior, rose to cross-examine. But he had a thankless task, for Jervis' evidence dealt almost entirely with observed facts which could not be disputed or even questioned; and when the learned counsel mildly hinted at errors of observation or mistaken inferences, Jervis blandly offered him the cast or the photographs, which the counsel smilingly waved away as matters outside the province of a mere lawyer.

The next witness came as a surprise to most of the persons present, including Andrew; for the name that was called was that of Elizabeth Kempster. As the lady stepped into the box and looked nervously at Thorndyke, a certain redness around the eyes and a handkerchief held in the hand suggested that the occasion was, for her, not a happy one.

When the preliminaries had been disposed of, Thorndyke opened his examination with the request:

"Will you kindly look at the prisoner, Mrs Kempster, and tell us whether you recognize him?"

The witness cast a deprecating glance at Andrew and replied:

"Yes, I recognize him."

"Can you tell us who he is?"

"I don't think I can," she replied. "He looks like my husband, Anthony Kempster, but from what I have just heard, he can't be."

"But, disregarding the evidence that you have heard, who do you say he is?"

"Well, he looks exactly like my husband."

"Have you previously identified him on oath as your husband?"

"Yes. I swore to him as my husband at the police station and in the police court. But," she added with a catch in her voice and an application of her handkerchief to her eyes, "I didn't know that I was letting him in for this."

"When you identified him at the police court, had you at any time any doubt that he was really your husband?"

"Yes. I did think, just for a moment or two, that I might have made a mistake. But then they found in his pocket-book a tradesman's bill addressed to A Kempster, Esq., and that convinced me that I was not mistaken."

"What was it that caused you that momentary doubt?"

"It was the way he spoke and behaved. He was quite polite to me, and he didn't reproach me for having given information against him. That was not at all like my husband. He was accustomed to talk loud and bluster when he was put out."

"And what about the voice? Was it exactly like your husband's?"

"No, it was rather like, but not exactly. I noticed then that it seemed a little different from what I remembered, and I noticed it again when he was giving evidence."

"I need not ask you whether your husband was in the habit of absenting himself from home, but I should be glad if you could give us some information as to a particular date. Do you know where your husband was on Good Friday in the year 1925?"

"Yes, I remember very well. He was in Wormwood Scrubbs Prison. He came out on Easter Sunday."

Here the judge interposed, though without any great emphasis.

"It is hardly necessary for me to remind learned counsel that it is not admissible to refer to previous convictions or delinquencies of the prisoner until the jury have given their verdict."

"That is so, my lord," Thorndyke agreed. "But the submission is that the prisoner is not the person named in the indictment and that the previous convictions of that person do not, therefore, affect him. And I may say that the point which I am trying to elicit is highly material to the defence."

"If you say that the point is material to the defence," the judge rejoined, "I must allow the questions to be put." Whereupon Thorndyke resumed his examination.

"Do you know how long your husband had been in prison?"

"Yes. Six months. I had notice when he was going to be discharged and I went and met him at the prison gate."

"Have you any doubt that the man whom you met at the prison gate was your husband?"

"No, none whatever. I recognized him and he recognized me, and I took him home and gave him a good dinner. Besides I had been present in the police court when he got his sentence."

"At the police court and in the prison, was he known by the name of Anthony Kempster?"

"No. When he was arrested, he gave the name of Septimus Neville, and he stuck to it. They never knew his real name."

"You speak of his real name. Do you know what his real name was, or is?"

"I am not sure. He married me under the name of Anthony Kempster, but I sometimes suspected that that was not his real name. He was very much in the habit of changing his name."

"Did you ever meet with the name of Barton in connection with him?"

"Yes. I think he had a cousin of that name. He was very secret about his letters, as a rule; but I happened to see one that he had left in the pocket of a coat that I had to mend for him, and I saw that it was signed: 'Your affectionate cousin, Andrew Barton.' But, of course, I didn't know that his name was the same as his cousin's."

This concluded Thorndyke's examination; and, as the prosecution had no inkling of the bearing of this witness's evidence on the issue, the cross-examination was tentative and brief. When it was finished and Mrs Kempster left the box, with a commiserating glance at the prisoner and a final wipe of her eyes, the court, and Andrew, had another surprise; for the witness who followed her was no less a person than Andrew's old friend, Mr Samuel Montagu.

The new witness, having given his name, deposed that he was a dealer in works of art and that his premises were in New Bond Street. He was a good judge of pictures – he had to be – and his own personal preference was for watercolour paintings, especially interiors and subject pictures of high finish and fine execution. When he had got so far, Thorndyke produced from under his bench a framed and glazed watercolour painting which was conveyed to the witness-box, and handed to the witness; who examined it with profound attention and evident interest.

"Have you ever seen that picture before, Mr Montagu?" Thorndyke asked.

"I have not," was the reply.

"There is, as you see, no signature to the picture. Can you give any opinion as to who the painter was?"

"I can. This picture was painted by Andrew Barton."

"You speak quite positively, as if you were certain."

"I am certain. I was for many years Andrew Barton's agent and dealer. Nearly all of his work passed through my hands, and I have always had a great admiration for it. I have two of his paintings in my permanent gallery and three of them in my private house."

"You feel that you can say quite definitely that this picture was painted by Andrew Barton?"

"Yes. Quite definitely. I have not the shadow of doubt."

At this point, Thorndyke sat down and Mr Horace Black rose to cross-examine. At his request, the picture was passed across to him and he examined it critically for a while before beginning. At length, he opened fire on the witness.

"You have stated, as if it were a fact known to you, that this picture was painted by Andrew Barton. Are you not offering us a mere conjecture as a statement of fact?"

"It is not a conjecture," replied Montagu. "It is an expert opinion, and a very expert opinion considering my great experience of Andrew Barton's work. And I feel perfectly certain that it is a correct opinion.'

"You are extremely confident. But, looking at this picture, it seems to me that there is nothing very highly distinctive about it. It seems to me to be a picture of the kind that is sometimes called photographic, such as could be produced by any skilful draughtsman."

"The people," said Montagu, "who call highly finished paintings photographic are people who don't know much about either painting or photography. There is no analogy between a work of imagination and a photograph."

"Still, I submit that a simple, realistic style like this could be easily imitated by any competent painter."

"That is not so," said Montagu. "A first-class professional copyist might be able to make a copy of this picture which would deceive any person but an expert. But imitation is quite a different matter from copying. To begin with, every artist has his own manner of thinking and working. Now the imitator would have to drop his own manner – which he couldn't do – and adopt, not only the technique but the mental and emotional character of the man he was imitating. And then, if he was trying to imitate a first-class artist like Andrew Barton, he would have to be a first-class artist, himself. But if he were, he wouldn't want to imitate anybody; and what's more, he couldn't do it, because he would have an unmistakable style of his own."

"And do you say that this simple, literal representation of an old woman making lace shows an unmistakable style which nobody could possibly imitate?"

"I do. I say that any genuine expert could pick out Andrew Barton's work at a glance. Of course, he was not like some of the present-day painters who play monkey tricks to give the art critics something to write about. It was genuine, honest painting done as well as he could do it; and nobody could do it better."

"We are straying away from the issue," said the counsel. "I am not contesting the quality of the work. My point is that you have sworn that this picture was painted by Andrew Barton, a fact which cannot possibly be within your knowledge since you admit that you never saw the picture before. Do you still swear that it was painted by Andrew Barton?"

"I said I felt certain, and I do feel certain; and I am ready to buy it for fifty pounds with the certainty of being able to sell it at a profit."

Here the counsel smilingly abandoned the contest and sat down. The picture was handed up to the judge, who inspected it with deep interest, and Mr Montagu retired triumphantly from the box.

The next name called was less of a surprise to Andrew, who had been following closely the drift of the evidence; and the name of Martha Pendlewick associated itself naturally with the picture. The old lady stepped up into the box with a bland smile on her face and, having curtsied to the judge – who graciously acknowledged the salutation – turned and saluted the prisoner in the same deferential manner.

"I want you, Mrs Pendlewick," said Thorndyke, "to look at the prisoner and tell us whether you recognize him."

"Lord bless you, yes, sir," said Mrs Pendlewick. "The poor young gentleman was lodging with me at the very time that the police arrested him. And a nicer and more considerate lodger no one could wish for."

As the old lady was speaking, the judge repeatedly glanced from her to the picture, which he was still holding, and back, apparently comparing the real with the painted figure; and meanwhile he listened attentively to the evidence. Then, at Thorndyke's request, the picture was handed down and presented to the witness, who nodded at it with a smile of friendly recognition.

"Have you ever seen that picture before?" Thorndyke asked.

"To be sure I have," she replied with a surprised air. "Why 'tis a likeness of myself a-making bone lace in my own kitchen."

"Do you know who painted that picture?"

"Certainly I do. 'Twas the young gentleman, himself, Mr Barton."

"Can you tell us when he painted it?"

"He took several days over it. I can't give you the exact date, but he finished it only a few days before the police made that unfortunate mistake."

"Can you say positively that you saw him paint the whole of it from beginning to end?"

"Yes. I saw him begin it on the white paper and draw it with a lead pencil. And then he put on the colours. It took him the best part of a week and he finished it, as I said, a few days before he was took away to prison."

Mrs Pendlewick's evidence was listened to with intense interest by the Court and spectators alike. But its effect on Mr Montagu was most remarkable. From his place among the "witnesses in waiting" he craned forward with bulging eyes to stare, first at Mrs Pendlewick and then at the prisoner. Evidently, he was in a state of complete mental bewilderment. He had sworn that the picture could have been painted by no one but Andrew Barton. But clearly it had been painted since Andrew Barton's death; and it had been painted by the Roman-nosed gentleman in the dock. He could make nothing of it.

His bewilderment did not escape the notice of Thorndyke who, even while he was questioning the witnesses, kept a sharp eye, not only on the jury but also on the spectators. For long experience had taught him that, in practice, the final test of evidence is its effect on the non-expert listener. Now, Mr Montagu was in a dilemma. The evidence of his eyesight told him that the picture had been painted by Andrew Barton. But it also told him that the man in the dock was not the Andrew Barton whom he had known. Yet there seemed no escape from Mrs Pendlewick's evidence that the picture had been painted by the man in the dock. It was a puzzle to which he could find no solution.

Thorndyke then noted Mr Montagu's state of mind and congratulated himself on having taken the precaution to put Montagu in the box before Mrs Pendlewick; for, evidently, if he had gone into the box after her, his evidence would have been worth nothing. He would never have sworn to the authorship of the picture. The observation, therefore, of Montagu's apparent immunity to the evidence of the change of personality came as a very useful reminder that that evidence had still to be driven home to the jury, and further, that it must be driven home to them through the evidence of their own eyesight. Fortunately, the next witness gave him the opportunity.

That witness was a quiet, resolute-looking gentleman who gave the name of Martin Burwood and stated that he was an Inspector in the Criminal Investigation Department of the Metropolitan Police. His duties were connected with the keeping of Criminal Records at Scotland Yard and especially with the Fingerprint Department.

"When the prisoner was arrested," said Thorndyke "were his fingerprints taken?"

"They were," replied the inspector.

"Were those fingerprints already known to you?"

"They were not. On receiving them from the prison I examined them and I then searched the files to see whether we had any duplicates. I found that there were no duplicates in the files."

"What does that prove?"

"It proves that the prisoner has never previously been convicted of any offence."

"Have you in your records any relating to a man named Septimus Neville? And, if so, of what do those records consist?"

"We have the records of Septimus Neville in the files. They consist of descriptive and other particulars, a complete set of fingerprints and two photographs, one in profile and one full face."

"Have you compared the fingerprints of Septimus Neville with those of the prisoner?"

"I have. They are not the same fingerprints."

"Are you quite sure that they are not the same?"

224

"I am perfectly sure. There is not even any resemblance."

"Is it possible that Septimus Neville and the prisoner can be one and the same person?"

"It is quite impossible."

"Have you compared the record photographs of Septimus Neville with those of the prisoner?"

"I have."

"Do you find anything remarkable about them?"

"I do. The photographs show that the two men are extraordinarily alike. They are so much alike that it is hardly possible to distinguish one from the other. I produce the photographs of both men."

He did so, and they were passed up to the judge, who inspected them with amused surprise. They were then handed round to the jury who, in their turn, viewed them with undisguised astonishment.

"You have shown us," said Thorndyke, when he had examined them and passed them on to the other counsel, "four photographs, two of each of these men. They appear exactly alike, but you say that they are the photographs of two different men. Do you swear that they cannot be four photographs of the same man?"

"I do. The fingerprints, which were taken at the same time as the photographs, prove conclusively that they must be two different men."

Thereupon Thorndyke sat down; and Mr Black, with more valour than discretion, rose to cross-examine. But it was quite futile; for the evidence was unshakeable and the officer was a seasoned and experienced witness. The usual questions were asked as to the possible fallibility of fingerprints, and received the usual answers. As a wind-up, the counsel asked:

"Do you swear that it is impossible for two men to have the same, or similar, fingerprints?"

"I swear that it is quite impossible," was the withering reply.

"And I suppose," the judge interposed dryly, "that we may assume it to be impossible for one man to have two different sets of fingerprints?"

225

The witness grinned and agreed that it was impossible; and the learned counsel, hiding his blushes under an appreciative smile, hurriedly sat down.

Then Thorndyke rose and, having announced that all the witnesses for the defence had now been heard, prepared to address the jury.

# CHAPTER SIXTEEN

## *Thorndyke's Address to the Jury*

---

"In view," Thorndyke began, "of the mass of evidence that has been produced and of its remarkable and convincing character, it seemed almost unnecessary that I should address you. But this is a trial on a capital charge and the prisoner's life is forfeit if it should be held to have been proved against him. I cannot, therefore, take any risks of a miscarriage. I shall, however, occupy as little time as possible. You are sworn to give a true verdict according to the evidence; and I shall confine myself to an examination of that evidence and to pointing out what has actually been proved.

"The prisoner is indicted in the name of Ronald Barton for the murder of Andrew Barton. The words of the indictment, therefore, contain four affirmative propositions:

1. That a murder has been committed.
2. That the person who was murdered was Andrew Barton.
3. That he was murdered by Ronald Barton.
4. That the prisoner is Ronald Barton.

"Now, in order that a verdict of guilty should be returned against the prisoner, it is necessary that each and all of those propositions should be proved to be true. If any one of them should be proved to be untrue, the case against the prisoner would fall to the ground. I am not referring to any legal questions which might arise in respect of defects

227

in the indictment; on which subject his Lordship will give you the necessary direction. I shall deal with the plain and simple issue, whether the prisoner is or is not guilty of the crime with which he is charged. To enable you to decide on that question, I shall ask you to examine critically those four propositions.

"First, has it been proved that a murder was, in fact, committed? So far as direct evidence is concerned, I can dismiss that question quite summarily; for no direct evidence was produced. You heard Sir Artemus Pope declare definitely that, not only did he find no positive evidence that deceased met his death by homicide, but that he found nothing that tended to suggest or raise any suspicion of homicide. There is, therefore, no direct evidence that any murder was, in fact, committed; and I submit that on that alone, the prisoner is entitled to a verdict of Not Guilty.

"We now come to the indirect evidence; which consists in certain considerations of motive and conduct. The motives that are suggested for the alleged murder are, first, that Ronald Barton stood to gain five hundred pounds by the death of Andrew Barton and, second, that Andrew Barton had in his possession certain valuable property which Ronald coveted and subsequently stole, and which was found in the prisoner's possession when he was arrested. It is further suggested that the conduct of the prisoner was such as to lead to the belief that he had murdered the man whose body was found at Hunstone Gap.

"And now we see the importance of the other three propositions. For if the person whose body was found was not Andrew Barton, then no insurance was payable, and the suggested motive ceases to exist. Again, if the prisoner is not Ronald Barton, he is entitled to no benefit under Andrew's will; and again the motive disappears. Further, if the prisoner is proved to be Andrew Barton, the property found in his possession is his own lawful property, and the other motive disappears.

"Thus, you will see that the issue that you are trying is really the issue of personal identity. The questions which you have to decide are: first, who was the person whose body was found at the foot of the cliff at Hunstone Gap? And, second, who is the prisoner? I will take these questions in their order.

"First, who was the dead man? Now, we have the evidence of Mr Cooper that two men were seen walking towards Hunstone Gap, and we may accept it as certain that the body which was found there was the body of one of these two men. For with that body was found the clothing of a man who corresponds exactly in appearance to one of them and who is known to have been in Crompton on that day and to have worn similar clothing.

"Of those two men, one had a broken nose and wore spectacles to conceal the disfigurement. The other had a normal and well-shaped Roman nose. The clothing was that of the man with the broken nose. But was the body also his? That is what you have to decide. Now I wish to impress on you the fact, which seems to have been somewhat overlooked, that that body was never identified. Mrs Barton saw it and was unable to say whether it was or was not the body of her husband, and there was no one else who was competent to give an opinion. The clothes which were found with it were the clothes of Andrew Barton. Of that there can be no doubt. And from that fact the reasonable inference was drawn that the body was that of Andrew Barton. But I repeat that the body itself was not identified.

"Later, that body was re-examined by Sir Artemus Pope and by Dr Jervis. Sir Artemus was naturally unwilling to pronounce on the identity of the body since his examination was not concerned with that question. But he admitted that the conditions which he found seemed to be irreconcilable with the personal description of Andrew Barton. On the other hand, Dr Jervis, who examined the body with the express purpose of ascertaining its identity, gave a clear, definite and emphatic statement that the body was that of a man with a normal and uninjured nose; and furthermore, he produced a plaster cast of the dead man's nasal bones, which was shown to you and from which, by comparison with the normal skull which was also shown to you, it was quite evident that the nasal bones of the deceased had never been broken until the chalk block fell on them. On these facts, Dr Jervis declared positively that the body could not possibly be the body of Andrew Barton. The evidence before you, therefore, of your own eyesight, confirmed by the testimony of an expert witness, is that the body found at Hunstone Gap could not possibly have been the body of Andrew Barton.

"But, so far, we have decided only who he was not. We have now to consider the question, who he was. And here you will see that I am not depending on the prisoner's evidence to decide questions of fact. That evidence is, of course, entitled to the same credit as that of the other witnesses; but I think you will agree with me that it will be more satisfactory if I can show you that the facts can be proved by independent evidence, reserving that of the prisoner to co-ordinate and explain facts that are otherwise difficult to understand.

"Now who was this dead man? We have agreed that he was one of the two men who were seen walking towards Hunstone Gap. All the known facts support this belief. Two men had been bathing in the Gap, for we find the nude body of one and the clothes of the other. The clothes were Andrew Barton's but the body was not his body. Then, since there were no other clothes, it is clear that Andrew must have gone off in the other man's clothes. That he could hardly have done so by deliberate choice but presumably by mistake, suggests that those clothes were, in size and appearance similar to his own. But the two men who were seen together were extremely similar in size and figure and were dressed in almost exactly similar clothes. Thus everything goes to prove that the body was that of one of these two men.

"Now of these two men, one is known, and has been proved to have been Andrew Barton. Who was the other? From the evidence of the only two witnesses who saw the two men, Mr Cooper and the waiter, Albert Smith, we know that the other man – Andrew Barton's companion – was extraordinarily like the prisoner; so like that both these witnesses instantly identified the prisoner and swore that he was the man whom they had seen. But the prisoner is indistinguishably like Ronald Barton. So like that Mrs Barton, when he visited her at her house, had no doubt that he was Ronald Barton, and still had no doubt when she was giving evidence in this court.

"The unavoidable conclusion is that the man who was seen with Andrew Barton must have been Ronald Barton. And this conclusion is strongly supported by the fact that Ronald and Andrew were cousins. It was a natural and probable circumstance that Andrew's companion should be his cousin Ronald.

"But if the body that was found was that of Andrew's companion, then it was the body of Ronald Barton; in which case it is unnecessary to point out that the prisoner cannot be Ronald Barton, but must be some other person.

"And now let us approach this question from another direction. The prisoner was arrested, in the first place, in the name of Anthony Kempster on an information sworn by Elizabeth Kempster, who identified him as her husband, Anthony Kempster, and swore to his identity as such. It is, therefore, obvious that the prisoner is either Anthony Kempster or someone who is indistinguishably like him. But who is Anthony Kempster? He is someone who is the indistinguishable double of the prisoner. But the prisoner is indistinguishably like Ronald Barton. Then it follows that Kempster must also be indistinguishably like Ronald Barton. As such indistinguishable likenesses are excessively rare, there is an obvious probability that these three men, Kempster, Ronald and the prisoner, are one and the same person; namely, Ronald Barton. And the fact that Kempster had a cousin named Andrew Barton confirms this probability so far that we may conclude confidently that Kempster was, or is, Ronald Barton.

"The question that we now have to decide is whether or not the prisoner is Anthony Kempster. For if we agree that Kempster is Ronald and the prisoner is Kempster, then the prisoner must be Ronald Barton. But we have evidence that Anthony Kempster served a term of imprisonment under the name of Septimus Neville. There is no doubt that Septimus Neville and Anthony Kempster are one and the same person, for we have the evidence of Kempster's wife to that effect. But we have the evidence of the officer from the Fingerprint Department that Neville and the prisoner cannot possibly be the same person. The prison photographs show these two men extraordinarily alike; so much so that it would have been hardly possible to distinguish one from the other. But their fingerprints are totally different. It is therefore certain that the prisoner cannot possibly be Septimus Neville. But since Neville and Kempster are one and the same person, the prisoner cannot be Anthony Kempster; and since Kempster is Ronald Barton, the prisoner cannot be Ronald Barton.

"So far, we have answered the question, Who is the prisoner? from the negative side. We have shown who he cannot be. He cannot be the person in whose name he stands indicted. Now let us approach the question from the positive side. Who can the prisoner be? Who is it possible for him to be?

"He is not Ronald Barton; but he is someone so like Ronald that those who knew Ronald well, including his wife, have mistaken him for Ronald. The prisoner and Ronald have that curious resemblance that is usually associated with what are called 'identical twins'. Now there is only one person who is known to us who has this strange resemblance to Ronald – his cousin, Andrew. The only possible inference seems, therefore, to be that the prisoner is Andrew Barton. For, if he is not, then he must be some third person who is indistinguishably like the other two. But this is against all reasonable probabilities. It is a sufficiently strange coincidence that we should have this pair of identical twins. It would be outrageous to turn them into identical triplets by postulating the existence of a hypothetical third person who is indistinguishably like them both.

"But we have still more convincing evidence that the prisoner must be Andrew Barton. We know that Andrew suffered from a depressed fracture of the nasal bones. Now, to the eye, the prisoner appears to have a well-shaped Roman nose. But the X-ray photograph shows that he has suffered, and still suffers, from a depressed fracture of the nasal bones; that the symmetrical appearance of the nose is due to a filling of a translucent substance, which must be paraffin wax since there is no other known substance which it can be, which fills up the deep notch caused by the injury and has restored the bridge of the nose. In short, the X-ray photograph shows us a condition of the nasal bones which is known to have existed in

Andrew Barton; which was peculiar to him, and by which he could be distinguished from all other human beings. Even alone, it would be enough to identify him as Andrew Barton.

"Thus you see that, without referring to the prisoner's evidence, the case against him has been completely disproved. With that evidence I do not propose to deal. It would be useless for me to occupy your time by flogging a dead horse. You heard his evidence and it will be fresh in your memories. All that it is necessary for me to do is to point out to you that, strange as was the story that he told you, it was an entirely consistent story and that you have every reason to believe that it was a true story. It did not conflict in any way with any other evidence that you have heard. On the contrary, its truth has been confirmed in the most striking manner by the evidence of all the other witnesses; not only of the witnesses for the defence, but also of those for the prosecution, and even by the able opening address of my learned friend, the counsel for the Crown. I shall, therefore, conclude by reminding you briefly of the facts which have been proved.

"The charge against the prisoner is that he, Ronald Barton, murdered his cousin, Andrew Barton. What has been proved is:

"First, that there is not the slightest reason to believe that any murder was committed by anybody.

"Second, that the body which was found was not the body of Andrew Barton.

"Third, that the prisoner is not Ronald Barton.

"Fourth, that he is Andrew Barton, the person whom he is accused of having murdered.

"Thus the charge set forth in the indictment has been disproved at every point and in every detail. It has been made abundantly and convincingly clear that the prisoner is innocent of the crime named in that charge; and I, accordingly, claim for him a verdict of Not Guilty."

# CHAPTER SEVENTEEN

## *The Verdict*

As Thorndyke sat down, a low murmur pervaded the court, and the judge glanced furtively and a little wistfully towards the jury. After a brief interval, Sir Oliver rose without alacrity and proceeded to polish his eyeglass with a thoughtful and somewhat hesitating air. As Thorndyke had really left him nothing to say, his reply could be little more than an empty formality, and he was apparently considering how he could best dispatch it when the foreman of the jury came to his relief with the intimation that the jury had heard as much as they considered necessary for their purpose. Thereupon, the Clerk of the court rose and inquired whether they had agreed on their verdict; to which the foreman replied that they had. The Clerk then put the momentous question:

"Do you find the prisoner Guilty or Not Guilty?"

"Not Guilty," was the reply, delivered with some emphasis; and even as the words were spoken, the court resounded with thunders of applause and Molly buried her face in her handkerchief. After a few moments, the judge held up his hand and the applause instantly died away, giving place to a profound silence. Then his Lordship leaned back in his chair and, regarding Andrew with a quizzical smile, addressed him thus:

"Mr Barton – I can safely address you by that name, though I will not venture to be more particular – the jury have found you to be Not Guilty of the crime with which you were charged. I consider it a very proper verdict and I concur unreservedly. You are accordingly discharged and are free to go your ways; and I hope that your troubles are now at an end. There are a few loose strands which you will have to gather up with the Insurance Society, and perhaps with the Probate Court; but they will probably present no serious difficulties. But, before you depart, I will counsel you most earnestly, the next time you are accused of murder or any other crime, to seek legal assistance rather more promptly than you did on the last occasion."

He concluded with a smile and a friendly nod; the gate of the dock was thrown open; the officer at Andrew's side wished him "good luck", and the prisoner stepped down to the floor of the court where Molly was waiting for him. While the judge had been speaking, she had risen and stolen across to the dock; and now, as he stepped down, she raised her eyes to his and silently held out her hands. Both were too overwhelmed for speech, or even to be conscious of the multitude of inquisitive eyes that were eagerly watching them. Passively, they allowed themselves to be shepherded by the discreet Jervis – who was acutely conscious of the curious though sympathetic spectators – out of the court and into a small room that opened off from the great corridor. Only then, when Jervis had slipped away with an excuse, did Molly trust herself to speak.

"Oh, Andy!" she exclaimed shakily, "is it really you? Can it really be you, or is this only a tantalizing dream?"

"It isn't a dream, Molly dear," he replied. "It is an awakening from a nightmare; a nightmare of my own creating. I am the very prince of idiots. Say your husband is a fool, Molly."

She laughed a little hysterically. "Shall I?" she said. "Then I will. Andy, you have, really and truly, behaved like a – perfect – old – *donkey*! But never mind that, darling. Only a few hours ago, I was a miserable widow. And now – "

She broke off with a sob and, laying her head on his shoulder, wept quietly and happily.

At this moment the door opened and Jervis entered, accompanied by Thorndyke, bearing the attaché case and the picture and followed

235

by Mrs Kempster. The latter, still red-eyed and somewhat emotional, advanced shyly and addressed herself to Andrew:

"I have come," said she, "to ask for your forgiveness for all the mischief I have made. I never supposed – "

"Forgiveness!" interrupted Molly, seizing both her hands impulsively. "Why, you dear creature, you have been our good angel! It was you who broke the spell and brought us all back to realities. We can never be grateful enough to you. And don't forget that you are our cousin."

Here the door opened again to admit two more visitors; none other than Sir Oliver and his junior, Mr Black. They both shook Andrew's hand heartily, and Sir Oliver, having carefully inserted his eyeglass, spoke for them both.

"We congratulate you most warmly, Mr Barton. You have given us a magnificent entertainment and we glory in our defeat. Your champion has displayed his usual invincible form; and we, the Philistines, have been smitten hip and thigh. But *not* with the jawbone of an ass."

# R Austin Freeman

## The D'Arblay Mystery
### A Dr Thorndyke Mystery

When a man is found floating beneath the skin of a green-skimmed pond one morning, Dr Thorndyke becomes embroiled in an astonishing case. This wickedly entertaining detective fiction reveals that the victim was murdered through a lethal injection and someone out there is trying a cover-up.

## Dr Thorndyke Intervenes
### A Dr Thorndyke Mystery

What would you do if you opened a package to find a man's head? What would you do if the headless corpse had been swapped for a case of bullion? What would you do if you knew a brutal murderer was out there, somewhere, and waiting for you? Some people would run. Dr Thorndyke intervenes.

# R AUSTIN FREEMAN

## FELO DE SE
### A DR THORNDYKE MYSTERY

John Gillam was a gambler. John Gillam faced financial ruin and was the victim of a sinister blackmail attempt. John Gillam is now dead. In this exceptional mystery, Dr Thorndyke is brought in to untangle the secrecy surrounding the death of John Gillam, a man not known for insanity and thoughts of suicide.

## FLIGHTY PHYLLIS

Chronicling the adventures and misadventures of Phyllis Dudley, Richard Austin Freeman brings to life a charming character always getting into scrapes. From impersonating a man to discovering mysterious trapdoors, *Flighty Phyllis* is an entertaining glimpse at the times and trials of a wayward woman.

# R AUSTIN FREEMAN

## HELEN VARDON'S CONFESSION
### A DR THORNDYKE MYSTERY

Through the open door of a library, Helen Vardon hears an argument that changes her life forever. Helen's father and a man called Otway argue over missing funds in a trust one night. Otway proposes a marriage between him and Helen in exchange for his co-operation and silence. What transpires is a captivating tale of blackmail, fraud and death. Dr Thorndyke is left to piece together the clues in this enticing mystery.

## MR POTTERMACK'S OVERSIGHT

Mr Pottermack is a law-abiding, settled homebody who has nothing to hide until the appearance of the shadowy Lewison, a gambler and blackmailer with an incredible story. It appears that Pottermack is in fact a runaway prisoner, convicted of fraud, and Lewison is about to spill the beans unless he receives a large bribe in return for his silence. But Pottermack protests his innocence, and resolves to shut Lewison up once and for all. Will he do it? And if he does, will he get away with it?

## OTHER TITLES BY R AUSTIN FREEMAN AVAILABLE DIRECT
## FROM HOUSE OF STRATUS

| Quantity | £ | $(US) | € |
|---|---|---|---|
| ☐ THE ADVENTURES OF | | | |
|    ROMNEY PRINGLE | 6.99 | 9.95 | 13.50 |
| ☐ AS A THIEF IN THE NIGHT | 6.99 | 9.95 | 13.50 |
| ☐ THE CAT'S EYE | 6.99 | 9.95 | 13.50 |
| ☐ A CERTAIN DR THORNDYKE | 6.99 | 9.95 | 13.50 |
| ☐ THE D'ARBLAY MYSTERY | 6.99 | 9.95 | 13.50 |
| ☐ DR THORNDYKE INTERVENES | 6.99 | 9.95 | 13.50 |
| ☐ DR THORNDYKE'S CASEBOOK | 6.99 | 9.95 | 13.50 |
| ☐ DR THORNDYKE'S CRIME FILE | 6.99 | 9.95 | 13.50 |
| ☐ THE EXPLOITS OF DANBY CROKER | 6.99 | 9.95 | 13.50 |
| ☐ THE EYE OF OSIRIS | 6.99 | 9.95 | 13.50 |
| ☐ FELO DE SE | 6.99 | 9.95 | 13.50 |
| ☐ FLIGHTY PHYLLIS | 6.99 | 9.95 | 13.50 |
| ☐ FROM A SURGEON'S DIARY | 6.99 | 9.95 | 13.50 |
| ☐ THE FURTHER ADVENTURES OF | | | |
|    ROMNEY PRINGLE | 6.99 | 9.95 | 13.50 |
| ☐ THE GOLDEN POOL: A STORY | | | |
|    OF A FORGOTTEN MINE | 6.99 | 9.95 | 13.50 |
| ☐ THE GREAT PORTRAIT MYSTERY | 6.99 | 9.95 | 13.50 |
| ☐ HELEN VARDON'S CONFESSION | 6.99 | 9.95 | 13.50 |

ALL HOUSE OF STRATUS BOOKS ARE AVAILABLE FROM GOOD BOOKSHOPS
OR DIRECT FROM THE PUBLISHER:

**Internet:** **www.houseofstratus.com** including synopses and features.

**Email:** **sales@houseofstratus.com**
**info@houseofstratus.com**
(please quote author, title and credit card details.)

## OTHER TITLES BY R AUSTIN FREEMAN AVAILABLE DIRECT
## FROM HOUSE OF STRATUS

| Quantity | | £ | $(US) | € |
|---|---|---|---|---|
| | THE JACOB STREET MYSTERY | 6.99 | 9.95 | 13.50 |
| | JOHN THORNDYKE'S CASES | 6.99 | 9.95 | 13.50 |
| | THE MAGIC CASKET | 6.99 | 9.95 | 13.50 |
| | MR POLTON EXPLAINS | 6.99 | 9.95 | 13.50 |
| | MR POTTERMACK'S OVERSIGHT | 6.99 | 9.95 | 13.50 |
| | THE MYSTERY OF 31 NEW INN | 6.99 | 9.95 | 13.50 |
| | THE MYSTERY OF ANGELINA FROOD | 6.99 | 9.95 | 13.50 |
| | THE PENROSE MYSTERY | 6.99 | 9.95 | 13.50 |
| | PONTIFEX, SON AND THORNDYKE | 6.99 | 9.95 | 13.50 |
| | THE PUZZLE LOCK | 6.99 | 9.95 | 13.50 |
| | THE RED THUMB MARK | 6.99 | 9.95 | 13.50 |
| | A SAVANT'S VENDETTA | 6.99 | 9.95 | 13.50 |
| | THE SHADOW OF THE WOLF | 6.99 | 9.95 | 13.50 |
| | A SILENT WITNESS | 6.99 | 9.95 | 13.50 |
| | THE SINGING BONE | 6.99 | 9.95 | 13.50 |
| | THE STONEWARE MONKEY | 6.99 | 9.95 | 13.50 |
| | THE SURPRISING EXPERIENCES OF MR SHUTTLEBURY COBB | 6.99 | 9.95 | 13.50 |
| | THE UNWILLING ADVENTURER | 6.99 | 9.95 | 13.50 |
| | WHEN ROGUES FALL OUT | 6.99 | 9.95 | 13.50 |

ALL HOUSE OF STRATUS BOOKS ARE AVAILABLE FROM GOOD BOOKSHOPS
OR DIRECT FROM THE PUBLISHER:

Tel:      Order Line
          0800 169 1780 (UK)
          International
          +44 (0) 1845 527700 (UK)

Fax:      +44 (0) 1845 527711 (UK)
          (please quote author, title and credit card details.)

Send to:  House of Stratus Sales Department
          Thirsk Industrial Park
          York Road, Thirsk
          North Yorkshire, YO7 3BX
          UK

# PAYMENT

Please tick currency you wish to use:

☐ £ (Sterling)    ☐ $ (US)    ☐ € (Euros)

Allow for shipping costs charged per order plus an amount per book as set out in the tables below:

CURRENCY/DESTINATION

|                          | £(Sterling) | $(US) | € (Euros) |
|--------------------------|-------------|-------|-----------|
| **Cost per order**       |             |       |           |
| UK                       | 1.50        | 2.25  | 2.50      |
| Europe                   | 3.00        | 4.50  | 5.00      |
| North America            | 3.00        | 3.50  | 5.00      |
| Rest of World            | 3.00        | 4.50  | 5.00      |
| **Additional cost per book** |         |       |           |
| UK                       | 0.50        | 0.75  | 0.85      |
| Europe                   | 1.00        | 1.50  | 1.70      |
| North America            | 1.00        | 1.00  | 1.70      |
| Rest of World            | 1.50        | 2.25  | 3.00      |

**PLEASE SEND CHEQUE OR INTERNATIONAL MONEY ORDER**
**payable to: HOUSE OF STRATUS LTD or card payment as indicated**

STERLING EXAMPLE

Cost of book(s):..................... Example: 3 x books at £6.99 each: £20.97

Cost of order:...................... Example: £1.50 (Delivery to UK address)

Additional cost per book:............. Example: 3 x £0.50: £1.50

Order total including shipping:.......... Example: £23.97

## VISA, MASTERCARD, SWITCH, AMEX:

☐☐☐☐☐☐☐☐☐☐☐☐☐☐☐☐☐☐☐☐☐☐☐☐

Issue number (Switch only):

☐☐☐

**Start Date:**              **Expiry Date:**

☐☐/☐☐                      ☐☐/☐☐

Signature: _____

NAME: _____

ADDRESS: _____

COUNTRY: _____

ZIP/POSTCODE: _____

Please allow 28 days for delivery. Despatch normally within 48 hours.

Prices subject to change without notice.
Please tick box if you do not wish to receive any additional information. ☐

House of Stratus publishes many other titles in this genre; please check our website (**www.houseofstratus.com**) for more details.